POWER OF THE CONCLAVE

BETH RAYMOND

Copyediting by Sylvia Cottrell, Ex Libris Editing

Cover design by Design for Writers

ISBN 978-0-9967323-3-8 (Trade Paperback)

ISBN 978-0-9967323-4-5 (Hardback)

ISBN 978-0-9967323-5-2 (Kindle)

to David
for still believing

SPECIAL OFFER

Sign up for Beth's no-spam newsletter and get an introductory short story and other exclusive information and content, all for free. Details can be found at the end of this book.

1

MASTER GERSEMI

HEADMASTER GERSEMI TAPPED HER FINGERNAILS AGAINST the table, one after the other, in a slow succession. It had been eighteen months. Eighteen *infuriating* months. How much longer must she wait for satisfaction?

Along both sides of the rectangular, polished wood table that filled the room, the ten purportedly esteemed members of her Directorate sat in silence. Most didn't have the courage to meet her glare. They were supposed to be the Masters that she, as Headmaster, could count on to ensure the proper administration of all of Corinas. Yet every time she met with them of late, they'd revealed nothing but more problems they seemed incapable of handling on their own. None deserved the silver whorls and stripes of rank that graced their gray robes.

The Conclave should have been in a far different position by now. They should have crushed the rebellion, eliminated their leadership, and scoured all remaining traces of it from every town. They should have executed the traitors in such a spectacle that no other woman of the Conclave would ever dare to consider rejecting her rightful role. Most importantly, they should have found Mathis—her Son—so he could fulfill his true destiny.

None of that had come to pass. Not even a tiny, single part. Instead, the rebels had gained strength while the Masters dithered, and here she sat in the Directorate's Room, once again, learning of another setback none of these women had prevented.

"Is that all?" Gersemi's tone made clear her disgust at the other Masters' incompetence.

Beryl, the Principal Master of Governance, sat to her right. Her shoulder-length brown hair, smooth and neat, framed her round face. She lifted her narrow eyebrows and gave a tiny shrug. "That's all they reported. They've dispatched a nearby Guard unit to confirm, but given our current situation, my recommendation is that we assume it is true and adjust accordingly."

Gersemi frowned. "To be clear, you've raised this report today as an urgent matter without confirmation? Why hasn't an Adept already determined if it is true?"

"An Adept performed a truth assessment on the citizen, of course, and she found his report to be accurate as far as he was concerned. But she could not establish from him alone whether what he reported as the truth in his own mind is, in actuality, the truth. We must learn more from others in Zanita; hence why a separate Guard unit is now investigating."

At the far end of the table, the Principal Master of Allocation and the newest member of the Directorate leaned forward, her long hair puddling against the table. She raised a hand halfway. "Headmaster?"

"Master Charla, I've told you repeatedly you don't need to raise your hand every time you wish to speak. You are all equal members of the Directorate," Gersemi said, though she wished it were not so. In the two months since she'd had no choice but to accept Charla's elevation—only because all the other candidates put forth for the position of managing the duties of the Adepts who lived within the Conclave itself had been even *less* capable— she had not once added anything of consequence to their deliberations.

Charla dropped her hand with a sheepish smile toward the

others. "Yes, Headmaster. I wondered—wouldn't it be faster for the Adept to reach out to the one assigned to Zanita? Certainly Zanita's Adept would know if a gang of rogue Guards had passed through town…right?"

Beryl shook her head. "There's no Adept in Zanita. It's been that way for years."

"…Oh." Charla returned her ignorant gaze to the table.

Gersemi sighed quietly. *Useless. Completely useless.* "So. As it stands now, we must wait to learn whether it is true that we've lost another Guard unit to the rebellion. How many is that now?"

"Twelve." Beryl tapped on the piece of paper before her. "Wait —thirteen, including this one."

"Thirteen," Gersemi snapped. "Thirteen units have abandoned their posts and their duty to the Conclave." What were the rebels promising them for such treachery?

"Thirteen we know of."

Gersemi clenched her jaw. "Thank you for that correction, Master Beryl. And as we sit here today, it appears there has been no progress whatsoever in finding any of them." The vein at the side of her forehead throbbed.

Jeyne, sitting to Gersemi's left as the Principal Master of Security, frowned at the accusation. Her hair, kept short above her ears, and upright posture made her seem almost a Guardswoman rather than a Master. "We're doing the best we can with the resources we've got. We've eliminated a number of places they could have gone to ground, and we positioned loyal Guards at those locations in case anyone doubles back. But Corinas is large, and searching every piece of the country is taking time. The heavy snows this past winter also slowed our search considerably."

"Excuses. It's summer now. How much more time do you require? The rebellion should not be so hard to locate, I would think, especially given that it seems to grow larger every day—for some reason no one has explained. *Why have they not been found?*" she demanded, clipping her final words in her fury.

Jeyne did not wither under Gersemi's assault. "With respect,

Headmaster, the rebels are not all in one place. If they were, you're correct—we would have found them by now. They wouldn't be able to hide the sort of traffic necessary to bring such a large group foodstuffs and other supplies. And, as you know, we've dealt with many rebel groups already."

Gersemi scoffed under her breath. Executions, while satisfying, did not help them solve the underlying problem. Not a single person in any of those groups had revealed in their truth assessments the location of the rebellion's leadership. Some honestly had no idea, while others gave false names they nonetheless believed to be true.

Jayne's attempt to assuage her ire had only fueled it. All the rebel groups they'd eliminated had been, in the end, inconsequential. None had been the one Gersemi sought: the one that had infiltrated the Conclave itself a year and a half ago. The one that harbored the traitors and the child Adept born outside the Conclave's control. The one that had manipulated her own Son when he was but a child, confusing him about where he belonged.

It was time to end this farce of a meeting. "That is all for today, Masters. We will meet again in a week's time. I suggest you have better information for me by then." Chairs scraped against the wooden floor as the women pushed back from the table. "Masters Jeyne and Beryl," she announced, "stay for a moment, please."

The two women lowered themselves back down into their chairs, glancing at each other. Everyone else hurried toward the door.

Gersemi folded her arms across the table and looked back and forth between the two. "Today, all I heard from you was more failure. We're no closer to capturing those we seek, nor to ousting the rebellion from our lands, than we were more than a year ago. In fact, we seem to be losing more and more of the citizenry to this absurd faction. Tell me, please, why I should keep you in your positions? I'm of half a mind to replace you both right now."

Jeyne's cheeks flushed. "As I've said before, many times, the rebels have scattered, and they've not returned to any of their known locales. I have all available resources searching for them. Unless you want me to move more Guard units from their bases of operation—something I would not recommend given the current problems with Governance—I'm doing all I can."

"The problems with Governance stem from the lack of Security and the ongoing issues in Generation," Beryl protested, glaring at Jeyne. "It isn't my fault that we don't have enough Adepts to go around. Half the Tribunals operate without an Adept for months at a time, and now many lack Guards, too. What are they supposed to do to keep the citizens in check?"

Gersemi observed the two women bicker and point fingers everywhere but at themselves. In truth, replacing either of them would be difficult, as both had been in their positions almost as long as Gersemi had been in hers. If things continued on like this, however, she'd replace them no matter the squawking she'd hear about it.

Admittedly, their problems stemmed in part from Gersemi's decision to recall all Adepts of the First Initiate back to the Conclave. Yet with the continued failures in Generation—which her Principal Master of Generation, Leyta, still had not remedied —they could not risk any delay in moving those girls into Seclusion. That was far more important to the future of the Conclave than any difficulties Beryl and Jeyne might face from having fewer Adepts in the field.

She rapped her knuckles sharply on the table to silence their argument. "I will give you both an opportunity to redeem yourselves. Master Jeyne: transfer a number of Guards to assist those Tribunals who lack regular Adepts." She held up her hand as Jeyne opened her mouth. "I understand it is not ideal. But we cannot let our cities run amok. I leave it to you to judge how many to transfer, but make sure you provide the Tribunals with enough Guards to maintain the peace."

"Yes, Headmaster," Jeyne said, her face no less red than it had been earlier, despite the fact that Gersemi was giving her far more leeway to do her job than she deserved.

"And Master Beryl, here is what I will do for you: I will allow field placement of Adepts from the Sixth Initiate."

Beryl gasped as Jeyne leaned back in her chair, her mouth agape. "The *Sixth*?" Beryl repeated. "Do you think they are ready?"

Gersemi raised her eyebrows. "I wouldn't have decided otherwise. Still, send them to more stable locations and rotate those from the Second and Third Initiates to places less so. I will also allow you to assign a Master to accompany each Adept from the Sixth who will be the one responsible for the child's care and continued training. The Tribunals have enough to worry about."

Beryl grinned. "That will do nicely, Headmaster. Thank you."

It had better, Gersemi thought. Adepts from the Sixth Initiate could only perform rudimentary truth assessments, but if Beryl failed even with these extra bodies, Gersemi would have better grounds to replace her. "That will be all, then. Next time, let's see improvements in your reports, hmm?"

"Yes, Headmaster," they said in unison.

She held up a finger. "Oh, one other thing," she said as if she'd only just thought of it. "There's still been no word whatsoever of the rebel Mathis?"

"No, Headmaster," Jeyne said in a measured tone, as if she were trying to determine what Gersemi wanted to hear. "Every Guard unit has his description, but the only leads we've received so far turned out to be dead ends. He's either altered his appearance, or he's being far more careful about remaining out of sight than we anticipated."

Gersemi hadn't really expected a different response to a question she'd asked many times before, but the asking would remind them that Mathis must remain a focus of their inquiries. They accepted her interest in the child Adept, and even the traitors, as those people belonged to the Conclave. They didn't realize that Mathis belonged to them, too.

Long ago, the Masters of Generation had seen the greatness within Gersemi. Though she hadn't known it at the time, they'd selected her to bear a Progenitor Son, something allowed to only a privileged few. Later tests showed he held within him an immense amount of residual Ability—more than any other Progenitor Son in hundreds of years. Gersemi had spent years secretly pouring through the old histories before she realized what that meant. Mathis's exceptionalism, passed on from her, meant he was destined to father the greatest generation of Adepts that had ever lived.

Gersemi had kept her research close, as well as the fact that she knew Mathis was her own. Not even Leyta—who presumably knew Mathis's parentage, given that she maintained the records of Generation—was aware of Gersemi's knowledge. Soon enough, Gersemi would reveal his importance to all, and they would finally understand her persistence.

But only if she could get him back. That he'd slipped away from her once before, when he'd been right under her nose…

Someone coughed. Jeyne and Beryl still sat before her, unmoving. She lifted her hand in a gesture of dismissal. "You may go."

"Thank you, Headmaster," the Masters chorused.

Finally alone, Gersemi tapped her fingernails against the table anew. She stared down its empty length, pondering her next move.

2

MATHIS

THE MOSQUITO BUZZED, ONCE AGAIN, NEAR HIS EAR. MATHIS scowled and swatted at the air above his pillow, displacing the insect. This time it returned almost immediately. Grumbling, he sat up from his bedroll. When he thought he heard it again, he smacked his hands together in its general vicinity. He squinted, searching his hands for any sign of a carcass, but by then the buzzing had started anew. He tried two more times before he decided his efforts were futile; it was too dark in his tent to see anything.

You all right in there? The silent question sounded in his mind alone.

Mosquito.

Ah. Want to go for a walk? I can't sleep anyway, and maybe the mosquito will go elsewhere while we're gone.

He grimaced, realizing in retrospect the noise he'd made trying to kill the stupid thing. *Did I wake you?*

No. I've been tossing and turning for hours.

Good. Not that you can't sleep, but—well, you know what I mean. And unlike most people he might say such a thing to, he was certain Alia did. *I wouldn't mind a short walk, so long as we don't wander too far from camp.*

That's fine. See you outside?

Mathis grabbed his boots and opened the flap of his tent. Outside, a swath of stars stretched across an inky sky devoid of any hint of a moon. He scooted to the edge of the canvas tarp that protected his gear from the ground and pulled on his boots. As he laced them up, the tent next to his wobbled, and a hand reached out to unlatch the flap.

Alia poked her head out from the tent and grinned in his direction. It no longer took him by surprise to see her with a full head of hair rather than the bare scalp she'd sported when they'd first met. Now, she didn't even have to rely on a wig to help with her disguise. Some medic Kelda came across had *inserted* real hair into Alia's scalp, giving her short, jet-black locks that were apparently here to stay. She gestured to the right with her thumb, questioning. He nodded.

He followed her past the other tents, making sure to step so he wouldn't wake up anyone else. At the perimeter of the camp, one of the two Guards on watch glanced their way. She lifted her chin in recognition, then returned her focus to the grassland beyond. So long as Mathis was with Alia, no one would stand in the way of her desire for a nighttime excursion.

Short grass in the early stages of summer growth brushed against his pant legs as they walked in silence. Alia would eventually talk about whatever was bothering her. He could read her pretty well by now, a combination of many months of close travel and all the time he'd spent communicating with her through his "minutia of Ability," as Kelda liked to call it.

Alia stopped and put her hands on her hips, tilting her head back up toward the sky. "Aren't they beautiful?"

"I suppose. Look the same as they always do."

"That's just it. They're so...*permanent*. No matter where we've been in Corinas, they always look the same. The Column is over there," she said, pointing to the left, "with the Basket right beside it." She turned. "And then there's the Arrow, which I think shows us the way home."

Mathis looked sideways at her. "Home?"

She wrapped her arms around her midsection. "I know how strange that sounds. I've never even been to the mountains! Still— I like to think of Brome as my new home, now. I guess I'm glad we're going to a place where we'll get to stay for a while. I'm tired of sleeping on the ground and wearing the same clothes for weeks." She plucked at the arm of her black jacket, a twin of his own.

"Realized you're not the adventuring type?" he teased, nudging her shoulder with his elbow.

"I'm not so certain I'd call what we've been doing 'adventuring,'" she groused. "Wandering from place to place, fixing what we can fix, and burying what we cannot? If that's what you consider an adventure, then I would rather stay home—wherever home might be." She looked up again at the sky.

Her reminder of what they'd found as they'd traveled Corinas extinguished his humor. True, a fair number of folks from the scattered rebellion had made their way safely to Brome thanks to their help. Those were good days when they'd come across people like that.

But on far too many occasions, they'd stumbled upon the aftermath of what he could only describe as a slaughter. When the Conclave decided someone—or some place—was disloyal, it did not discriminate when it came to eliminating the perceived threat. Entire villages had been wiped out.

He wondered if the Masters yet realized how badly their attempts to destroy the rebellion had backfired. With all the indiscriminate destruction, they'd displayed to all how little they cared about the people of Corinas. Support for the rebellion had only grown, with many citizens now willing to question the Conclave's role in their lives—an act of defiance practically unheard of mere months ago. Even the Conclave's own Guards were defecting to the rebellion, including, on a few notable occasions, entire units whose commanders had simply had enough.

"I spoke to Tovi again this evening," Alia said, returning his attention to her. "I bet we'll get to Brome sooner than planned. She said the pass was clear."

"Captain Levina assumed it would be, so far as I know, so I don't think it will make a difference to the schedule."

Alia sighed. "We've been moving so *slowly* these last few weeks."

"For good reason," he said, scratching at his short beard. The rest of what had been Captain Keya's group wasn't exactly fit for travel. Holed up in an abandoned safe house since they'd lost their leader in a nasty skirmish against the Conclave's Guard, their numbers had continued to decline due to illness and injury. They were lucky any of them had survived, and Captain Levina didn't want to lose any more.

"You're right," Alia said solemnly, rubbing her hands against her upper arms. "Let's keep going."

Mathis kept a watchful eye on their surroundings, though more out of habit than because of any true concern that something might lurk in the darkness. His primary task was, after all, to protect Alia from harm, and he'd done a pretty decent job of it. While he liked to think it was due to his skill, he recognized the involvement of a good measure of dumb luck, too. The Conclave would not have abandoned their efforts to find—and destroy—Alia. An Adept like her wasn't supposed to exist, let alone work for the rebellion.

Granted, she wasn't the Conclave's only target. Several rebels were on the Masters' list of wanted individuals, including Mathis himself. Those who didn't know his true identity assumed he was on it due to his involvement with the failed attempt to rescue Alia's friend from the Conclave. That was fine by him. The fewer people who knew he was the son of an Adept, the better. It wasn't something anyone with sense would be proud of.

"I'm quite looking forward to seeing Tovi again. Nyona, too.

Aren't you?" Alia asked. "We've been away from them so much longer than we ever expected. I'm sure they feel the same way."

Anxiety tumbled Mathis's stomach. The last time he'd seen Nyona, they'd admitted to having feelings for one another. But that had been over a year and a half ago. In all that time, they'd exchanged nothing more than superficial words through Tovi or Alia, and the passion he'd once felt had long since dissipated. They'd now been apart longer than they'd been together, and it wasn't as if they'd ever really been *together*. A few rushed kisses did not make a relationship, and nineteen months was a long time to be away from someone he'd only just gotten to know.

"Hello?" Alia looked up at him, an annoyed expression painting her features.

"Sorry. Yes. It will be nice to see them after all this time." His words sounded stilted and false to his ear.

She raised her tattooed eyebrows. "You do realize you can't really lie to me anymore, right?"

"It *will* be nice," he protested. "Just…awkward."

"I understand." She patted his arm.

He was happy to let it go, though he doubted Alia really understood the conflict that roiled inside him. As long as he'd known her, she'd never shown an interest in any man—or woman, as the case might be. With no experience like that, how could she appreciate the apprehension that came with the expectation of seeing a former love?

A shriek pierced the night's solitude. Heart racing, he whipped around, expecting to see an attack on the camp. Instead, weapon-less rebels scampered around a tent that had erupted with a fierce orange glow. "Fires," he muttered, for once using the curse quite literally. "We'd better go help. Come on."

They hurried back, but by the time they arrived the others had already put out the flames. A half-charred tent had partially collapsed in on itself, and a few people were salvaging what they could. Captain Levina observed their activity with her arms folded across her chest. Next to her, the former Master, Kelda, wrung her hands together. "I so hope nothing is damaged. Have you found it yet?" she called to those rummaging amidst the tent's remains.

Captain Levina rubbed at her forehead wearily, leaving behind a black mark of soot. "What were you thinking, lighting a candle? What happened to your glow lamp?"

"It's dead."

"Kelda," Alia reproached. "You should have asked me to recharge it. It would have been no trouble at all."

"Now that we're so close to Brome, I would prefer that you not use your Ability for something so trivial. How could I live with myself if the Conclave found you because of my dead lamp?"

Captain Levina raised an eyebrow. "Because your candle catching this whole grassland on fire wouldn't have drawn their attention?"

"Well, if you put it that way—" Kelda cut herself off, eyes lighting up when one of the rebels came out of the tent holding a blue leather satchel. "That's it!" she cried, nearly ripping it from the woman's hands. She pawed through the bag, then let out a relieved sigh. "Everything seems to be fine. I'm so glad. Some of this scholarship took me months and months to piece together. I don't know what I would have done if it had been lost."

"Maybe you shouldn't keep it all in one bag if it's that irreplaceable," Captain Levina commented. She yawned. "All right, people," she announced. "Excitement's over. We're still leaving early, so get whatever last bit of sleep you can. Kelda, you can stay with me. We'll clean the rest of this up in the morning."

"I don't know how I can fall asleep after all that," Alia said as they walked back to their own tents.

"Best to give it a go," he reminded her. "Even a few minutes will be better than nothing. Sounds like the Captain's planning on keeping us on schedule tomorrow, so it'll be a long day."

"I don't mind a little exhaustion if it means no more delays. Just think: this time next week, we'll have real beds again. We can catch up on our sleep then."

"True," he said, anxiety flaring anew at her reminder of the imminent end of their journey. Even if he'd not been anxious about reuniting with Nyona, he wouldn't have been as excited about reaching Brome as Alia. Despite everything that had happened over the past nineteen months, he'd grown used to life out in the field, and he liked not quite knowing what to expect each day. He wasn't certain how he felt about being stuck in the same place for who knew how long—and up in the mountains, no less.

Also, out here, Captain Levina allowed him a great deal of freedom and responsibility even though he wasn't an officer. When he told people what to do in relation to keeping Alia safe, they usually followed his orders. They weren't a real Guard unit, after all, with a normal chain of command. That would all change once they were in the relative safety of Brome. They'd assign him to some unit, and he'd be, once again, just an individual member of the whole. He'd have no real responsibility—and certainly no authority.

"Well, good luck getting some rest on the ground tonight," Alia said cheerily before she ducked into her tent.

He entered his own tent and pulled off his boots. Sleep would be damned near impossible, but he should try to take his own advice. He lay back down on his bedroll, pulled the blanket up to his chin, closed his eyes, and tried with little success to calm his churning thoughts.

At least the stupid mosquito was gone.

3

ALIA

ALIA YAWNED AND STRETCHED, MARVELING AT THE FEEL OF A real bed. During her travels, the only chance she'd had to sleep in a true bed were those rare times when they'd spent a night in a better-furnished safe house or with someone sympathetic to the rebellion. Most often, the only thing that had been between her and the ground was a bedroll with a thin cushion that had diminished over time into near nothingness.

Now that she was in Brome, she had not only her own bed but also her own room. It was tiny, but at least she didn't have to pack it up each day. Beside the bed, the only furnishings were a round side table and a small wardrobe. A glow lamp emitted a constant dim light. Without it, the room became unsettlingly dark.

She rolled over to her other side. A thin line of light peeked from under the door, but no sounds came from the other side. Everyone must have already left for the day. Kelda, not wanting to spend her first day in meetings, intended to collect Tovi first thing for lessons, and Nyona had planned to go into town early to speak to Mathis.

Alia hoped their talk would clear the air. Yesterday's reunion had been awkward, with both Mathis and Nyona exchanging only a few words. That couldn't go on forever. She hoped that whatever had happened between them in the past would not cloud their friendship going forward. They were all on the same side after all.

She held a finger on the glow lamp to adjust its light gradually so as not to blind herself. When she noticed the time on the small clock next to the lamp, she groaned. The meeting would start soon, and she'd be late if she didn't hurry. One night of soft pillows and warm blankets and she had already reverted to old habits.

Part of her wanted to skip the meeting, no matter Levina's insistence that she attend. She wasn't an officer, so there was no real reason for her to go to a meeting meant for them. Levina only wanted to introduce her to those in command she'd not yet met, and that could happen any time.

Still, she understood the importance of first impressions, especially when she already had so much to overcome. It was one thing for the rebels to accept a child Adept who'd never once stepped foot inside the Conclave; it was something else entirely for them to accept a Sempiternal who had lived most of her years as the enemy. Ignoring Levina would not be a good first step along the path of acceptance.

She fluffed the pillows and propped them up against the headboard, then folded the crocheted throw and draped it over the bottom edge of the bed. If her friend Sarabie were still alive, she'd have laughed to see her efforts. Her chest tightened at the thought. Back when they were roommates in the Conclave, Alia had halfheartedly made her bed only to avoid the Masters' wrath. Now that she had her own room again, she would keep it neat by choice.

As expected, no one was in the larger bedroom Nyona and Tovi shared, nor in the small common area. Large glow lamps, the sort that provided heat as well as light, hung from the ceiling. They were dreadfully expensive, but they made all the difference in this strange, windowless home built within the protection of a natural cavern. Thick rugs also helped insulate them from drafts that might otherwise creep through the wooden floorboards.

She went into the tiny washroom and splashed her face with cold water pumped in from a natural spring located somewhere farther back in the cavern. It was a bit disconcerting to know that on the other side of the wall, mere inches from where she stood, was a dark, open space that continued deep into the mountain. Nyona promised the space narrowed considerably, and they had checked to make sure no animals had burrowed within before they'd begun construction, so there was nothing to worry about coming from that direction. Still, Alia was glad to be on *this* side of the sturdy walls.

Her jacket hung from a hook near the front door. After the meeting, she'd find warmer clothes. She'd abandoned all of her winter gear months ago, as the temperature had shifted in the lowlands and doing so lightened her pack. Up here in the mountains, however, her thin jacket was insufficient, no matter that it was technically summer.

The front door did not take her straight outside—it instead butted up against a narrow passage through the rock. At the far end, a tepid natural light guided her way. Once outside, the sun was nowhere to be seen, hidden somewhere behind the gray stone cliffs that towered above the entrance to the cavern on three sides. Giant fir trees of indiscernible height and trunks the width of at least two spans of her arms further shrouded this end of the valley. Kelda claimed they were older than Corinas itself, a prospect Alia found hard to believe, no matter their size.

She wrapped her arms around her midsection, shivering, and nodded a silent greeting to the two Guards who stood watch at the edge of the forest. Other than those two, nothing suggested there was anything of interest over here. From a distance, even the narrow passage to the cavern looked like nothing more than a small black scar in the rock. It was all part of the rebellion's effort to keep their Adepts hidden away in case of an attack. It was overkill, most likely, but she would not second-guess the Captains' precautionary measures. They would know better than she how to keep them safe.

Brome itself was past the forest—or, at least, the place they were calling Brome. The true Brome, the one that appeared on all the maps as a cautious reminder, was far to the east. If anyone from the Conclave caught word that the rebels were gathering in "Brome," they would naturally look first in the abandoned ruins of the place where they'd destroyed the prior generation's attempt at rebellion.

Anyone who stumbled upon this place, however, would realize immediately that it was not a typical mountain enclave. Massive wood-and-steel gates, with walls and watchtowers on either side, blocked the entrance into the valley. Inside the gates, the rebels had cleared away the trees and used the lumber to erect buildings with sharply pitched roofs, none of which reached over two stories, and all too new and too well-constructed for a mountain village. No true village would ever need those three long barracks, either.

Then there were all the people. So many Guard units had defected to their cause—at least twenty, by Nyona's most recent count—there was no more room for them within the gates. Instead, the Captains had sent growing numbers to hide in the passes and the lower valley to serve as the rebellion's first lines of defense.

Here, the gray cliffs rose to the same dizzying height as near the cavern, encasing most of Brome in a natural barrier. There was no rope long enough to allow a safe descent. A row of two-story buildings lined the base of the cliffs, indistinguishable from one another except for the color of their doors. The one in the middle with the yellow door, and two Guards standing before it, was her destination.

A tall, slender woman jogged up to the yellow door, and with barely a pause, yanked it open. Alia hurried her own steps, reminded that she too was running late.

As she approached the command center, both Guards eyed her up and down, suspicion writ large on their faces. Had no one told them to expect her? "Good morning," she said in her most pleasant voice, hoping they would grant her entry without too much trouble. "My name is Alia. I'm here for the officers' meeting."

"We know who you are," one of the men said, his expression unchanged. "You're late."

She maintained her smile as she pulled open the door, knowing it would do no good to berate his rudeness, especially in front of the other Guard. She'd grown used to citizens no longer jumping to do her bidding as they'd once done based on the mere appearance of the white robes she'd worn as an Adept of the Conclave, but displays of outright hostility were another matter.

Those two were probably like many others in the rebellion who thought she was nothing more than a plant, biding her time to turn them all in to the Conclave. No matter her actions, they couldn't believe she'd switched sides. Her Sempiternal status didn't help matters, she knew. An Adept's power was supposed to wane toward the end of adolescence. To those already suspicious of her motives, that she still had her Ability at twenty years of age only proved she must be working on the Masters' behalf.

Alia followed the sound of voices to a large room crowded with women. Levina and Jana sat at a table at the front with some other women Alia recognized from yesterday's introductions as Captains. A chair was open in the front row, but Alia didn't wish to put herself that much on display. She glanced around, searching for somewhere else to sit, and tried to ignore the curious stares.

Across the room, Marta waved and gestured to an empty chair next to her and Ciara. Their twin blonde curls and similar features made their mother-daughter relationship obvious to anyone who cared to look. How had she ever missed it? She'd spent so much time with them both before she'd learned the truth and never once considered the possibility. For those living in the Conclave, the impossibility of ever knowing which Master was an Adept's mother was taught as a fact, and she'd accepted that falsity without question.

Alia avoided thinking on the topic as far as her own circumstances were concerned. Kelda was convinced that Alia's mother, whoever she was, was dead. Once the Conclave learned Alia was a true Sempiternal, they'd not have allowed her mother to live, even though the damage, so to speak, was already done.

"You're just in time," Marta said as Alia sat down next to her. "The last officer has arrived. Have you met Lieutenant Elcy? She's quite brilliant, I think. I wouldn't be surprised if they made her a Captain one day."

Alia shook her head. "No. Yesterday was pretty much Levina introducing me to some other Captains and catching up with people." The lanky woman who'd rushed into the command center before her sat sideways in a chair a few rows ahead of them. With smooth, freckled skin and brownish-red hair, she didn't seem much older than thirty. Maybe that was the usual age for a Lieutenant; Alia had paid little attention to the command structure of the rebellion thus far. She, and the other former members of the Conclave, were mostly kept outside of such matters.

Jana rapped her knuckles on the tabletop. "Let us begin, please." Voices quieted at her request. Alia realized the Captain's short brown hair was similar to her own, and wondered if Kelda had mimicked Jana's hairstyle when directing the medic who'd given Alia her own head of real hair. "First of all, we are happy to welcome—finally—Captain Levina, and those of you who traveled with her to Brome," Jana continued once the chatter of the room had ceased. "Your efforts out in the field were well worth the delay in your arrival." Levina lowered her chin in a single nod to Jana's praise.

"For those of you who do not know Alia," Jana continued, "please take the time to introduce yourselves. We will be inviting her on occasion to these meetings to add to Marta and Ciara's contributions. We expect all of you to treat her with the same respect you give to them."

Alia's cheeks flushed as the eyes of every person in the room turned her way. Some of the women's stares were blatantly distrustful despite Jana's pronouncement. A sudden urge to look into their minds jolted her. Her Ability thrummed just beneath the surface, and it would take no effort at all to unleash it. None of them would have any idea that she'd pried into their thoughts— not even former Masters like Ciara and Marta would notice anything was afoot.

Her increased skills weren't merely because she was Sempiternal, though it was a factor. She'd always been able to do more than other Adepts in her Initiate, including Marta, before feeling fatigued. Yet it was Kelda's scholarship that had taught her how to harness her Ability in new ways. Tasks that had once taken a great deal of effort, like a truth assessment, now came as easily as turning on a glow lamp.

As the women's attention turned back to the Captains, the urge to read their innermost thoughts faded. What good would it do? She didn't need to confirm the truth of what they thought of her from their minds when it was already obvious on their faces.

After more introductions, Levina launched into an abbreviated version of their travels. She concluded with the story of when they'd found what remained of Captain Keya's group. "They ran into a loyalist Guard unit south of the mountains a few weeks before we caught up to them. I'm sure you've all heard by now that Captain Keya and most of her staff didn't make it. They also lost about two-thirds of the unit. It's amazing we found any survivors at all."

"South?" someone in the third row asked. "What were they doing down there?"

"They were coming from the southeast, with plans to head north, but then the Conclave sent that surge of Guards to the middle of the country. Captain Keya had no choice but to detour. We were supposed to meet her at the western pass." A collective murmur of understanding percolated through the room.

"Captain Keya was with us from nearly the beginning," said Jana, "and we will miss her talent and dedication as we plan our next steps." She shuffled some papers on the table. "Now, let us turn to a report of what's going on in Valen."

Ciara sat taller in her chair. "Has Hasso returned?"

Alia had assumed the medic—or former assassin, if she were to speak in terms of prior alliances—was lurking somewhere in town. It would be interesting to see him after all this time. At least his glower of distrust would be a familiar sight.

"Not yet, though he should be here soon." Jana lifted an unfolded piece of paper. "His report is what we'll discuss next."

Alia stifled a yawn as the meeting dragged on and on. She idly picked at some balled-up fabric on the edge of her trousers, then scrutinized her fingernails. Aside from the Captains making sure everyone knew who she was, her presence at this meeting was pointless. She couldn't contribute as an officer, no one asked her any questions, and she already knew about most of what they were discussing from her communications with Tovi and her own experiences traveling the country.

She perked up when Jana directed a question at Marta. "How many Adepts does the Conclave have at present?"

"There are nine Initiates, but they aren't equal in number. The First and Second have only fifteen to twenty Adepts each, and the Eighth has less than ten. So…" She looked up toward the ceiling's rough-hewn timbers. "Perhaps one hundred and twenty?"

"In all nine?"

"I don't know how many there are in the Ninth because they weren't in active service when I left. That wasn't the sort of information anyone shared with new Masters."

Alia resisted looking at Marta; her friend's own twin daughters, born several years ago, would be in that Initiate. Did she ever think of them? Perhaps not. Like all Masters, Marta would not have expected to know her children.

"So, there could be another twenty from the Ninth?"

Marta shook her head once. "I doubt it. I'm guessing there's no more than ten. It doesn't really matter for our purposes—anyone in that Initiate wouldn't be ready for the Masters' use."

"It's still too many," protested a young woman with long black hair who sat near the corridor. "As I've been saying, the better course is to continue stealing away their muscle. What good are their Adepts if they have no Guards left to act on their will?" A fair number of other women signaled their approval by smacking their hands against their thighs.

Levina patted the air before her to quiet the room. "Lieutenant, we are all in agreement that we need to adjust our plans. We're in active war with the Conclave, and citizens are finally standing up for themselves. We will not waste this momentum. Rest assured we will take all your suggestions into account."

"Our voices should be more than a 'suggestion' in whatever this new plan is," the Lieutenant grumbled, while those seated next to her nodded in agreement. "Many of us have been in this fight a long time. We have a right to know what you're planning."

One Captain, a thin, delicate-looking woman whose name Alia didn't remember, scowled. "You forget yourself, Lieutenant," she said sharply. "As your commanding officer, I will tell you what you need to know when you need to know it, and no sooner."

Levina leaned back in her chair and put her hands behind her head. "That's true. Also, in full disclosure, we're still working out the specifics. I did only arrive yesterday." She grinned lazily, and her pale attempt at humor nevertheless lightened the tension that had developed in the room.

"There is nothing more to discuss today," Jana said. "Next week, we should be able to report more about our plans. In the meantime, please make sure your units continue their drills. The time for us to act is now, and we need to be prepared to do whatever it takes to win this war against the Conclave. Will you be ready?"

The crowd of officers roared their affirmation, and Alia couldn't help but join them.

Whatever it takes.

4

MASTER GERSEMI

GERSEMI CLOSED HER EYES AND PINCHED THE BRIDGE OF her nose with her thumb and forefinger. "Just have out with it, Master Charla," she said, wondering once again why she'd agreed to allow this ball of nerves into the Conclave's Directorate. Managing Adepts' use of Ability within the Conclave should not have been as difficult as she made it appear.

"We finally reached Master Cecily."

"And? Did she find it?"

Charla tucked her hair behind her ears. "No."

"That is unfortunate, but not unexpected." Cecily's young Adept, from the Sixth Initiate, would have had little experience in locating sources of unauthorized use of Ability. At least she could detect it. Gersemi made a mental note to see if there might be someone else to investigate the area south of Valen, near the mountains. If they were lucky, perhaps the traitor had finally made herself known. She was bound to slip up, eventually.

"Yes, but—" Charla's eyes darted from Gersemi to the floor and back, over and over.

"Is there something else?"

"Master Cecily went to investigate it by herself, as she thought it might be unsafe for Adept Khyana to be out in the open without a proper Guard unit."

No wonder Cecily hadn't found the source. What did she think she would accomplish without her Adept? "And?" she prompted, when it became plain there was more to the story.

"She did not leave Adept Khyana under the Tribunal's supervision. Instead, she left her in the care of two families who had fostered for us before. She thought having two watching over her would be better than one."

Apprehension cascaded through Gersemi in a cold rush. "*And?*"

Charla swallowed. "When she returned this morning, Adept Khyana was gone."

Gersemi inhaled and then exhaled slowly, trying to keep the promise she'd made to herself not to lash out when someone gave her bad news. She'd had a lot of practice of late. "What do you mean, 'gone'?"

"She's...disappeared. No one has seen her since last night."

"What of the families?"

"Both claim they thought the other had her overnight."

"And the Tribunal?"

"They knew nothing of Master Cecily's plans. They did send out Guards to search once they learned what had happened."

A low rage began to build within Gersemi despite her best efforts to keep her feelings at bay. She'd only allowed field placements of Adepts from the Sixth Initiate to appease her Directorate after she'd recalled everyone from the First. Valen, a seaport on the north coast of Corinas, should have been a safe place for a young, inexperienced Adept; as a town built on the stability of trade, the rebellion had made no inroads there. *Or so we thought.*

Why would Cecily ever leave her charge with ordinary citizens? One could *never* trust mere citizens with an Adept's care, even citizens who had fostered male children. Losing a boy usually was of no consequence. But losing an Adept, especially now...

Gersemi folded her hands on top of the file she'd intended to read before Charla's arrival. She straightened her back and focused on her breathing before she spoke again.

"You and Master Beryl shall arrange for both families to be brought to the closest town with an Adept for truth assessments. When that is complete, have them dispatched."

"Yes, Headmaster." Charla pulled out a small notebook from the pocket of her gray robe and scratched a quick note.

"Master Cecily is to return to Corval at once. I am relieving her of her duties, effective immediately, and once she returns, I intend to bring her disassociation to a vote. Someone who has failed so spectacularly in her primary duty no longer deserves to be a Master of the Conclave."

Charla looked up, her eyes wide. "Yes…yes, Headmaster," she stammered.

"Did anyone else in Valen see anything, anything at all, that might help us find Adept Khyana?"

"Not that anyone has admitted. We could send someone to perform truth assessments if you think it best—"

"No," Gersemi interrupted. "I will not send another Adept anywhere near Valen. It's obviously been compromised."

Charla nodded. "Okay. I will arrange what you've requested right away. Unless there is something else?"

"Yes. I don't want a mere handful of Guards searching for Adept Khyana. I want *all* of Valen's Guards out looking for her, as well as all those posted within a week's travel. It's only been one night, so the rebels couldn't have taken her far. Make that happen, and also tell the Tribunal it is to hear no petitions until I instruct them otherwise. Let the citizens of Valen see how well they can manage without Guards and Tribunal both." Soon enough, they'd be begging for the Conclave's return, no matter what dirty promises the rebels might have made.

Charla scribbled in her notebook. "Yes, Headmaster." She looked up and tilted her head to the side. "Wait. You think the rebels have Adept Khyana?"

Gersemi scowled at the woman's idiocy. "Did you think she

wandered off on her own? She's a child of the Sixth Initiate. Before this assignment, she'd never stepped outside the Conclave. Of course the rebels have her. They've made their interest in acquiring our Adepts quite plain." She waved her hand through the air in a curt dismissal. "See to my demands. I will expect an updated report this afternoon."

Once she was alone, it took all her mental strength to beat back the anger coursing through her veins. The rebels must think because they convinced the traitor to switch sides, others would do the same. It was a fool's errand, but that described the rebellion to the last. Even if they managed the impossible, a single Adept operating on the behalf of their cause—or two or three—would never be a match against the might of the Conclave's own.

At the far end of her reception room, bright beams of summer sun cast through the window. Gersemi sighed. Now was not the time to dwell on dark thoughts. The Conclave would withstand this time of turmoil. An institution that had survived prior rebellions, including one forged by the most powerful of Sempiternals long ago, had nothing to fear from a band of misfit citizens and their pet Adepts.

Charla's unexpected visit had wasted time she'd wanted to use to prepare for her meeting with the Xeydeyan emissary who had arrived a few days ago. Xeydeya, a small country far across the sea to the north, was a backward little place that boasted nothing comparable to Adepts. She'd never been there herself—no Adepts ever left Corinas, and few Masters did, either—but nothing she'd heard of it sounded at all appealing, even those aspects that weren't obvious exaggerations. Metal buildings stretching into the sky higher than the tallest tree? Pure fantasy.

She read the latest intelligence report Jeyne had put together for her in the file. The emissary, who was also a prominent merchant in her own right, appeared in Corval once a year or so. Gersemi found her odious, yet she always granted her requests to meet as it benefitted the economy to maintain positive relations with an important trade partner. Without Xeydeya, Corinas would have none of the steel it needed for cooking implements, weapons, and other such important items. Until she could find a way to bypass their monopoly on the raw materials and know-how necessary to make steel, she was stuck putting up with these yearly intrusions.

Someone knocked at her door. "Yes?"

A eunuch in a sharp black uniform with a silver insignia embroidered on his dress coat stepped inside. His name escaped her, as he'd only recently joined her retinue, though she remembered him by how short he was compared to his peers. "Apologies for the interruption, Headmaster, but it is time for your meeting."

"One moment." She skimmed the rest of the page before pushing herself up from the chair. The emissary might be beneath her, but there was no reason to give offense by making her wait.

The eunuch accompanied her down to the main floor and her private foyer next to the Public Room. "I will remain here, Headmaster, in case you need anything. I took the liberty of doubling the usual complement of Guards, as well."

She raised her eyebrows. It had been some time since one of her eunuchs had taken some initiative. "Thank you…?"

"Enece, Headmaster."

"That's right. Thank you, Enece. I'm sure this won't take long at all." She patted her hair, ensuring the pins still held it in place, then opened the door to the Public Room.

Typically, they reserved use of the Public Room, with its wide-open floor space before the dais and rows of stair-stepped mahogany benches along the sides, for the one or two occasions a year when the Directorate met with those citizens of Corinas worthy of such attention. Its magnificence became even that much more apparent without a crowd.

A tall woman with dark hair braided into intricate loops that cascaded past her shoulders turned from a painting of a mountain landscape. Instead of wearing a robe like a proper government representative, she wore loose black trousers and a belted green jacket. "Headmaster Gersemi," she said with a broad smile and barely a trace of an accent. "Thank you for meeting with me. It is good to see you once again."

Gersemi inclined her head the barest acceptable amount, then gestured to the closest bench. "It is good to see you as well, Kalisfena Tatyn." The Xeydeyan custom of using two names for one person in formal address always felt strange to her ears. However, she usually only had to do it once, and today was no exception.

"Please, Headmaster Gersemi. As I tell you each time we have the fortune to meet, you may call me Kalisfena. All my friends do." The emissary lowered herself onto the edge of the bench and folded her slender hands on her lap. Each finger, including her thumbs, bore a silver ring, some plain and others set with gemstones. Thick steel bands encircled her wrists over the close-fitting sleeves of her jacket. It was an obnoxious display of riches, made even more obvious by the contrast of the bright metal against her amber skin.

Gersemi faked a smile. She fanned out the folds of her robe to exhibit the silver-threaded embroidery of her rank that nearly obscured the underlying gray fabric. "To what do I owe the pleasure of your visit today?" she asked in a perfectly diplomatic tone.

Kalisfena's expression grew forlorn. "I wish I were here on more pleasant business. I'm afraid, however, that I must inquire about some troubling rumors we've been hearing about Corinas all the way up in our little neck of the world. I'm hoping you can clear things up for us."

"I can't imagine what you might be referring to," Gersemi replied nonchalantly. She pulled at a loose silver thread on her robe and flicked it to the ground.

Kalisfena's eyes darted to the discarded thread and then back to Gersemi. "Well, you see, several of our merchants have not been receiving prompt payment from some of those in Corinas. From the Conclave itself, of course, there has never been a problem. But, you see, it is the smaller customers. We have continued to extend credit as a gesture of our continued esteem, but we simply cannot keep doing so if it is possible payment won't be forthcoming for the foreseeable future." She blinked her long, black lashes.

"Goodness, that sounds awfully dramatic," Gersemi said with a small laugh. "I'm certain your people would have been paid in due course. But, seeing as how you have raised this issue with me directly, send me an accounting and I will be happy to arrange for your merchants to be paid what they are owed from the Conclave's own coffers. It will be nothing to us." That should be more than enough to send her on her way.

"That would be most appreciated, certainly." The emissary leaned forward. "But, you see, we are concerned there is a...shall we say, *larger* problem afoot in Corinas. I know you've had...troubles...with a rebellion since we last met, but it seems that the Conclave is...shall we say, losing some control over the situation."

Wouldn't you love that, you smug little bitch. "You've been misinformed," Gersemi said through a tight smile. "While we've had some upstarts making noise of late, rest assured we are dealing with them accordingly. It is nothing that should trouble you and yours."

"Hmm, yes. That is good to hear. However..." Kalisfena paused and lightly tapped a long finger against her painted lips. "There is something more. I'm sure it is nothing but a silly sailor's tale. You know how such men can be. But still, if I can be so bold, I must ask so that I might reassure my people."

"By all means," Gersemi said, clasping her hands together lest one reach out and smack the fake concern off the woman's face.

"You see, we have heard stories of an Adept no longer in your control who has maintained her Ability for longer than she should." Kalisfena tittered and shrugged. "I am embarrassed to even voice such an absurdity. It will go a long way if I can report back to my people that you, the Headmaster of the Conclave, confirmed this tale as false."

"Of course it is false," Gersemi lied.

Kalisfena tilted her head and stared with dark eyes for several long seconds. "I am glad to hear it, as will my people be." She placed her hands flat against her thighs and stood. "Well, that is all I wished to speak about today. I will send you the names of the merchants who have not been paid, and the amounts they are owed. I appreciate you taking the time to meet with me today, and for setting my fears at ease, Headmaster."

"Oh, that's too bad. I'd so hoped you could stay for a longer visit." She regretted the words as soon as they'd left her mouth, dreading what might happen if the woman were to change her mind.

"One day, Headmaster, I hope we will have the opportunity. For now, I thank you once again for speaking with me. I look forward to returning to Xeydeya with the news of our continued friendship with Corinas. I am certain it will bring great joy to my people."

"I'm sure."

Gersemi dropped her mask of pleasantry the moment Kalisfena turned her back. The emissary usually displayed a certain amount of attitude, but she'd always shown the proper deference to the power of the Conclave, as Ability was not something any other country could replicate. Today was something different. If it wouldn't inevitably spark an international incident, Gersemi would have summoned an Adept to perform a truth assessment on Kalisfena right then and there. Instead, she waited until the woman left the Public Room, as if nothing were amiss.

Back in the foyer, Enece waited where she'd left him. "Find Master Jeyne and Master Beryl," she barked. "Tell them to meet me in the Directorate's Room. Now."

"Yes, Headmaster." He managed the quickest of bows before dashing out the door.

She stood alone, considering her options. If Xeydeya —*Xeydeya!*—thought it could gain some advantage under the circumstances…well. It was time to end this rebel farce once and for all.

5

MATHIS

THIS CLOSE TO THE MIDDAY MEAL, THE BARRACKS WERE crowded with men lounging about or changing out of sweaty training gear. Most were still strangers to Mathis. Everyone kept saying that the defection of so many of the Conclave's Guards was good for the rebellion, almost as if repetition would guarantee its truth. Maybe they were right, yet he found it difficult to trust people who'd sought his death not long ago, no matter that Tovi had purportedly confirmed their loyalties through truth assessments. He'd seen the spark of recognition in some of their eyes when they'd heard his name.

He slid his newly cleaned boots under his bunk. At least they'd added him to a unit made up of long-time members of the rebellion. Lieutenant Elcy wasn't half bad, and from what he'd heard from the others, she'd more than proved herself out in the field. She wasn't some suck-up who'd risen in the ranks despite having no talent.

Levina wants to see you. Can you get away?

I'll be right there, he responded.

Alia's habit of jumping into his head whenever she felt like it had not ceased upon their arrival in Brome. *It's easier,* she'd responded blithely when he'd asked why she persisted. She wasn't necessarily wrong, though it would be nice if she gave him some choice about it. At least he no longer visibly reacted to her intrusions. The last thing he needed was for more people around here to suspect he might be more than he appeared to be.

Outside, human activity bustled underneath the thin light of the sun that had finally appeared over the cliffs. Usual rank-and-file types hurried about on tasks unknown, while a few officers, unburdened by any real tasks, moved at a more sedate pace. A long line had already formed outside the mess hall, which wasn't large enough to accommodate the population of all three barracks at once. His stomach rumbled at the reminder of food. Hopefully by the time he was done with whatever Captain Levina wanted of him the lunch crowd would have thinned.

Over in the small training area, a few units continued their morning drills despite their obvious exhaustion. He rolled his eyes at the futility of their efforts. Those aimless movements would never help them become better fighters. Their Lieutenants should stop ordering such repetitive nonsense, let their people get something to eat and some rest, and then try some more focused exercises in the afternoon.

Not that anyone would ever ask him for his advice. Even in the rebellion, only women could become officers of the Guard, and the Captains had made it quite clear over the years they would not make an exception for him. It was their loss; he'd do a far better job than those idiots over there.

Up ahead, Nyona emerged from one of the small shops that had sprouted up amongst the residences, a bulging canvas bag slung over her shoulder. She didn't notice him, and he didn't try to gain her attention. Their reunion two weeks ago had been a mishmash of awkward pauses and stilted conversation. Since then, they'd barely spoken to one another despite having decided—at least, he'd *thought* they'd decided—to try to get to know one another again, with no expectations. She'd been his friend before there was a hint of anything else, and if they could get past all this frustrating unease, maybe they could be friends once again. Maybe.

What's taking you so long? Can you not get away?

Calm down. I'm almost to the command center.

We're not there. We're at Kelda's.

Thanks for letting me know. He shook his head in annoyance. It wasn't as if he could read her mind, even if she could read his.

I'm not reading your—oh. Sorry. For once, he detected a hint of genuine embarrassment on her part before she left his mind. Their connection through Ability was so strong now it was hard for her not to read more of him than she intended. He didn't blame her for that, and he had nothing to hide. Still, he hoped Kelda's research would soon reveal something he could do to grant him some privacy.

The row of two-story buildings at the base of the cliffs were identical except for their doors. He knocked on the one with a blue door, which was three doors down from the command center's yellow.

"Come in!" someone called.

The front room on the lower level of this building served as Kelda's office, with a huge desk piled with papers, several chairs, and half-full, floor-to-ceiling bookshelves. Kelda was not there, however; she was probably off with Tovi somewhere. Instead, besides Alia and Captain Levina, he found Ciara, who also lived in the building, and Captain Jana. He darted a glance Alia's way. Would it have been so hard to say *all* these people wanted to meet with him?

"Welcome, Mathis," Ciara said. "Would you like something to drink?"

"Nah, I'm fine. You wanted me?" he asked Captain Levina. Whatever this was, it seemed best to get it over with quickly.

"Yes. Have a seat."

As he started to sit down, Hasso sauntered into the room. Startled by the medic's entrance, Mathis dropped against the edge of the chair. This time, he didn't spare Alia his glare. He hadn't seen the man since the fight in Corval almost two years ago, and him being here was something she damn sure should have mentioned to him as part of her summons. He might no longer blame Hasso for his foster parents' executions, but that didn't mean he had to like the man.

The former assassin sat down next to Ciara. She smiled and looped her arms around one of his, pulling him close. "Hasso returned to us late last night," she explained to no one in particular.

"Yes," said Captain Levina. "Mathis, how much do you know of what Hasso's been up to?"

Mathis scooted back in his chair. "Nothing." A sinking feeling in his stomach told him he'd soon be wrapped into it, whatever it was. The man's intelligence always affected Mathis's duties, and usually not in a good way.

Captain Levina raised her eyebrows. "Nyona didn't say anything about it?"

He pursed his lips and shrugged. His situation with Nyona wasn't something he was about to get into in front of the Captains.

"Hmm. Well, Hasso will bring you up to speed. I'll explain the mission after."

Mathis perked up. Sure, a clean, warm bed and regular cooked meals were nice after being on the road for so long, but he'd soon die of boredom here. A mission outside Brome would also take his mind off his fractured relationship with Nyona.

Hasso's quiet voice was the same as he remembered. "I received a report from one of my sources that Valen possessed an Adept for the first time in years. The Captains sent me up there to confirm and to see if her presence had anything to do with us."

Valen abutted a stretch of northern sea famous for its calm, making the town a common port of call for foreign merchants. Mathis had been there a few times as a child, and he remembered it as a crowded, damp coastal town that smelled of fish and brine. If that was where this mission would take him, he was far less enthusiastic about the prospect.

"True enough, an Adept was there, though I was surprised to find she was probably Tovi's age, or even a little younger. She had a minder, but she still shouldn't have been outside the Conclave."

Mathis furrowed his brow. "Why not?" Tovi had managed just fine out in the real world, despite all the threats against her. Some privileged Adept of the Conclave had nothing to fear in comparison.

"An Adept normally doesn't receive her first field assignment until she's at least ten years old," Alia answered. "Her training's not really complete until then. In the Conclave, an eight-year-old Adept would only be able to perform the most rudimentary of truth assessments, if she could do it at all."

"I watched her for several weeks," Hasso continued. "She didn't seem to do anything noteworthy; she took part in a few petition days, but otherwise remained out of sight. About two weeks ago, the Master she came with left town and headed west, toward one of our waypoints. She didn't go that far. She stopped in some little farming village and returned to Valen the very next morning. That same afternoon, she and the entirety of Valen's Guard paraded out down the eastern road. Since then, there's been no sign of the Adept."

Captain Levina nodded. "While we don't think the Adept is in Valen anymore, it's possible she still is, or that the Conclave will send someone else to take her place. We need Hasso elsewhere, so we are sending Lieutenant Elcy to Valen to investigate further. You will accompany her so we may receive real-time reports through you and Alia. When you get closer to Valen, Lieutenant Elcy will adopt the role of a merchant, and you will act as her security personnel. Neither role should prove difficult, although remember that a description of you—outdated as it may be—is floating around out there. Don't shave off that beard."

Mathis frowned. He'd been a bodyguard in truth, but a Lieutenant pretending to be a merchant was only asking for trouble. "I seem to recall a time when an officer acted as a merchant on a mission, and it didn't turn out so well," he said. Nearly two years ago in Corval, such a ruse had resulted in the deaths of his sister, Sonya, several other rebels, and the person they were trying to rescue from the Conclave. Granted, his sister's spontaneous decision to claim merchant status to the Conclave had been her own, but her choice had nonetheless proved disastrous. Mathis himself had been lucky to get out of the Conclave alive.

Captain Jana's face softened. The long scar on her cheek, once angry and red, had faded to a pinkish-white, yet it would always be a reminder that Mathis himself didn't always make the right choices. His failed attempt at a diversion had led a unit of the Conclave's Guard right to his own, and many had paid the price. "Valen is a city specializing in trade. Merchants are everywhere. Lieutenant Elcy will not bring to you the same attention as a merchant entering the Conclave would."

He shrugged, uncomfortable with the downcast atmosphere he'd created. He imagined that Captain Jana, more than anyone else, missed Sonya, as she'd been grooming her for years despite his sister's utter lack of leadership ability. "When do we leave?" he asked.

"Today." Captain Levina leaned back in her chair and placed her hands behind her head with her elbows out to the sides. "If you leave soon, you can clear the high pass before dark. We expect the mission should take about six weeks. Return to your barracks and pack quickly; Lieutenant Elcy already has her orders and will meet you when she's ready to go."

"All right," he said, knowing he had no real choice in the matter. Who cared if there was one more Adept out in the world? The rebellion's luck in finding malleable Adepts had ended with Alia, and they'd stopped trying long ago. It wasn't as if she and Tovi had made much of a difference to the rebellion, anyway. Two Adepts alone could never defeat the Conclave.

Alia accompanied him back outside. "You could have given me a heads-up about all that," he muttered.

"I know. Sorry."

He recognized her apology as sincere—a consequence of

spending so much time in each other's heads, he supposed. "It's been a while since we've had to do this from afar."

"At this point, I don't expect we'll have much trouble connecting once I find you. And I don't think that will be difficult, either, as I'll generally know where you should be."

"Still, we should set a time to connect. I don't want any surprises, especially once we're in Valen."

"Hmm. How about two hours after sundown, every third day? We can up the frequency once you get to Valen if there's a need."

"That'll do," he replied. The line outside the mess hall had diminished, and he didn't see Lieutenant Elcy loitering outside his barracks, but he didn't really have time to sit down for a meal. He'd grab something quick along with some travel rations, then get to packing.

"Kelda means to find you before you leave, so keep an eye out for her. She's with Tovi, so you'll be able to say goodbye to her, too. I take it you'd rather not have me ask Nyona to meet you there?"

Time spent in each other's heads, indeed. "Nah."

"Do you want me to tell her anything later?"

"You can tell her…" He paused. "Tell her I'll see her the next time around, I guess."

6

ALIA

"THERE IT IS AGAIN!" EXCLAIMED TOVI.

Alia opened her mind again, more for the sake of the child's feelings than because she expected to notice something. Every other time over the past few days when Tovi had claimed she'd detected a spike of Ability, Alia, far more practiced in such things from her time in the Conclave, had felt nothing at all. They were all well convinced it was nothing but Tovi's imagination.

This time, however, Alia caught a quickly fading remnant of Ability from somewhere to the north, in the direction Tovi had described. Her stomach twisted.

"You felt it that time, didn't you?"

"Yes." She smiled for the child's benefit as her insides churned.

"I *told* you so," Tovi crowed, pumping her fists into the air in a gesture more becoming of a Guardswoman than an eight-year-old child. Her dark curls bounced on her shoulders and her wide green eyes danced with excitement. "Who do you think it's coming from?"

"I don't know." Unlike what she would have expected from a trained Adept, the Ability she'd detected had been...evanescent, somehow. Might it be the missing Valen Adept, lost and injured?

Might it be another child like Tovi, born outside the Conclave and arbitrarily launching Ability into the ether without an awareness of her actions? Or—the worst possibility of all—could it be an Adept imperfectly trying to mask her activity from the rebellion? Perhaps after all this time, the Conclave had recognized the value in using methods they'd once kept secret.

Nyona's smile seemed equally forced as she gathered Tovi close. "I think that's enough for today, love. Why don't you go find Kelda and let me and Alia talk?"

"Okay. Alia. When you talk to Mathis later, tell him about that branch that almost fell on you today in the forest. Don't forget!" she admonished.

"I will." The child's innocent enthusiasm contrasted sharply with the nearly overwhelming worry that had descended upon Alia.

Once the front door closed, Nyona turned on the sofa to face Alia. "Did you truly feel something? You weren't just humoring her?"

"I did. There wasn't much by the time I caught it, but I definitely felt someone using Ability."

"From where?"

"I couldn't tell—it was that fleeting. It was almost like someone was trying to hide themselves. We should ask Kelda about it. We haven't tested what leaks out if one of us fails to mask our use all the way."

"How would she have learned to do it? It took Kelda a long time to figure out such a thing was even possible."

"Yes, but honestly, wouldn't someone in the Conclave know about the teachings in the book the Masters themselves banned? They must be aware of the technique."

"You're probably right." Nyona gripped her hands together. "But that means they could be at our doorstep, and we'd never know."

"This wasn't at our doorstep. It was coming from the north, somewhere near Valen, I think."

Nyona propped her arm on her leg and leaned her head against her hand. "That's still too close."

Alia nodded. "We should let Levina and Jana know right away. I can also contact Mathis; it's not anywhere near the time for us to talk, but I can see if he's available. Maybe he and Lieutenant Elcy can investigate to see if it might be coming from that Adept they're looking for."

"I'll go deal with the Captains now. You should stay here and monitor the area, in case it comes again. You'll be able to pinpoint where it's coming from and if it's coming from more than one Adept. That is much more important than wasting your time reaching out to Mathis. Until we know more, he wouldn't be much help, anyway."

Nyona's curt dismissal of Mathis's capabilities was curious, to say the least. Alia wasn't certain what exactly had transpired between them—she'd purposely tried to avoid reading much about it in his mind—but something clearly had gone awry. Long ago, before the Captains had split them into separate travel groups, Alia had been confident that Mathis and Nyona were paired, or at the very least headed in that direction. Now, Nyona acted as if they weren't even friends.

Alia, on the other hand, now considered Mathis to be one of her dearest friends, and she missed him quite a lot. She'd grown used to seeing him every day, and the ease of their mental communication had drawn her closer to him than to anyone else. He'd also been quick to speak up for her to those in the rebellion who feared her Sempiternal status. Since he'd left, she'd noticed the stares and distrust increase. It needed checking, but she hadn't figured out how to do so without making it worse.

Turning her mind away from such useless thoughts, she pulled her legs up onto the sofa and stuffed a pillow behind her back. This would be like monitoring for unauthorized use of Ability, something she'd done plenty of on behalf of the Conclave. It was one of the many ways the Masters exerted tight control over their Adepts. *Masters harness Ability*, claimed the edict, which prohibited an Adept from deciding for herself when to use the energy stored within her mind. If the Masters caught an Adept doing so, her punishment was swift and unpleasant, as Alia could attest to personally. And if an Adept failed to report any unauthorized use she detected, the same punishment awaited her.

Although hiding her use of Ability from anyone who might be searching for it now came as second nature, she would take special care today. If the Ability from the north was directed toward Brome, she could not risk disclosing her own reconnaissance through careless error. If she slipped at all, she opened herself up to a coordinated attack. She wasn't about to let the Conclave's Adepts overwhelm her again and turn her mind into a quivering, useless mess like they had during the botched attempt to rescue Sarabie.

That they'd been able to do it at all, even once, had been a stark lesson that being Sempiternal didn't make her omnipotent. True, a seemingly limitless pool of Ability lay within her, ready for use at the blink of an eye. And she would never lose that Ability, unlike a regular Adept, who would have passed into Seclusion long before she reached Alia's current age. Yet her advanced skill was more of a reflection of the additional experience that comes from age and, more importantly, Kelda's scholarship. It was not something inherent within Alia herself. At the end of the day, she really was no different from Tovi—merely older.

She closed her eyes and rested the palms of her hands against her knees. Measuring her inhalation and exhalation in silent counts of three, her mind calmed and focused on the task at hand. To perform a general search such as this, she cast her Ability out like a fisherman's net, controlling its slow northward expansion. She concentrated her efforts in the general area from which she'd detected the fleeting trace of Ability, then settled in to wait.

After what seemed like hours, with no more hint of Ability to the north, she let go of the effort. The risk of detection increased the longer she maintained her search, and at this point, she was second-guessing whether what she and Tovi had noticed was real. She drew her Ability back within herself so as not to cause a detectable ricochet of energy, then opened her eyes and stretched her arms up into the air, releasing some of the tension in her upper back.

Someone knocked on the front door. "Coming," she called. The door was set with an automatic lock, which she found to be quite a nuisance. It seemed a ridiculous precaution; if the Conclave attacked and got all the way to the end of the valley to this cavern, a lock would not make much of a difference. Even more annoyingly, the lock was imbued with Ability in such a way that she could not manipulate it with her own.

Marta stood in the dark passage with her hands clasped together before her stomach. Her blonde curls cascaded over the ivory blouse she wore down to the waist of her long green skirt. "I need to talk to you."

"Of course," said Alia, her brows drawing together. She held the door open as her friend passed into the house, then let it close by itself on its weighted hinge. The lock latched anew. "What's going on?"

"I'm going out on a mission tomorrow. I'm terribly nervous, as I've not been out of the mountains since I arrived. But that's not the worst of it. They are sending Tovi with me."

"*What?*" Alia was certain she'd misheard. "Did you say Tovi?"

"Yes."

"Whatever for? Where are you going? Does Nyona know?"

Marta held up a hand to her rapid-fire questions. "She's screaming at Levina and Jana right now about it, but it will do no good. Kelda agrees it must be done. They say we won't be on our own. And that we won't be gone too long—"

"What is the plan? And why is this the first we're hearing of it?" Alia interrupted, aghast that the Captains and Kelda, in particular, would be willing to subject Tovi to such danger out of the blue.

"Kelda suspects the Ability you observed is coming from the Adept that disappeared from Valen. They want us to go up there to see if we can find the source. We are supposed to act as Master and

Adept, ask around in some villages west of Valen to learn what we can, and come back. Nyona demanded she go instead of me, but Kelda said she couldn't play the role of Master convincingly because she would show too much familiar care toward Tovi."

"That's the stupidest plan I've ever heard," Alia spluttered. "Mathis and Lieutenant Elcy are already in Valen; they are far closer to where those spikes are coming from than we are. They should go look, not you two." She shook her head, trying and failing to see the logic of such an asinine decision.

"It needs to be someone who can act as an authority of the Conclave in case we find the Adept. I was a Master for a little while, remember? As much as I hate to admit it, it makes sense to send me."

"If they want authority, they should send Ciara. She was a Master much longer than you, and she has more experience than you do in pretending to be something she's not." Alia snapped her fingers. "This Adept probably would recognize you, too, and know you were with the rebellion now."

"They're not going to send Ciara out on a mission. They need her and Kelda close for counsel. And even if they did, that wouldn't help Tovi."

"Why not? Hasso could go with Ciara when he returns from whatever it is he's doing. Or someone—anyone—else."

"If we truly want to find the source, someone has to go who can detect Ability."

"Then they should send me instead," Alia said, frustrated that Marta's logic kept defeating suggestions that would keep Tovi in Brome. "I'm better able to take care of myself than a child."

"They can't afford to lose you," Marta said quietly.

Alia pressed her lips together. Marta's words rang of truth, though the Captains had never expressed it. Unlike Alia, Tovi's Ability would one day fade, and her value to the rebellion would diminish. Guilt over something Alia had never wanted nor asked for flooded her, and she picked at a chapped bit of skin on her lower lip with fidgeting fingers. "None of this makes any sense.

You've kept Tovi safe and hidden away all this time, and now they want to send her out to find what might be a hostile Adept. Any true Adept and Master would know in a moment you were not who you claimed to be."

"That's what Ciara said. She disagrees with all of this, but I think they aren't listening to her for much of the same reason they aren't listening to Nyona."

Of course, mothers would not want to send their children into danger, no matter their age, but that did not mean their protests were without merit. "There must be a way to change their minds," Alia said.

"I don't think so, especially not when Kelda supports them. Orders have already gone out to those who will be traveling with us, and we're to leave at sunrise."

The lock on the front door rattled, then clicked. Nyona stormed inside, dragging Tovi by the hand. She stopped short when she noticed Alia and Marta on the sofa. "She's told you, then." Her face was flushed, and it seemed she barely held tears at bay. "This plan is *madness*."

"Mama, everything will be all—" Tovi started, but Nyona sliced her hand through the air in a sharp gesture.

"Hush!" Tovi flinched and looked down at her feet. Alia had never seen Nyona treat her daughter so curtly.

"I take it there was no talking them out of it," Marta said glumly.

"No. None. Ciara tried to as well, but Kelda—*Kelda!*—agrees with it, and her opinion apparently carries more weight than the rest of us altogether. Even if it were a good plan, which it is not, there is no reason for such a rush. But they claim it can't wait, and that it must be you two." Her voice shook. "They even had the gall to pull rank and tell me my 'attitude' was out of line. My attitude? *I am Tovi's mother!* I don't care what they say, they cannot so easily dismiss me. Tovi will not be going on this fool's mission without me, and that's final." With that, she towed her wide-eyed daughter into their room and slammed the door.

7

MATHIS

Throngs of shoppers crowded the marketplace next to the docks, passing from one temporary stall to another filled with the wares of small-time merchants. Today's mid-afternoon crowd was larger than usual, probably on account of the morning arrival of another giant Xeydeyan trading vessel. Four such ships had come and gone in the two weeks since they'd arrived in Valen, and each time, a predictable crowd of gawkers gathered.

Mathis bit into some sort of yellow fruit he'd bought from a nearby cart. He chewed the sweet, thick flesh, then wiped juice from his chin with the back of his hand. After a few more cloying bites, he tossed what remained of it off to the side, resolved never to buy one again. A gray-and-white gull swooped down and grabbed the remnant in its beak before taking back off into the air, surrounded by others noisily vying for its catch.

He leaned against the wooden railing in front of the shop Lieutenant Elcy had insisted on visiting today. She'd already visited most of the shops in town, it seemed, all in the guise of a wealthy merchant. She claimed her visits were all regarding the missing Adept, but Mathis had his doubts. Merchants weren't the only ones in this town who might have relevant information, yet she hadn't seen fit to talk to anyone else. His role as a merchant's body-guard—and her direct orders—prevented him from doing much digging on his own.

With nothing to do but wait for his Lieutenant, Mathis resumed his idle observation of passersby. Near the cart where he'd bought his own failed snack, a young, plainly dressed boy seemed far too interested in what a few shoppers might have in their pock-ets. As Mathis considered whether it was worth it to shout out a warning, the door behind him banged open, startling away the potential thief.

Lieutenant Elcy strode, scowling, from the shop, followed by a flustered-looking woman. "Merchant Maryla," the woman called, wringing her hands. "I'm certain I can find what you seek soon. It could even be this very day! My Xeydeyan contact is most resourceful, and I'm certain…" Her voice trailed off as Lieutenant Elcy continued into the street, her dark-green merchant's robe swirling around her ankles.

Mathis jogged to catch up to her. "I see things went well," he joked.

She wrinkled her pert nose. "She wasted my time. That merchant from yesterday promised me up and down and left and right that this shopkeeper was the one I sought. She wasn't. She didn't know a damned thing."

Mathis lengthened his stride to keep even with her brisk pace. "She didn't know anything about—" He glanced around. Busy with their own tasks, no one seemed to pay them any mind, but he lowered his voice just in case. "The person we're looking for?"

She stopped in the middle of the road and held up a hand to shade her eyes as she peered toward the docks. "Wouldn't you think everyone should be off that ship by now?"

He frowned slightly at her obvious attempt to avoid answering his question. "I guess."

"That shopkeeper said no other Xeydeyan ships were scheduled to come in for two more weeks."

"So?" he asked, confused.

"If she's not on this one, then she's not coming," she muttered almost to herself.

"Who?"

"Come," she ordered, ignoring him once again. "Let's not waste any more time out here today." Without waiting for him, she continued toward their inn, maintaining with seeming ease the straight, upright posture common amongst women of a higher class. As the crowd thickened around her, Mathis had no choice but to abandon their conversation and act as a proper bodyguard. In his annoyance, he probably elbowed a few people out of their way harder than necessary.

Resentment boiled underneath his skin at the confirmation of what he'd already suspected, although he should be well-used to being kept in the dark by now. This mission obviously was about something more than finding out what happened to a missing Adept. For all he knew, that something more was the *only* reason for the mission. It wasn't as if they were making much progress with the stated purpose.

Was this why Alia had been nothing but cagey of late? Given the way they communicated with each other, she couldn't completely hide her underlying worry from him, yet she refused to admit to it. When he pressed, she claimed they needed to keep their conversations short to reduce the chance of being overheard. The excuse was garbage; Alia had long ago mastered the technique of hiding her use of Ability, and Kelda had taught him a thing or two to do on his end, too. Now, her reticence made sense. Shorter conversations meant she wouldn't inadvertently reveal to him whatever else it was about this mission he wasn't supposed to know.

A few blocks past the marketplace, their inn rose four stories above the street, taller than any of the surrounding buildings. Overlapping wood shingles, weathered and gray, covered the sides. Nearly all the inn's windows were open except for those at the top left corner. Lieutenant Elcy had demanded they keep their windows locked as an absurd precaution; no one would ever scramble their way up the side of the building to get into their room.

Mathis opened the door to the inn and surveyed the common area before they entered, as any bodyguard worth his pay would do. Only a handful of people were present, and they paid him no mind as they conducted hushed meetings at corner tables. He nodded toward Lieutenant Elcy and held the door open for her. Affecting the attitude of an egotistical merchant, she swept by him and granted the innkeeper the barest of greetings before beginning the long march up the stairs.

When they reached the top floor, Lieutenant Elcy let out a sigh of relief. His breathing was slightly elevated, though he pretended the effort of climbing four flights of stairs had no effect on him. He unlocked the door, then grimaced when a wave of heat escaped. They'd forgotten to close the curtains again, leaving their suite that much more exposed to the effects of the summer sun. He crossed the room and threw open the windows wide to allow what little cooling ocean breeze there was that day to flow inside.

Lieutenant Elcy yawned and lowered herself into one of the polished wooden chairs arranged around an ornate white marble table, then poured herself a glass of pink wine from a carafe that kept its contents chilled no matter the temperature of its surroundings. Everything about this inn was expensive, from the furnishings to the food and drink, but she hadn't blinked at the extravagance. This inn was *the* inn for the merchant class, and she'd insisted they must lodge there for their cover story. That she wasn't concerned about the cost must mean the rebellion had been saving money for far longer than he'd thought.

Now that she was relaxed, maybe she'd answer his questions. "So back to what I was saying before—" he started.

"Did you hear anything new today?" she interrupted, as if he'd not spoken at all.

Mathis bit back an angry retort. She wasn't a bad Lieutenant per se, and his time with her on this mission had been fine for the most part, but her continued avoidance of his questions today had

tested his patience. He resolved to return to his own line of questioning once he answered hers. "Another version of the story that
it's us responsible for the Adept's disappearance. I overheard it
from some citizens waiting to buy food at one of the carts."

She rolled her eyes. "Wonderful. How does this one go?"

"The way they tell it, a small band of rebels broke into the
Tribunal's estate in the dead of night and stole away the Adept."

"That's not new," she said, waving her hand in dismissal.

"I'm not finished," he snapped, annoyance building anew.

She raised her eyebrows. "By all means, then. Please continue."
She took another sip of her wine.

He tried to settle his anger, knowing it would do him no good
if his outbursts caused her to assert her rank more fully. "They say
that after we kidnapped her, we killed her and sent parts of her in
different boxes back to the Tribunal."

Lieutenant Elcy sat up straight in her chair. "What? That is
beyond ridiculous."

"Yup. I also heard a few things about Adepts in other towns
going missing, too, but I wouldn't put much stock in that. I
imagine there are just stories of Valen's Adept floating around and
catching on from place to place."

"How widespread is the rumor about the boxes?"

"Seems to be limited for now, but I imagine that'll change with
that kind of detail. People love a good story, and this one is pretty
lurid."

"The citizens here should know better than to believe such a
tall tale. We're not monsters! The rebellion has never killed children—that's solely within the Conclave's purview."

"We *have* stolen Adepts."

She shook her head. "That's different. They are on our
side now."

"These people don't know that, not for certain. I'm sure many
are convinced we've taken them against their will."

"Still. Even if they are, that should prove we aren't in the business of killing the Adepts we allegedly steal. What in the world—"

A polite knocking at the door cut off the rest of her words. Mathis hastened to the door, keeping his free hand on the hilt of the knife he carried strapped to his side. If the person outside was a legitimate visitor, seeing a bodyguard prepared with a weapon should cause no alarm. And if they weren't...

Out in the hallway stood a tall woman wearing the green robe of a merchant. Absurdly braided loops of black hair were piled atop her head, and she had more rings on her fingers than any person with sense would ever wear in public. She gave him a disarming smile. "Why hello there," she said with a slight accent. "I am looking for Merchant Maryla."

"State your name and business, and I'll see if she's willing to take a visitor," he said gruffly. Lieutenant Elcy had spoken to more than her fair share of Xeydeyan merchants in the past few weeks, but none had ever deigned to come to her.

"I am Kalisfena Tatyn, and if I'm not mistaken, her business is with me."

Lieutenant Elcy appeared behind him, nearly shoving Mathis aside. "Kalisfena Tatyn? I am whom you seek. Please, won't you come in?"

Is this the person she's been looking for? Perhaps now he might learn what was going on. Lieutenant Elcy couldn't send away her "bodyguard" without raising suspicion.

"Sit, please," Lieutenant Elcy said with extreme deference, gesturing toward one of the chairs at the table. "Thank you for coming here. I would have come to you, certainly, only I was having difficulty finding you."

Mathis squirmed at the level of obsequiousness she showed the foreign merchant. He'd never seen her act like this, not even around the Captains. The fact that she didn't bend over backwards to please those in power was one of the things he'd respected about her.

"It is no trouble at all," the merchant said with a smile, "and I think it is better here in any case. There are many merchants with whom I might meet in this inn, so my presence is not so unusual.

If I granted you—to all appearances, a merchant of no repute whatsoever—an audience…"

Lieutenant Elcy lifted a hand up and nodded. "Of course, of course. I should have thought of that."

Kalisfena Tatyn seemed to smile genuinely then, and her prominent cheekbones lifted almost to her eyes. "So. Knowing we are whom we expect each other to be, why don't you tell me your true name? Your Captain Levina did not tell me whom she would send."

"Of course, Kalisfena Tatyn. I am Lieutenant Elcy, and this is Mathis. He is one of ours, obviously," she said with a small laugh.

Mathis hoped he kept his face devoid of the astonishment he felt at the casual way in which Lieutenant Elcy had revealed their identities to this stranger, and with the windows wide open, no less. How did she know this merchant was who *she* claimed to be, and that no one else listened?

"I am pleased to meet you, Lieutenant Elcy, and you as well —Mathis, it is?" She looked him up and down, then tilted her head slightly to one side as she considered him. "I trust you have been using a different name here. You don't *quite* match the description of the person with that name for whom the Conclave has such great interest, but the similarities are uncanny."

The implied threat stood the hairs on Mathis's arms on end, yet Lieutenant Elcy seemed unfazed. "To be sure," she said. "Fortunately, as he plays the role of my bodyguard, I do not need to use his name all that often, anyway."

"That is satisfying to hear." The merchant clasped her hands before her chest in a rather theatrical fashion. "I apologize that I have kept you waiting for so long. I was away on other business and only arrived in Valen this morning."

Her apology rang hollow to Mathis, but Lieutenant Elcy gobbled it up. "I thought as much," she said with a smile.

The merchant traced an idle pattern against the tabletop with a long index finger. Light reflected from her rings against the ceiling.

"I did not expect you would arrive so soon. I do hope my people have been accommodating in my absence."

"Yes, Kalisfena Tatyn," Lieutenant Elcy said, her head bobbing up and down as if she wanted nothing more in life than to appease this woman. "Our room and board has been more impressive than expected. We greatly appreciate it. And the delay has truly been no problem, as we are not here only on business with you and yours."

"Oh?" The merchant's finger paused.

Mathis surreptitiously tried to catch the Lieutenant's attention; whatever arrangement the rebellion had with this woman, it clearly wouldn't extend to their search for the missing Adept. His efforts proved futile.

"I'm sure you know that Valen's Adept disappeared recently," Lieutenant Elcy said, getting right to the point she should never have raised. "We came early to investigate her disappearance."

Kalisfena Tatyn's finger resumed its lazy dance. "Ah, I see. And have you been able to satisfy your curiosity?"

"Not really. Most of what we've heard are rumors about ourselves—well, not about me and Mathis personally, but about the rebellion being responsible for her disappearance. We've found nothing legitimate to explain where she is. I'm beginning to think the Conclave removed her of their own accord and are trying to pin it on us. It wouldn't be the first time they've tried to shift the blame."

Kalisfena Tatyn switched to toying with one of the many metal bracelets at her wrists. "Hmm. The Conclave is loath to admit the rebellion has any Adepts at all. It is better for them that way, don't you think? If your citizens learned the truth—really learned the truth—then they'd know it was possible for an Adept's power to persist into adulthood, rather than losing this power as the Masters promised. I'm certain you can understand how...discomforting... that might be for them. I imagine it would be similar to how your man here must feel right now. He seems about to burst. Speak, if you so please." A hint of a smile played at the merchant's lips as she turned her gaze on him.

"Thanks," he said with thick sarcasm. That this woman had been highly involved in the rebellion for years without him ever knowing of her existence bothered him more than he cared to admit. "Lieutenant, what in fires is going on?"

Kalisfena Tatyn laughed. "He is not aware? You brought him to meet with me, and he is not aware?"

Lieutenant Elcy at least had the decency to blush. "It is not something widely shared. I'm not certain..." She grimaced and sighed. "Fine. I'll deal with the Captains on this. Mathis, Kalisfena Tatyn funds the rebellion. Without her, there would be no Brome. There probably wouldn't have even been a Morell," she said, referring to the town where the rebellion had originated. "We'd already planned to meet with her when news came of the Adept. The Captains decided to have me look into the latter as I was already planning to be here."

"She paid for Brome?" he said, pointing to the merchant. He didn't believe it. No one was *that* rich.

"It is not only me," Kalisfena Tatyn responded. "I am simply, as you say, the representative of a larger group."

He still didn't want to believe, but...it would explain much. For as long as he'd been a part of the rebellion, they'd never suffered from a lack of funds, even after the complete destruction of Morell and subsequent cessation of wages they'd all once received as purported members of the Conclave's Guard. It struck him now as naïve to think the rebellion would ever have had enough money on their own to build what he'd seen in the mountains.

Still—placing so much reliance on an entity outside of Corinas did not seem like the best idea. Kalisfena Tatyn and her compatriots could abandon them whenever they felt like it by crossing the ocean and turning off the spigot of coin behind them. "What's in it for you?" he demanded. Lieutenant Elcy glared at his tone, but after so many lies, he had stopped caring what she thought.

Kalisfena Tatyn tilted her head, causing the large silver earrings hanging from her ears to jingle. "We have a common goal, yes?

You are not the only ones with grievances against the Conclave. Xeydeya would gladly welcome the leaders of the rebellion in their place. So. We help." She smiled in what appeared to be an attempt to absolve his suspicions.

It didn't work.

The Captains had better know what they're doing.

8

ALIA

"Alia? Are you ready?" Nyona asked from the other side of the door.

Alia kicked away the blankets. She'd meant to get up the first time she'd woken to the sounds of movement beyond her door but must have fallen back asleep. "What time is it?" she called.

"Two hours past sunrise."

"Oh." She hadn't slept in as long as she'd feared, then. "You want to go now?"

"Yes," Nyona said, irritation clear in her voice. "Are you coming or not? I want to catch at least one of them before their day becomes busy."

"Yes, yes. Calm down. Let me change."

Nyona had been damned near impossible of late, though Alia couldn't blame her. Since the moment Tovi left over two weeks ago, Nyona's sole focus had been the safe return of her daughter. Each time Tovi reported to Alia about the mission's progress, Alia asked how she was doing, if she felt safe, and when they might come back, knowing these were the questions Nyona wanted answered most. Each time, Tovi insisted her mother need not be so concerned, but the placations of an eight-year-old girl understandably hadn't eased Nyona's tension.

Several days ago, Marta and Tovi had arrived at a small village to the north called Eads under the guise of a traveling Master-and-Adept pair. That was where they had expected to find the source of those intermittent surges of Ability, but by the time they had arrived, all detectable activity had ceased. Alia herself hadn't sensed a thing for days—not from Eads, nor from anywhere else nearby.

Nor had Marta managed to suss out any information from the villagers about Valen's missing Adept. No one admitted to an earlier presence of an Adept, and because Eads had no ties to the rebellion, Marta didn't think they would lie to someone they believed to be a Master. The villagers had also showered Tovi with an absurd level of honor, the sort normally only seen in places quite unused to an Adept's presence. Tovi had offered to do truth assessments to make sure, but they didn't dare allow her to use that much Ability so close to Valen. For all they knew, Valen's Adept was still with the Tribunal, lying in wait as part of some elaborate trap.

Last night, Nyona had resolved to convince the Captains there was nothing more for Marta and Tovi to accomplish on this mission, and that it was time for them to come home. They'd put her off yesterday, citing their busy schedules. There had been an uptick in officer meetings, especially of the upper ranks—none of which they'd made Alia attend, fortunately—yet it still seemed Levina or Jana could spare Nyona a few moments of their time. Alia agreed to accompany Nyona today in the hopes that her opinion might help sway the Captains' decision. Every day Marta and Tovi lingered out in the field for no reason only added unnecessary risk.

Dressed in dark leggings, a long purple tunic, and a jacket, Alia checked her reflection in the small mirror she'd obtained from a supply shop in town. She ran her fingers through her short hair in an attempt to flatten the spots that were sticking up from sleep, then opened her door.

Nyona paced in the common area. "Finally. Let's go."

Outside, Alia shivered despite her thick jacket. Now that summer was in decline, it took far longer for the valley to warm than it had when she'd first arrived. Maybe there was a way to use her Ability to help keep warm...no, that was a silly thought. It would take too much effort when all she really needed to do was wear more clothing. As a Sempiternal, she wasn't at risk of burning out her Ability from overuse like a normal Adept, but that didn't mean she should use it frivolously.

She sighed in annoyance. Some of the Conclave's teachings remained embedded in her consciousness no matter how much time had passed. In some ways, life had been much simpler then. As an Adept of the Conclave, she'd known what the Masters expected of her, even though she'd rebelled against it at times. They'd mapped out her whole life for her, and her responsibility to the Conclave and Corinas was clear. Had she been an Adept like all the rest, she'd be a Master by now, having given birth to a new Adept after her own Ability faded. A shiver unrelated to the cold passed through her. Now that she'd experienced a new kind of life, she couldn't imagine such an existence. The freedom she felt now was more than worth the danger inherent to the rebellion.

They hoped to speak to Levina first, as she had more influence over the other Captains than anyone else, including Jana. Fortunately, they found her in her office at the command center, perusing some papers while sipping her morning tea. She looked up from her desk when they walked in unannounced. "You're up early," she said to Alia. "I'm guessing it must be something important if Nyona managed to get you here before noon. Have you heard something new?"

"No, and that's the thing," Nyona responded, her words spilling out in a tumbling torrent. "The spikes of Ability ended before they even arrived at Eads, and they've not returned. Marta concluded that no one in the village is a threat, and they've not learned anything about the missing Adept, either. There's no point in them remaining out there any longer, where anyone might come across them and realize they aren't who they claim to be. Or worse—think that they *are* part of the Conclave and insist on escorting them back to Corval. Plus, summer is waning, and the snows will begin falling soon in the passes. We think it is time for you to order the mission complete. Alia could then tell Tovi today to start for home." Nyona took a breath and let it out slowly. Her cheeks were rosy from her rushed monologue.

Levina tapped the sides of her cup with her fingers, staring into its contents. She said nothing.

Nyona looked meaningfully at Alia, tilting her head toward Levina. "I agree with Nyona," Alia blurted before Levina could render her judgment. "Tovi and Marta have done all they can out there. They should come home."

Levina lifted her gaze, and Alia knew her answer before she said the words. "They will remain where they are for now. We have already decided."

Nyona's jaw dropped at Levina's matter-of-fact response. "Why?"

"Due to some recent developments elsewhere, I may need Marta to meet someone at the waypoint near Eads. They need to stay the course until we know for certain."

"How long will it be until you know?"

Levina leaned back in her chair and folded her arms over her chest. "I can't say with certainty; depends on what other intelligence we get." She placed both hands flat on her desk, looking between two messy piles of paper. "Now, if you'll excuse me, I need to finish preparing for my meeting."

"But—"

"Goodbye, Nyona," Levina said, her head already bent over another page.

Once they were outside and well past the earshot of the Guards at the door, Nyona turned to Alia, her face flushed and expression hard. "I should have fought harder against this inane plan in the first place. They're using her, just like the Masters would have. They don't care what happens to her."

"That's not true, and you know it," Alia chided.

"We need to speak to Kelda. They'd have not sent Tovi away if not for her agreeing to it. If we can convince her it's time for them to come back, maybe she can change Levina's mind about whatever else it is they think they need Marta for."

"Well, we all agreed someone needed to investigate those spikes of Ability to see if they were a threat. Tovi's nearly nine years old, and she's had far more training than any Adept her age. She's so strong; she can handle anything that might come her way. I certainly didn't know as much when I went on my first placement. I'm sure it was the same for you."

Nyona snorted. "When we went on our first assignments, there was not a war going on. It's different now, no matter her skill."

"What are you talking about? This rebellion has existed for years."

"Not like this. The Conclave would snatch her in an instant if they found her. Who knows what they might do. She is in danger every day she remains out there. I should have never let them send her away from me," she said, her voice breaking.

Alia put her arm around Nyona as they continued to walk. Of course Nyona would think of Tovi as nothing more than a child who needed her mother to feel safe. Maybe if Mathis were with Tovi she'd feel less anxious; despite their falling out, Nyona still trusted him, of that Alia was certain.

"There she is!" Nyona exclaimed, pointing. Kelda shuffled across the clearing toward her house, her arms filled with books. Long gray hair fell loose over her shoulders, making her appear more like a peasant grandmother instead of the rebellion's foremost academic. "Let's go."

Kelda's expression turned quizzical as they approached. "Is everything all right?"

"You need to help us convince Levina it is time to bring Tovi home," Nyona said without preamble. "They'll listen to you."

"Oh, dear." Kelda shifted her burden in her arms. "Why don't you come along to my office and tell me what is going on?"

As they walked, Nyona relayed their conversation with Levina, finishing as she held open the blue door to Kelda's residence. "Isn't it obvious that they should return? A Guard can stay back to meet with whomever they're meant to meet."

Kelda dumped the books onto her desk, catching one as it tried to escape off the edge. "If Levina's mind is made up, I can't say I'll be able to convince her otherwise."

"You convinced her to send Tovi away!"

"I did no such thing. I merely *agreed* it was necessary." She turned and placed some of the books in a rare empty spot on her bookshelves. "Believe me, I wish there had been a better option. We had little choice." She shook her head and turned back around to face them. "That said, why don't we wait for Tovi to check in today, and see if things are the same. When are you expecting her to contact you?"

"Within the hour. Do you know whom they might want Marta to meet with? That, more than anything Tovi might say, seems to be driving Levina's decision."

"I don't. I've been so busy with my research that I've not attended many meetings." She finished shelving the books. "I was going to arrange for some breakfast. Would you like to join me?"

Alia's stomach growled at the suggestion of food. "Yes, please." Nyona merely shrugged.

Kelda disappeared farther back into the house. She soon returned with Calio, the blond eunuch who'd once served Sarabie and now served Kelda, Ciara, and when she was here, Marta. "Hello," he said with a smile as he lay a covered tray on the desk with a slight rattle. The red tattoo on his right hand would forever mark him as once being a servant of the Conclave, but here in Brome, few understood what it truly meant. "It is good to see you this morning. Do you have news of Marta?"

"I'm afraid not," said Alia.

"Ah. Well, please enjoy your meal. I will let you get back to your discussion."

Kelda lifted the tray cover to reveal a typical mountain breakfast: chunks of brown bread, a thick slab of butter made from the milk of the cows kept farther down the mountainside, the small violet berries harvested from the brambly bushes in that same area, and tea. "I will say, while we would have supported Calio had he chosen a different path once he joined the rebellion, I'm glad he decided to continue to serve in this fashion," Kelda said. "I've missed having help all these years."

They ate, though Nyona only nibbled at a little bread. After Calio cleared away the tray, Alia and Kelda passed the time by chatting of inconsequential topics and Kelda's latest hypotheses. Nyona sat in a chair off to the side, peering out the window in silence.

"Alia, she's very late. Can you try to reach her instead?"

Nyona's voice startled Alia, and she looked up from the book Kelda was showing her. The simple clock hanging on the one wall not occupied by bookshelves filled with tomes of various sizes showed that nearly two hours had passed. Her brows furrowed. "You're right. She is."

"Is it really so unusual for a child to be late for something?" Kelda asked with a comforting smile.

"Tovi's never once been this late. In fact, the one time she couldn't reach me, she contacted Nyona instead."

"Yes," said Nyona. "And I've heard nothing."

Kelda gazed past Alia's shoulder. "Have they taken her, then?" she said almost to herself.

"I'm sure the Conclave does not have her," Alia blurted, glancing toward Nyona, whose face had drained of color at Kelda's quiet suggestion. "Let me reach out to her. I haven't needed to do so as she's been so punctual, but I am certain I will find her in no time. Perhaps she and Marta have found something, after all, and that's why she's late. I'm sure everything is all right."

Kelda nodded, yet her eyes remained sad. "Then by all means, proceed."

Alia didn't like that look in Kelda's eyes. She folded her hands in her lap and began.

∽

Alia drew back her Ability as quickly as she could before opening her eyes. Nyona and Kelda hovered in front of her. There was no good way to tell them this news, so she just came out with it. "Someone has taken Tovi from Eads. Marta, too, but they aren't together."

Nyona's hand flew to her mouth, her eyes filling with tears.

Kelda's lower lip twitched. "Did she say what happened?"

"I couldn't find Tovi right away, so I looked for Marta instead. I found her away from the village, toward the coast. She couldn't relay much as someone was watching her, but the gist of it was that she and Tovi were taken in the middle of the night, and separated almost immediately. She didn't get a good look at who took them, but she assumes Guards. Tovi hasn't contacted her since."

A wild, animal fear displaced Nyona's tears. "She could be dead, then!"

"Uh-uh," Alia shook her head. "She's not."

"How do you know?" Nyona demanded.

"Because I've not felt it." Alia and Tovi had connected through their Ability so often that she had complete confidence she would know if Tovi passed. It wouldn't be like when Sarabie died—they'd been actually linked at the time, making it feel as if Alia herself were dying. Nonetheless, there was no way Tovi could cease to exist in this world without some aspect of her Ability ricocheting back toward Alia as a requiem.

Tears welled anew in Nyona's eyes. "She must be hurt. Otherwise, she would have called out to me—or to you—the moment they took her."

"That's true," Alia admitted reluctantly before she fished about for an alternative reason for Tovi's lack of communication. "Wait —what if they're using maypop on her, like the rebels did with us before to keep us unconscious? There was no long-term harm from that." She hoped that wouldn't remind Nyona of how the rebels had later implanted both Alia and Tovi, yet even so, all that remained from that unfortunate experience were the faint scars at the backs of their necks.

Nyona leaned forward in her chair with her hands clasped between her knees as if she might be sick. "I knew they would find her one day," she said as she rocked back and forth. "And I let her leave, anyway."

Kelda wrung her hands. "I must tell Levina what has happened. This cannot wait."

"Of course. Do you mind if we wait here for a bit? I'll take Nyona home soon, but..." she gestured toward her friend, who clearly was in no condition to trek all the way back to the cavern.

Kelda nodded. "Stay however long you need."

After she had left, Nyona continued to rock back and forth, periodically sniffling. Alia didn't know what she could say to comfort her. Her insides twisted with guilt over Tovi's disappearance. The Captains had sent Tovi instead of her because they thought the child more expendable. Their precaution in her favor now seemed almost prescient.

"You have to tell Mathis," Nyona said in a monotone.

Alia had only recently revealed to Mathis that Tovi was out on a mission at all, and only by accident. His response upon learning she'd been trying to keep it a secret from him had not been pleasant, and she could only imagine how he would react to this news. "I will. He's expecting me to contact him later tonight."

"Tell him now. He deserves that. He loves her." Nyona's voice cracked.

The child's mother looked as if death itself might overtake her at any moment, and here Alia was wallowing in her own guilt. If this was something that would help ease Nyona's mind, however small it might be, then she would set aside her own reluctance. "Okay. I'll see if I can reach him now."

Mathis greeted Alia's contact with surprise. Sounds of a crowd were distracting him. *Is something wrong?*

It would be best to just come out with it; nothing could soften this blow. *Yes. The Conclave has taken Tovi.*

Outrage surged toward her, threatening to burst through the careful mask she maintained around their Ability. *Stop it!* she ordered, frightened by his intensity. *Calm down, or you'll expose us both!*

For once, he did as she requested—or at least enough to avoid certain disaster. *How?* he asked once he'd regained some control.

I don't know. What matters is that they were taken late last night and then separated. Marta is near the coast, west of Eads, but she doesn't know where Tovi is.

Is she…?

No.

Then where is she?

I don't know.

Then how—

I'm certain she's not dead. Trust me on this.

Mathis's attention drew elsewhere. *Hold on.* He pulled away, forcing Alia to twist the thin thread of Ability that connected them so as not to lose it. In so doing, she could see through his eyes despite losing direct access to his thoughts. They'd practiced this a few times, although today he didn't seem aware of it.

He stood on a crowded wooden dock. Several women appraised Mathis as he passed them by, and probably not because they were considering him for service on one of their boats. To his left, a large ship painted with intertwined spirals of green and black that extended into broad stripes obscured whatever activity might be occurring out in the water. It was by far the biggest vessel moored at the docks; the boat a few berths ahead of it, crawling with at least twenty sailors, was tiny in comparison. A flag with three large black stars centered against a field of emerald green flew from the ship's main mast. The flag of Xeydeya.

Lieutenant Elcy, dressed in the green robe of a merchant, stood at Mathis's side. She spoke to a tall woman with amber skin and long, braided black hair. Even from Mathis's perspective, Alia noticed the fine quality of the woman's loose trousers and belted green jacket. The Lieutenant and the stranger seemed friendly with each other; it would take more Ability than Alia was willing to expend to hear their words. She guessed this was the Xeydeyan merchant Mathis had mentioned yesterday—the one funneling money toward the rebellion.

Lieutenant Elcy gestured toward Mathis. The foreign merchant simpered at him and reached out to stroke his bicep with long, elegant fingers that each bore a silver ring. She then threw her head back in laughter before turning to shake the Lieutenant's hand. After casting a final smile Mathis's way, she walked up the plank to the Xeydeyan ship, waved once, and disappeared from view.

The Lieutenant turned a bemused look toward Mathis that quickly shifted to one of concern. He raised a finger to his temple and tapped. She nodded in understanding.

Alia had never been to Valen, nor had she perceived the seaport through Mathis's eyes until today, so she tried to take in as much as she could as they hurried away from the docks. Stalls of fresh fish and not-so-fresh vegetables, fruit, bread, and the occasional homespun craft filled a busy marketplace. Proper shops lined the sides, but with his attention focused straight ahead, she couldn't tell what they sold.

Mathis and Lieutenant Elcy entered a tall, gray building. They rushed up a flight of stairs two at a time. At the topmost landing, Mathis unlocked a door. Suddenly, Alia's vision of the world around Mathis ceased as his mental connection returned strong and true. *Sorry. Business.*

I saw, she said sheepishly. *I didn't intend to.* Annoyance flitted past her.

Where is Marta again? West, you said, near the coast?

Yes.

They're probably taking Tovi by sea, then. They'll want to get her behind the walls of the Conclave as soon as they can.

Alia nodded to herself. *Probably. That would be far quicker than going overland, and they're not likely to run into anyone from the rebellion.*

By sea it is, then.

Alia didn't like the way that sounded. *What do you mean?*

We're done with Valen. We found no true news of the missing Adept, and that merchant you saw was the one Lieutenant Elcy's been meeting with. She's gone now, so we have no reason to stay here. We will go find Tovi instead. I'll tell her the Captains ordered us to.

*What? You can't...*Alia protested, but only half-heartedly. He and Lieutenant Elcy were close to Eads, so the Captains were certain to make such an order a reality anyway. She could even suggest it to make sure they did.

Mathis's smug satisfaction at her acquiescence blended with the sharp tang of impending retribution. Alia knew that once he'd found the Guards who'd taken Tovi, he intended to leave no survivors.

9

MASTER GERSEMI

ALONE IN HER SLEEPING CHAMBER, GERSEMI ADMITTED TO herself that everything was falling apart.

They'd received nothing but bad news for months, and none of her actions in response had stemmed the tide. More and more citizens were leaping blindly into the rebellion's waiting arms, including an astonishing number of the Conclave's own Guard. After everything the Conclave had provided for those people, she couldn't fathom their betrayal, especially now that there was real work to be done.

Maybe if the Conclave could pay them more, they wouldn't be so quick to abandon their posts. The rebels must have offered them something more than vague promises of "freedom"—whatever that was supposed to mean. The notion of having to purchase her own Guards' loyalty filled her with loathing, yet if she had the funds, she would do it. They needed bodies to fight against the rebellion more than she needed her pride.

If only we had the funds, she thought darkly as she pulled the brush through her long, wavy hair. Customs enforcement, normally a major source of revenue, was down, and within the country itself there'd been a marked drop in tax collection. She blamed both on the rebels' machinations; they likely were stealing the money for themselves and using it to pay off her Guards. Her Principal Master of Finance, Ryna, had added more staff to both functions, but even if they did their jobs—instead of failing like everyone else—the Conclave could not redistribute that revenue for months. By that time, anyone whose loyalty she could buy would be long gone.

They Xeydeyans were also to blame for the empty coffers. They had significantly increased the tariffs on their exports, including for orders placed long ago. While this inimical action affected all citizens, it had hit the Conclave especially hard. They'd spent months negotiating contracts for more modern arms for use against the rebels, and they were close to running out of the basic steel necessary to replace their conventional weaponry. The Conclave had had no choice but to accede to Xeydeya's exorbitant demands.

Adding insult to injury, the Xeydeyans had slowed much of their overall trade, citing the purported "instability" in Corinas resulting from the continued rebellion. Although the rebels had caused no real trouble in the major port cities, Xeydeyan merchants had stopped making calls to most destinations except for those closest to Corval, and the frequency of their vessels had plummeted. Many of the secondary traders had followed their example, leaving Corinas's goods stuck at the docks, rotting away. The chorus of outrage from her own merchants had grown increasingly loud.

Yet all of those problems combined were nothing compared to the problem of her missing Adepts. No—not a problem. A nightmare.

Gersemi set the brush on her dressing table and stared at her reflection in the mirror. Her hair had more strands of silver than brown now, the transformation having accelerated over the past few years. Soon enough, there would be nothing left of her youthful color. A few more wrinkles appeared at the corners of her eyes, and there was no question now that the two uneven, vertical creases between her eyebrows were permanent. No Headmaster in the history of the Conclave had been in her position as long as she had, and it showed.

She slipped underneath her bedcovers and touched the glow lamp mounted against the wall, plunging the room into darkness. Despite her best efforts to fall asleep, her mind would not rest, tumbling over and over facts and circumstances that, for now, remained out of her control.

Twenty-seven. Twenty-seven missing Adepts, primarily from the north, and no one could tell her how the rebels had managed it. They'd lost the entirety of the Sixth Initiate, all girls so young they should have never been outside the Conclave in the first place. Half the Fifth was also missing, as were Adepts from the Fourth, Third, and Second.

This afternoon, Beryl had reported that yet *another* Adept had gone missing while traveling back to Corval. She'd relayed the news with stoicism when she should have been on her knees, begging for Gersemi's pardon. The Principal Master of Governance's responsibilities included placing Adepts in the field *and* returning them safely home. Beryl had failed to perform her duty almost beyond comprehension, yet the others in the Directorate acted as if she were not at fault. Of course she was! The coordinated abduction of so many Adepts—including fifteen on all the same night two weeks ago!—wouldn't have occurred if Beryl had kept a handle on their Tribunals.

After that horrendous event, Beryl should have been the one to realize the need to recall every last Adept from the field, and once again, she'd abdicated her responsibility. Gersemi had given the orders without hesitation despite Beryl's mewling protests. Never had the Conclave left the cities and towns of Corinas without the services of Adepts, but they had no choice. The Conclave required Adepts to survive, and she would not sit around and let the rebels pick them off, one by one. Because of her prompt action, their remaining Adepts would soon be safely home, and here they would stay until the Conclave defeated the rebellion for good.

Her hands balled into fists. News of what the rebellion had accomplished would soon spread throughout the country if it hadn't already. It was already well known the rebels had two Adepts, though the Conclave had done its best to squelch rumors that the traitor and the child were in any way unique. Once knowledge of the rebellion's latest thefts became widespread, however, it would only encourage people to believe the rebellion had outsmarted the Conclave. Such thoughts already percolated amongst the populace, which was why so many had abandoned their rightful government.

Where were they? It was one thing to keep hidden one or two Adepts, but twenty-seven? Jeyne, her Principal Master of Security, had been using her limited resources to search the countryside to no avail. There'd been no signs of them at all: no rumors of frightened girls in the company of rebels, no discarded white robes along a forest path, no hints of Ability where no Adept should be. Yet Gersemi wasn't ready to accept that this wasn't due to incompetence. After all, if only Jeyne had found where the rebels had holed up, none of this would have happened.

Impossibly, the rebel leadership remained hidden despite Jeyne's claim she'd searched tirelessly. She'd even sent people to look in the mountains after hearing the rebellion might operate in the area, but all that her people had found were small groups of ignorant villagers and bored Guard units chasing the same false rumors. None of her spies ever seemed to report useful intelligence.

However, Jeyne's failures gave Gersemi the perfect excuse to remind people of the importance of finding Mathis. He must know where in Corinas the rebels had absconded to—with luck, if they found him, they'd find everyone else. In the last few weeks, on her instruction, a renewed description of Mathis had gone out along with a generous reward for news leading to his capture. Perhaps if she'd done that to begin with, he'd have already been found.

She closed her eyes and took a deep breath, then another,

letting her lungs fill and deplete slowly as she tried to let go of her worry. In the dead of night, there was nothing she could do to improve their situation, and she desperately needed the refreshment of sleep.

~

What petals remained on the flowers in Gersemi's private garden had lost much of their color. Soon it would be autumn, which in a normal year was a time of jubilation. In a normal year, the city of Corval would mark the season with the three-day Festival of the Flame, which celebrated the founding of Corinas. In a normal year, the Conclave would be preparing to start Generation ceremonies for those former Adepts who had ascended to Seclusion. And in a normal year, with a little luck, most of those former Adepts would become pregnant before winter's arrival, ensuring the continuity of the Conclave's power.

This was not a normal year, as it had not been last year, or the year before that.

"I still don't understand," Gersemi said out loud.

Her Principal Master of Generation, Leyta, sipped her tea, then wiped at her lips with the back of her hand. The dark circles under her eyes were more pronounced today, and her long, unkempt brown hair and obvious exhaustion made her appear almost a peasant woman despite her robe with the ornate silver designs indicating her high rank. "Frankly, I don't, either. The first two from this Initiate to go through Generation produced Adepts without any difficulties, and Marta even gave us two. We've examined the rest quite thoroughly and can find no reason to explain these continued failures. At least there is no sign of the plague, thank goodness."

Gersemi's lips twisted at the mention of Marta, a once-promising Master and now just another casualty of the inexplicable, infuriating pull of the rebellion. "It seems to me that something is inherently wrong with this Initiate, aside from the obvious rot of a Sempiternal. You told me Marta's twins were unplanned, and then there was the whole debacle with Sarabie. It seems Kati is the only one who's given us what we expected of her."

"Well, yes, I suppose, if you phrase it that way. Still, even Marta and Sarabie became pregnant on the first try. As for the rest...we've swapped the men around, pulled some fosters back we'd intended for other uses, and even allowed more than the usual number of ceremonies. And still—nothing. I fear what will happen if this goes on much longer."

"Are you not the Principal Master of Generation?" Gersemi snapped. "It is your job to know, not fear."

Leyta plunked her cup onto a saucer with a clink of porcelain. "I'm doing all I can," she protested. "This situation is unprecedented. Never in our recorded history has there been such a lack of Generation."

"The Provenance is whole?"

"It was the last I checked." Leyta blinked rapidly. "Surely, we would well know if it were not."

Gersemi nodded her agreement. The Provenance's very existence was one of the most guarded secrets of the Conclave. Members of the Directorate only learned of it upon rising to their rank. Still, if it were damaged in any way, Adepts would struggle to use their Ability, and that was something all Masters would notice, even if they did not know the cause.

As Headmaster, Gersemi was primarily responsible for keeping the Provenance safe, a duty that extended back to the founding of Corinas and the First Adept. When she was younger, she'd gone down to check it once a month, at least, as doing so allowed her to feel, for just a moment, a hint of her former Ability. As time went on, however, she found the chore to be tedious, the reminder of what she'd lost too painful to revisit regularly. She'd sent Leyta in her stead for years, now.

Gersemi reached for her own cup. She held it in both hands and inhaled the warm scents of cinnamon and mint before taking a sip. "It sounds like you are telling me there is nothing more you can do."

"Besides keep trying? No. We can't…magic up Adepts," Leyta said, wiggling her hand in the air to indicate some inexplicable flight of fancy.

If they'd found Mathis by now, they might not be in this predicament. She was certain he could overcome whatever problem existed amongst this Initiate. Yet she was glad not to waste him on this unworthy group, all born shortly before she'd become Headmaster. Her predecessor had made many mistakes. She would not repeat them.

Shriveled petals, the useless debris from a beautiful past, dotted the dirt around the thick, thorny trunks of her garden's rosebushes. "I have decided," she announced. "Spend no more time on this Initiate. There obviously is some taint running throughout them, and quite frankly, we're fortunate your efforts have not propagated it further. We will be better off once we've rid ourselves of the whole lot."

Leyta pursed her lips. "This is a decision the entire Directorate should consider. Disassociating seventeen young women from the Conclave who might still produce Adepts seems a terrible waste."

The woman did not yet understand. "You've been trying with them for over two years, have you not?"

"Yes."

"And you have permitted them well beyond the usual two attempts, have you not?"

Leyta's shoulders fell. "Yes."

"Then there is no reason to consult with anyone else. You are the Principal Master of Generation, and you have informed me that, after many, *many* attempts at Generation, these seventeen girls could not fulfill their duty to the Conclave. We no longer need to pretend the situation will change. Get rid of them. Now."

Leyta frowned, her eyes downcast. "I can start, but it will take some time to complete. We're not prepared to disassociate so many at once. It will take several months to complete even the minimum training necessary to make sure they can lead productive lives outside the Conclave. I'll have to figure out the best way to deal with their memories; the Adepts we have in Generation cannot process them all at the same time. I will also need to find individuals to monitor them once they begin their new lives. People we can trust."

Gersemi sipped her tea. She *still* did not understand. "I will not waste what few resources we have on all that nonsense. I am not seeking their disassociation."

"What other choice is there? I can't keep them sequestered away here for the rest of their lives."

"No, you cannot." Gersemi looked into her eyes. They were the same mud-brown color as her hair. "That is why I have directed you to get rid of them."

The color drained from Leyta's face. "You can't possibly mean—"

"Make sure it is done without pain," Gersemi spoke over her protest. "They deserve that, at the very least, for their earlier service. Consult with whomever you need to and begin immediately."

"S-such a thing has not been done since the Great Uprising," Leyta stammered, the blood rushing back to her cheeks in mottled red patches.

Gersemi let out a sharp laugh. "It clearly was *not* done well, otherwise we would not have a Sempiternal running around out in the open today. But that raises a good point. If you know of any men who share any lineage with this Initiate, get rid of them, too."

Leyta's face somehow flushed even more. "Headmaster, that may very well be half of them."

"Then so be it," she said with a wave of her hand. Once they had Mathis, they'd have no need for anyone else. Her Son would ensure the strength of Adepts for generations to come. "Do you understand my orders?"

"Yes. I disagree entirely, but I understand."

"Then why are you still here? I expect a report from you within the week."

"It will be done, Headmaster Gersemi," Leyta said with a stilted formality that made her only appear churlish. She gathered herself up from her chair, loudly scraping the legs against the stone, and bustled out of the garden, her anger plain in every line of her body.

Gersemi took another sip of tea. It mattered not. Leyta could disagree all she wanted, so long as she obeyed.

10

MATHIS

MATHIS SCRATCHED UNDER HIS NOSE, THEN SPIT AWAY A flake of salt that fell on his lips. He no longer tried to keep his beard clean, as crust would only build up again within a few hours due to the near-constant sea spray.

A shadow at the periphery of his vision to the east caught his attention. Shading his eyes from the sun's glare, he peered across the waves. *Kelp. Or more sea junk.* Nothing to get excited about. He was starting to wonder if they'd ever find the child he'd once promised to protect.

In the past week and a half, they'd searched nearly twenty small trading and fishing ships along the northern coast of Corinas under the auspices of customs enforcement. None had harbored Tovi. While they'd had to chase down a few, none truly had resisted their efforts, either. Even the massive Xeydeyan ship they'd come across had paused to allow the customs officer to review some paperwork, though they couldn't actually inspect it on account of some old trade agreement with the Conclave.

He'd expressed his surprise at the ships' cooperation to the Shipmaster after their first few boardings. "Oh, they try to avoid us, to be sure," she'd said, her deeply tanned skin wrinkling around her eyes as she smiled. "But if they're caught, they know how to play the game. If they cooperate, see, we'll complete our work quickly and get out of their hair. They've got schedules to keep, and they don't want to be hung up by bureaucracy. So, they let me and mine crawl through their hulls, and their Shipmasters even smile along like idiots when we find they carry improper goods."

"Why do they even bother carrying that stuff if they're so willing to dump it?"

She snorted. "There are far fewer enforcement ships operating these days. Budget cuts, you see. And of what's left, I'm guessing a good third of us are aligned with the rebellion in some fashion. These vessels play the odds. Most of the time, they win."

A wave threw up a larger-than-usual burst of spray. Mathis wiped his face, his eyes stinging.

"Heads-up!" A sailor up the mast pointed to the east, where a small ship stood in stark contrast against the waves.

"Move to intercept!" the Shipmaster called, lifting her spyglass. Sailors hurried to manipulate the rigging and sails so their ship followed the Shipmaster's command.

With increased speed, wave after wave crashed against their hull, causing it to bounce and lurch. Lieutenant Elcy wouldn't be happy right now. She'd spent most of the last ten days in their cabin below, hobbled by pervasive seasickness.

As they got closer to the other ship, he realized that the glints he'd dismissed as sunlight reflecting off the ocean were coming from the ship itself. "Heyo," the Shipmaster said with surprise, lowering the spyglass. "Looks like we've got a live one." She handed the long tube to Mathis.

He closed one eye and focused his other through the viewing hole. His heartbeat quickened. Several women in gray robes stood against the ship's railing. Light caught at the silver designs covering their sleeves and chests. A few people in the black uniforms of the Conclave's Guard milled around on the deck behind them.

"You should probably stay below for this one," the Shipmaster warned.

"If Tovi's on that ship, it'll come down to a fight. You'll need me for that."

The Shipmaster grinned, revealing a dimple in her left cheek. "That's what I like to hear. Go let your Lieutenant know. Things could get...interesting."

"I'll be right back." He hurried to the front of the ship and half-jumped, half-slid down the ladder to the first level of the hold, the prospect of finding Tovi lending renewed vigor to his limbs. Now more than ever, he wished he could contact Alia on his own so she could scan the ship herself for signs of the child. The best he could hope for was the unlikely chance she might reach out to him herself before it came time to board. But after over a week of no contact at all, as she'd warned might be the case, he doubted he'd be so fortunate.

The deck, which was still above the waterline, consisted of the Shipmaster's quarters, a tiny kitchen and eating area, and the small cabin he shared with Lieutenant Elcy. He opened the door to the cabin, and a waft of fresh vomit reached his nose. She glanced up from the metal bucket she held between her knees, her face paler than it had been in days. "Another ship?" she asked in a raspy voice.

"Yeah. And this one's got Masters on it. Three, by my count. This could be the one."

"Three? Why would there be three out here?" She wedged the bucket between the bunk post and the wall. "We must proceed very carefully." With obvious effort, she began to stand. About halfway up, she paused and sat back down, swallowing.

"You're in no condition to do much of anything, it seems. Stay here. Next time you see me, maybe I'll have Tovi, too."

"You're not going anywhere near that ship," she said with more force than he expected given her condition. "They're looking for you, too."

Everyone kept saying that to him as if it would somehow give him pause. Yet he'd been all over Corinas for nearly two years, and no one had even stopped him for questioning. These Masters would never consider that he might be here, on one of their own customs-enforcement ships. Besides, with his full beard and ragged, wind-blown hair, he looked nothing like the already inaccurate descriptions he'd heard of himself.

"I mean it, Mathis. Go tell the Shipmaster you're sitting this one out, then come back down here."

"Sure," he lied. *As if I would stay back for this.* He cared not a whit about disobeying her, especially given that the only reason they were out here at all was because he'd claimed Alia had said the Captains had ordered it. Might as well add this minor infraction to the heap of trouble he'd be in eventually. It would all be worth it once he found Tovi. *I still can't believe the Captains were so stupid as to send her away.*

Back above deck, several of the sailors, fighters all, hunkered behind some storage crates, busy strapping knives around their calves and hiding others underneath their sleeves. His own knives were always on his person, except for when he slept, as he wasn't simultaneously responsible for manning the ship. He would feel better with a sword, but that wasn't a weapon someone on a customs ship would ever carry.

As the ships moved closer to one another, Mathis needed no mechanical assistance to see that two of the women in Masters' garb were older, probably in their late thirties or early forties, with silver decorations on both the sleeves and bodices of their robes. They huddled together with what he assumed was their own Shipmaster, who gestured toward his ship. The third Master was young, with only a few stripes of silver crawling up her sleeves. She stood apart from the others, scowling at his ship's approach.

Once the two ships came within hailing distance, his Shipmaster stood up on the lower rung of the railing. "Customs enforcement!" she called cheerily. "Permission to board?"

"This is not a merchant ship, as you can rightly tell," the other Shipmaster retorted. "This is a Conclave vessel."

"Oh, I understand you *appear* to be a Conclave vessel. But I take my orders from the Conclave, too, and my orders are to search every ship I come across to make sure proper duties have been paid. Doesn't matter if you're a local fisherman's weather-beaten rowboat, a wealthy Xeydeyan merchant ship—or one that looks like a Conclave transport." She shrugged and smiled. "If you let us on, and you are what you claim to be, then you can be on your way shortly with my apologies for the hassle."

Once, a Shipmaster would have been a true Master herself, with complete authority over everyone on her ship. That time had long passed, so they waited for the women in gray-and-silver robes to confer with one another. As the seconds ticked by, Mathis's fingers twitched against his legs. Tovi had to be on that ship. It would explain the presence of so many Masters.

One of the older Masters turned and nodded to their Shipmaster. "Permission granted," the Shipmaster called, disapproval clear in her tone. "Be quick about it."

"Not a problem," Mathis's Shipmaster said with aplomb. "Carry to."

The winch creaked as it unwound to lower a small rowboat into the water. Mathis and the rest of the boarding crew clambered down and rowed over to where the other ship had dropped its own rope ladder. The inspection team went up first, followed by the customs officer.

Mathis's stomach twisted with revulsion as he passed the Masters. The younger one with short blonde hair, glaring with her chin held up in a caricature of haughty authority, further inflamed his loathing. His lip curled, and he turned away to join the others in their perfunctory search before he said something stupid.

After a few minutes, the customs officer gestured toward the hatch. "Can someone unlock this, please?"

"I don't think so," the young Master snapped, stepping forward. "There is nothing that concerns you below."

Another of the Masters gently pulled the young woman back. "It is all right, Master Kati," she said. "They may search below. They won't leave, otherwise, absent us exercising our authority in a manner most displeasing. I don't think that will be necessary today; they are merely performing what they believe to be their duty."

"But—"

"I said, they may search," the older one repeated with some heat in her tone. "I expect we will receive a robust apology once they have." The blonde one backed off and stood with her arms crossed over her chest like a petulant child.

Six Guards accompanied the inspection team down into the hold. Mathis resisted the urge to check his weapons. His eyes adjusted to the dim lighting, revealing a small space with narrow bunks along each side, three-high, and a small collection of crates in the middle. Beyond all that was a wall blocking off whatever space remained of the hold, accessible by a bolted door.

His fingers tingled, like they did when Tovi tried to contact him. She could not simply leap into his head like Alia could, but there were signs. *She's in there. She must be.* Without hesitation, he opened his mind to the contact.

Who are you?

Mathis fled immediately from the unfamiliar connection, his heart pounding in his ears so loudly he could barely hear the useless chatter of the people around him as they searched the crates. His foolish response to his stupid fingers had put them all in danger. He hoped beyond hope that whoever reached out to him wasn't beyond that door, but he knew that to be nothing more than wishful thinking. The contact had been too strong, and too immediate, to come from anywhere else.

He didn't have time to warn the customs officer before one of the Guards fiddled with the lock on the door and lifted the bolt from its socket. Three Guards entered the room first. Mathis lingered behind, heart hammering, hoping to remain unnoticed until he could get off this boat. He should have listened to Lieutenant Elcy.

"Get moving," a Guard grumbled, shoving him forward.

Four girls wearing pristine white robes stood near the pointed bow of the ship, in living quarters richer than most would enjoy on land. Thick rugs covered the floorboards and four real beds were lined up against one side of the ship, and the opposite side hosted a sofa, chaise, and a few chairs. Two of the Adepts bore haughty expressions similar to the young Master's, while another, much smaller than the rest, was half-hidden behind them. The last one, a redheaded teenaged girl, scanned the inspection team with an assessing gaze. When her eyes reached Mathis, her lips parted.

Fires. The sinking feeling in his stomach grew.

The customs officer looked his way. He gave the tiniest shake of his head. Tovi was not here. "Thank you," the officer said to their escort. "I believe we can dispense with searching further."

"Damned right you can," a Guard behind Mathis muttered under his breath.

"Our apologies, Honored Ones, for disturbing you," she said.

Mathis turned, wanting nothing more than to leave this ship before anyone put two and two together. He hoped the others would get the hint from his haste. Fortunately, the Guards seemed more than willing to hurry them along, and soon enough, Mathis pulled himself up onto the deck.

"That's the one!" a woman cried out.

Before he'd gained his footing, several Guards grabbed him, twisting his arms behind his back. With a growl, Mathis struggled against their grip as they hoisted him upright and shoved his face against the mast. One held a knife to his throat, forcing him to still himself, as another roughly patted down his arms and legs, tossing his own weapons to the side one by one as she found them.

"What is the meaning of this?" came the outraged shout of Mathis's Shipmaster as sounds of fighting carried from below decks.

He huffed against the pressure of the knife as the three Masters peered around the Guards who held him fast. "I thought he looked familiar," one murmured. "We are fortunate Adept Kora thought so, too."

"He looks like the sort of degenerate who would be friends with Alia and Marta," the young Master said with a snort.

"Yes, Master Kati," the first Master said patiently. "Take care of this, yes?" she said to no one in particular as she turned from him.

As the Guards dragged him away from the mast, Mathis renewed his struggle with vigor. One staggered away from him after he elbowed her in the face, and he upended another onto her back. Right as he was starting to think maybe, just maybe, he'd break free, he felt a sharp pain at his neck, and then everything went black.

11

ALIA

"Nothing."

Nyona wilted at Alia's announcement of another failed attempt to find Tovi or Mathis. Ciara, who sat beside her on Kelda's new forest-green settee, put her arm around her. "I'm sure she'll find her soon," she said in a comforting tone.

Alia wished she could share in Ciara's confidence. Every day for weeks now, she'd used her Ability to search back and forth along the northern coast of Corinas to no avail. Every time she tried to push her search farther out to sea, her efforts quickly fell apart. All Adepts accepted that the energy of the ocean's waves somehow interfered with Ability, but Alia had hoped being Sempiternal might make a difference. Other than perhaps being able to push out a little farther before the inevitable occurred, it had not.

Her overland searches had been similarly fruitless. She'd checked the various travel routes between the northern coast and Brome almost every day with nothing to show for it. Once, she'd even risked sending a delicate touch of Ability toward the Conclave, as Tovi had been missing long enough to have reached Corval, but she'd encountered some sort of shielding that had caused her to retreat in a panic lest she herald her presence. Kelda had buried herself in research ever since, trying to figure out how they'd created such a barrier.

That strange shielding suggested even more strongly that Tovi was already within the Conclave's walls. Mathis himself must have realized that by now; too much time had passed for her to still be out on some ship. Soon enough, he would have to abandon his search and come home. And once he was back on dry land, she'd find him—and warn him of what to expect upon his return.

Levina and Jana had been furious when they'd learned he and Lieutenant Elcy had gone out to sea to search for Tovi on their own, and nearly as upset to find Alia had not informed them of it right away. Alia hadn't mentioned it at first because she didn't want to get Mathis in trouble for starting a search in advance of the orders she was certain the Captains would give. When they'd given those orders to someone else instead, she'd had no choice but to tell the Captains the truth.

Nyona rubbed at her temples. "She's been gone so long. I don't know what else to do. If she's in the Conclave, I don't know how we get her out unless the Captains launch a full-on assault, which they will not do any time soon. And if she's not, then that means...that means..." She looked down at the floor.

Ciara patted her hand. "Don't think of that. We know she still lives. Alia would have felt something, otherwise. You should feel fortunate to have such comfort," she said with a sad smile.

Alia's cheeks flushed at the unsaid implication concerning Ciara's own daughter. She had no way to reassure Ciara that Marta lived, and Ciara knew as well as everyone the opposite was most likely true. Having already given birth to twin Adepts, the Conclave would have no reason to keep Marta alive. Today, she hadn't even looked for her, not wanting to waste the energy on what was most likely a pointless task. Yet, for Ciara's sake, she found herself still wanting to try. "Why don't I try to find Marta this time? Perhaps I'll get lucky."

Ciara's eyes lit up with anticipation. "Oh, if you wouldn't mind—"

"Let the girl rest, Ciara," Kelda chided, never lifting her eyes from the book she was reading at her desk. "She's been searching all morning."

"It's no trouble," Alia said quickly. Frequent use of Ability didn't cause her the extreme level of weariness other Adepts experienced. It had been that way for as long as she could remember, and now she understood why. The Conclave taught that Ability was a finite resource, and that using too much could result in losing it altogether. For most Adepts, exhaustion protected them from burning out. Alia's Ability, however, would never dissipate while she lived, so her body needed no such precautionary measures. "I'll do it now, before lunch."

She closed her eyes and tried to erase the memory of Ciara's hopeful expression. If Alia had been searching for Marta only a few years ago, it would have been easy to find her on account of the connection they'd shared as members of the same Initiate. Now that Marta no longer had any true Ability of her own, that connection had faded. Her personal signature—as every Adept possessed—now differed from what Alia had known when they were children, which made finding her out in the world that much more difficult. She held no hope she would find her today, but at least she could tell Ciara she'd tried.

Accessing the tiniest thread of Ability, she cast her thoughts northward. She quickly scanned the areas she'd searched many times before, then decided to push out to sea as far as she could. Right as she was about to give up her efforts, a ping of Ability, not unlike those she'd once detected near Eads, caught her attention. It seemed to come from a spot on the ocean farther out than she remembered searching before—faint, just a coin dropping on a stone floor a thousand miles away. Adrenaline surged through her. She couldn't help but hope it might—somehow, impossibly—be Tovi.

When she sensed the disjointed Ability again, she pounced and latched on, holding it fast. It was fragile and fragmented, and she couldn't sense anything more from it before her connection failed other than that it came from an Adept. Of that, she was certain.

Another ping of Ability lurched forth. She managed to catch it at the last moment. This one had more structure to it than the last, but the signature was not Tovi's. Disappointed, yet curious, Alia carefully traced it back toward its source. At the end of the thread, she felt an acute sense of desperation mixed with futility, and glimpsed a mixture of fragmented mental images of dark and light, green and black. She tried to probe a bit more, hoping to learn who this Adept might be, but the ocean's interference shattered the connection once again.

Alia waited, and waited, and waited some more. No more pings came forth. The Adept must have finally traveled beyond even Alia's range. She opened her eyes and exhaled. "I found someone."

Kelda's eyebrows shot up. "What?"

"Marta?" Ciara asked at nearly the same time.

"No. Not Marta."

"Tovi?" Nyona chimed in.

"No."

"Mathis?"

"No," Alia said, annoyed with their rapid-fire inquiries. "It was no one I knew." She described what she'd observed. "The images were so scattered. I'm not sure they were even real, but the Adept's anxiety definitely was."

"We've been getting all those reports about the Conclave recalling their Adepts to Corval," Ciara pointed out. "I doubt the Masters have told them why. Maybe she thinks the order is unique to her."

Alia shook her head. "Her emotions were much more... visceral than I'd expect if she were only worried about some punishment from the Masters. Also, she was at the very edge of where I could reach. I think she was going north, not east."

"North..." Ciara stood with a thoughtful look and walked

over to one of the bookshelves. She ran her finger across some of the books' spines, then crouched before a lower shelf.

Kelda glanced over at Ciara as she tapped her pencil repeatedly against the desk. "I'm sure she was headed east. The ocean is disorienting. It might not have even been a true signal, but rather your own Ability reflecting back to you."

Alia wrinkled her nose. "Is that even possible?"

"Theoretically."

She wished Kelda would stop playing with her pencil. The sound set her nerves on edge. "I'm positive it was someone else. Those images didn't come from me."

"Well, stranger things have happened. I wouldn't worry too much about it unless you detect something like it again." Kelda set down her pencil at last. "Ciara, what are you doing?"

"Ah! Here it is." She removed a medium-sized tome from the shelf and flipped through the pages. "Yes, this is the one I was thinking of."

"What are you looking for?"

"Those colors Alia saw. Green and black." She turned the book around and held it out for Alia. "Might it have been this?" A green-and-black motif filled half the page, with tiny, spidery text underneath it.

"Yes, I think so," Alia said with some surprise. "Especially this part, here." She pointed to the part of the design where the spirals morphed into stripes. "Isn't that what the Xeydeyans paint on their ships?" She was not a student of livery by any means, but it would be hard for anyone in Corinas not to be familiar with the pattern cast upon the ships of their major trading partner. She'd also seen such a vessel through Mathis's eyes, when he and Lieutenant Elcy had met with that Xeydeyan merchant right before he'd gone off on his own.

"Yes," said Ciara with a pained expression, tilting the open pages toward Kelda, who had come to peer over her arm. "They've always been envious of our Adepts. The instability in Corinas might have given them the perfect opportunity."

"Wait a minute." Nyona held up her hand. "Are you trying to say the *Xeydeyans* might have Tovi?"

"And perhaps that missing Adept from Valen, too. For all we know, they might even have more. It would better explain why the Conclave has recalled all its Adepts."

"Well, now, let's not jump to any conclusions," Kelda warned. "Let me speak to Levina and Jana about this. They will have a better feel for what the Xeydeyans might be up to than any of us."

"But the Xeydeyans are helping the rebellion," Alia said, confused by the implication in Ciara's words. "Why would they take Tovi?"

"Maybe they didn't realize she was one of ours. She and Marta were out playing Adept and Master, after all." Ciara grimaced. "I do hope we have not laid the blame for their disappearance at the wrong feet. We will have lost a great deal of time if so."

Nyona clasped her hands under her chin, her expression full of worry. "If Tovi were in Xeydeya, shouldn't she have reached out to us by now to let us know she is safe?"

"Perhaps they implanted her."

Nyona's eyes went wide. "If they took her for their own use, why would they do that? That doesn't make any—"

Shouts erupted outside, and the women rushed to the window. A crowd had gathered in the clearing near the main gate.

"Is it an attack?" Ciara asked.

"No weapons," said Alia, straining to see through the murky glass.

Nyona grinned. "Maybe it's Tovi!" she exclaimed, as if the last fifteen minutes of their conversation had not occurred. She sprinted out the door without bothering to wait for anyone else.

Alia, Ciara, and Kelda were near the back edge of the crowd when Levina emerged with her arms around a tall woman with auburn hair. *Lieutenant Elcy.* With a catch in her breath, Alia scouted for Mathis. Could Nyona have been correct after all?

"Something's not—" Ciara started, then touched Alia's shoulder. "We'll be right back. Stay here."

"Okay." Alia did not wait for her and Kelda to leave before she latched onto her Ability and reached out for Mathis. There was no immediate reply. *Where are you?* she thought, confusion and frustration warring inside her.

A snippet of conversation distracted her from her search. "Lieutenant Elcy's lucky to have made it back," one woman said to another, who nodded sagely.

Alia recognized them both as lower-ranked officers. "I'm sorry to interrupt, but what do you mean, she's lucky?"

One raised her eyebrows. "You didn't hear? There was a fight on a Conclave ship. Our people got slaughtered." The woman spit off to the side. "More reason why we need to stop dallying around up here. The fight is somewhere else."

Alia's stomach dropped. "Sl—slaughtered? Everyone?"

"Not everyone, obviously. Lieutenant Elcy made it back, along with a few of her people."

"Did Mathis?"

The second woman shook her head. "They took him. That's what I heard, anyway."

"Thanks," Alia said, the words dry in her mouth. The Conclave had Mathis? Dazed, it took a bit of time to find where Ciara and Kelda had run off to. They stood next to Levina and the returned Lieutenant near the front entrance of the command center.

The Lieutenant was finishing up a story when Alia approached. "I don't know," she said in response to someone's question, and ran her thumb along a large, purplish bruise at her jawline. "Like I said, I was below decks the whole time. The fighting seemed to start pretty quickly, though, so they must have recognized him right away." Her face screwed up into a scowl. "Many people died because he wouldn't follow a damned order to stay behind."

"Might they have had an Adept on board?" Levina mused. "Maybe they did a truth assessment on the lot of them and knew they were affiliated with us before they boarded."

Kelda shook her head. "Impossible over water."

"What of the Shipmaster?" Ciara interjected. "Are we certain of her loyalties? Perhaps she told them Mathis was with her."

Lieutenant Elcy snorted. "If she did, that was a stupid move on her part, seeing as how now she's dead."

"If she was an informant for the Conclave, her death wouldn't change the fact that our entire operation might be compromised."

"Anything is possible, I suppose," Kelda admitted. "Yet I can't imagine she was not true to our cause. She's been with us for ages. And remember, the Conclave has made no secret of the fact they wanted Mathis. His description was all over the country, and it wasn't too far off from reality, if you ignored his beard. I think this was simply dumb luck on their part, facilitated by Mathis's decisions to ignore orders many times over. He wasn't supposed to be on that ship in the first place."

"How long do you think they'll keep him alive?" Levina asked Kelda.

"Not very long. He might be a Son of an Adept, but in their eyes, he's also a traitor. He might already be dead."

Alia's heart sank. This, she could not deny.

12

MATHIS

MATHIS SAT ON THE EDGE OF THE BED, MASSAGING HIS shoulder with one hand. Yesterday's efforts to break down the thick wooden door of his room had been futile, but he had no choice but to try, anyway. If he allowed himself to remain captive for much longer, his chances for survival would drop to zero.

That he was even still alive at this moment, weeks after capture, puzzled him. When the Conclave's Guard had seized him on that boat, he'd figured they'd execute him on the spot. He'd expected the same once they reached Corval. Yet here he was, alive and well. They'd not tortured him, and other than a few rudimentary questions from some of the Guards early on—which had been easy to ignore—they hadn't even asked him about the rebellion. In fact, they'd mostly left him alone.

He scratched at the fresh stubble at his cheek. Two days ago, he'd woken groggily to find himself clean-shaven. They'd obviously drugged him to accomplish that feat, though they shouldn't have bothered. Without a razor, it would only grow back. The sooner that happened, the better. At night, he could see his reflection in the windows, and he looked like a damned child.

Maybe that's an apt description, he thought sourly. He'd acted much as one when, convinced of the superiority of his own intuition, he'd walked himself and others right into a trap. If he'd had any sense at all, he would have listened to Lieutenant Elcy and remained behind on the customs ship. He fingered the still-healing wound at the side of his throat, which fortunately hadn't been too serious.

The others who had boarded the Conclave ship with him hadn't been so lucky.

He didn't like to think the only reason he'd survived the fight on the ship might be because of his true parentage. Alia had told him what the Masters did with their sons. He wasn't going to stick around to be castrated, or, even worse, turned into a stud for washed-up Adepts.

Still, no matter the risk to his person, he could never leave without Tovi. She had to be here, somewhere.

He walked over to the row of windows along the far wall. The Conclave stood at a point on the southern edge of the island city of Corval, and little of the city itself—or the rest of the Conclave—was visible from here. Some might find the never-ending view of the eastern sea's greenish-blue waters charming, but for him, it was frustrating. His room was high enough up that if it had faced the city, he could better plan how to escape.

Someone knocked at his door. The courtesy lacked any sense; he had no power to prevent their entry. He didn't respond. They knew he was there.

A latch on the door clicked, and the door eased open. A burly Guardsman, taller than Mathis himself, peered inside and glared when his eyes met Mathis's. "He's at the window," he said to someone behind him.

"Let's go, then," a woman grumbled.

The two Guards entered the room. Mathis stepped away from the window and held his arms out to the side as the female Guard patted him down. It was a stupid exercise—there was nothing in the room he could fashion into a weapon—but it was easier to let them search him than protest. He'd tried that at first, with nothing to show for it but bruises and the humiliating memory of being trussed up like an animal for slaughter.

"All clear," the woman called, as if anyone thought the result might be different.

The young Master with short blonde hair strode inside, the one who acted like she owned the place although her robe lacked the decoration the Conclave bestowed upon its Masters of rank. Mathis had heard her name several times, but to him, she'd always be the Master responsible for his capture. That was all he needed to remember of her.

She glanced about with obvious disdain, turning up her small, pert nose. "You are to be granted a great honor today. I can't possibly imagine why a rebel would deserve such a thing."

He gasped, as if this were the best news he'd had in years. "An honor? I can't wait!"

A scowl transformed her face to that of a spoiled child denied a favored toy. "I can see why Alia took up with the likes of you. She, too, lacked proper respect. Good riddance, I say."

"Who?" he asked innocently, knowing it would further anger her.

The Master sniffed. "Don't waste your time playing coy with me. We all know you know Alia. Marta, too."

He shrugged and shook his head. "Sorry, don't know who you're talking about." He snapped his fingers and opened his eyes wide. "Wait a second. Maybe one of those names *is* familiar. Isn't Alia that super-powerful Adept that decided she wanted nothing to do with you? Oh yeah, that's right. *Everyone's* heard of her," he needled.

The woman's cheeks bloomed with color and she stepped forward, her hands balled into fists. "She is *not* 'super-powerful,' she is a malcontent, and—"

"That is quite enough, Master Kati."

Mathis glanced to his left. An unusually tall Master stood just inside the doorway. Intricate patterns of silver whorls and stripes embellished her robe from the cuffs of her sleeves to the hem that almost touched the floor. Even her brown, wavy hair had strands of silver throughout. Two other Masters and a wall of Guards blocked the hallway behind her.

"Headmaster! I...I was only—" Master Kati stammered.

"I know precisely what you were doing. It is unnecessary, and, I daresay, counterproductive. You may leave."

The young Master, her cheeks even more flushed than they'd been before, bowed her head with abject subservience. "Yes, Headmaster. My apologies." She clamped her lips together and scurried out of the room.

Mathis swallowed around the lump that had appeared in his throat. At the first reference of "Headmaster," he thought he'd misheard. The Headmaster of the Conclave—the woman responsible for everything wrong in Corinas, the woman who'd ordered her Guards to kill people he knew and loved, simply for daring to want a better life—would never come to visit a rebel prisoner personally, no matter his parentage.

Yet here she was.

His head pounded as the Headmaster observed him in silence. He kept his gaze forward as her eyes traveled across every inch of him, as if she thought she'd find some sign of the rebellion hidden in his skin.

Finally, her emerald-green eyes met his own. Nearly his height, she didn't have to tilt her head up that much. "Mathis," she said with an unusual emphasis on the first syllable. "I am Headmaster Gersemi, and with me are Masters Beryl and Jeyne, members of my Directorate. I apologize for not coming sooner. I trust you have found your accommodations comfortable?"

Her pleasant tone, the sort one would use with a valued guest, set his nerves even more on edge. "I've been in worse."

She laughed with a gentle lilt. "I can only imagine. Rest assured this is temporary. Once things...settle...I hope to move you someplace where you'll have more freedom."

Mathis refused to let her fake charm discomfit him. "I'll have more freedom when you let me go."

Headmaster Gersemi smiled, her eyes twinkling in the reflected light of her robe. "Oh, I'm afraid we cannot do that. We have been looking for you for a long time. Much longer than you realize."

Discomfited by her far-too-familiar tone, he glanced away. If it were possible, he'd have sworn the other two Masters were as bewildered by it as he.

"Where have the rebels taken our Adepts?" the Headmaster asked.

He returned his attention to her, taken aback by her sudden change in topic. "I don't know what you're talking about."

"Mathis, please," she said, shaking her head. "We know you are with the rebellion, and highly placed."

He snorted. *This* he could handle. "You think I'm highly placed in the rebellion? Some intelligence you have. No wonder the Conclave is losing its grip on Corinas."

The Headmaster's smile remained in place, but her eyes tightened. "You may not realize that some here watched with their own eyes as you tried to kidnap one of our own—watched as you fought our own Guards, leaving behind your prey and companions to die. These were not the actions of someone who lacked the trust of those women who play at command."

Her barb caught in the guilt he still felt about the failed rescue attempt of Alia's friend. Sonya's decisions had bungled the entire mission, but she'd paid for her arrogance with her life. Part of him would always wonder if he might have changed her course, and the futures of the others who had died, if he'd tried harder to convince her to stick to their original plan.

Having spent most of his life masking his emotions, he was at least certain none of what he felt showed on his face. "I hear I have a common look. People get confused all the time."

"Hmm. I think you are confused to think you are common. Do you not realize your supposed friends have been lying to you? Your loyalty to them is misplaced."

"My loyalty is just fine where it is, thank you."

She shook her head, her eyes full of unwanted pity. "You poor thing. So confused and deluded. They never told you who you truly are, did they?" She held up both hands in front of her. "Of course they would not; it would ruin all their plans if you'd known. Your so-called 'Captains' depend on your ignorance. But believe you me, your place is not with them. It never was."

Confirmation of why he still lived bloomed then, and it had nothing to do with him being a "highly placed" rebel. They knew he was a child of an Adept. Of *course* they did, and it had been foolish of him not to accept this reality. In their minds, he was the Conclave's property to do with as they wished. For now, that included letting him live when any other rebel in his shoes would have been dead long ago.

Yet they appeared to have no idea of *his* own awareness of what he was.

There must be some way to use this to my advantage.

"I don't know what you're talking about," he repeated.

"Perhaps that is so, but we will save that discussion for another time." Headmaster Gersemi tilted her head to one side. "For now, let's try a different question. Where are the rebels hiding?" She asked it as if she requested the most mundane of information, like whether it was raining outside.

"Like I said. Don't know what you're talking about." He could continue saying this all day if she persisted.

She gestured lazily to the side with her fingers. The Guards behind her shuffled their positions. "I had hoped it would not come to this, but we will do as we must. You are privy to needful information, and while I'm certain that, in time, you would give it to us willingly, we cannot wait."

A red-haired girl dressed in a white robe entered the room and stopped near the protective barrier of Guards. Mathis recognized her as the Adept from the ship, the one who'd tricked him into making contact. His heart began to pound as he realized the Headmaster's intent.

He had no memory of ever having an Adept rifle through his

head for answers he'd rather not give. Alia had never performed a truth assessment on him, nor had Tovi. What would it feel like? Would it be like when Alia appeared in his mind unprompted? Or when he let her see the world through his eyes and ears? *It is no matter*, he thought, calming himself to prepare for what he imagined was to come. She would not gain access to his mind so readily this time.

The Adept closed her eyes.

A feathery presence tickled his mind. It took little effort to bat away the girl's first attempt to reach inside, as well as her second, third, and fourth. As the minutes ticked by, and the others watched the Adept with increasingly concerned expressions, Mathis grew confident she would learn nothing from him that day.

Her presence retreated. He couldn't help but smirk. They'd tested him, and he'd won.

The Adept whispered to the Master closest to her, the one with the short black hair who looked half a Guardswoman despite her silver-and-gray robe. That woman nodded. "It must be done, Headmaster."

Master Gersemi furrowed her brow and sighed. "I understand. Proceed."

Before Mathis could do much to react, Guards swarmed him. They pushed him toward the corner of the room and forced him into the wooden chair. Someone wrenched his arms behind him, and at the same time, straps cinched tight across his calves and thighs. The final indignity came in the form of a leather band across his forehead that fixed his head against the chair's high back. He struggled against his bonds as the Guards backed away.

The Adept kept a wide berth as she walked around him. He jerked as her cool fingers pressed against his sweaty temples. Before he could react much further, her presence slammed into his mind like an anchor plunging into the calm ocean's depths.

Scrambling, he threw up everything he had in an attempt to

defend himself—everything Alia and Kelda had taught him, as well as everything he could think of on his own.

It wasn't nearly enough.

The Adept tore away his protections over, and over, and over.

Exhaustion loomed.

Images of the rebels' location and details of his search for Tovi leaked from his mind in steady drips: Brome, with its cliffs jutting far above the enormous evergreen trees, the clearing before the command center, the mountain pass. Valen, the inn, the customs ship, and this same Adept, staring at him instead of Tovi. Panicked, he lashed out, desperate to stop his thoughts from escaping to his enemy. His mind tumbled with chaos as he fought wildly against the Adept's intrusion. For the tiniest of moments, it seemed the pressure in his mind eased.

Blink.

Excitement and fascination replaced his alarm. Headmaster Gersemi stood in the middle of the circle in which he sat, turning slowly. He'd never been so close to her before, and he couldn't tear his eyes away. Her robe, thick with silver whorls and scrolls, was unlike that of any other Master. He waited as she considered each of the young Adepts in the room. When his turn came, he held his breath, anxiously hoping she would find no fault. After what seemed a lifetime of scrutiny, the Headmaster smiled, and his heart nearly burst with pride.

Blink.

Youthful female chatter emanated from a large, cavernous room. The floor sloped down toward an empty platform, and Adepts sparsely filled the rows of concentric benches before it. He walked down the center aisle, glancing wistfully at the First Initiate in the topmost rows. Alia, dressed in the same stark white robes as everyone else, sat alone, oblivious of his gaze. He shivered at the sight of her bare scalp, then hurried to his seat.

Blink.

Sarabie stood naked on the platform, her pale skin augmented with patterns painted in red dye. The corners of her lips trembled, and tears stained her cheeks. In the silence, a Master pulled a red robe over Sarabie's head, while a second Master lifted a silver-and-red-jeweled crown from a velvet pillow.

Blink.

Master Marta lectured at the front of the room. She might only be newly a Master, but everyone knew she embodied incredible achievement, even if they weren't certain why. He hoped some of it would rub off on those lucky enough to be present that day.

Blink.

The alarm bell clanged over and over. His roommate cowered in the corner with her arms covering her head. Clasping his hands against his fear, he risked a glance out the door. Two Masters, surrounded by Guards, strode down the hall, barking orders to close their doors and activate the rarely used locks. He hurried to do as they commanded, his fingers shaking as he turned the contraption. Had the rebels truly invaded the Conclave itself—his home, his refuge, his *everything*? If they found their way into his hall, or *fires*, into his room, he didn't know what he could possibly do—

The visions recoiled from Mathis's mind as swiftly as they'd entered. Red-faced, the Adept stumbled away from him. Masters flocked around her, chattering in a frenzy, ignoring him as he tried, panting, to make sense of the tangle of memories that were most definitely not his own.

13

ALIA

ALIA STIFLED ANOTHER YAWN. EVERY DAY, SHE WATCHED THE waves, searched the horizon for land that didn't exist, and watched the waves some more. Other than a brief squall two days into their journey, they'd not even encountered any autumn storms that might have made life on a ship more interesting.

She'd been excited for this mission at first, and had leaped at the chance to take part. Their journey was pregnant with expectation: they would travel to Xeydeya, find Tovi, and bring her home. They hoped to find the other missing Adepts, too, though no one had made clear to her what they were to do in that event other than making sure the Xeydeyans were not planning to use them for their own purposes. Given the rebellion's reliance on Xeydeya's financing, they couldn't exactly walk in and make demands.

She'd also expected this trip would restore to her the sense of freedom she'd lost since her arrival in Brome. Her time traveling with Mathis and Kelda and the others had been arduous, but she'd become self-sufficient in a way she'd never thought possible. She'd learned to hunt, cook, mend clothing and bodies, and even fight. Not that she enjoyed doing all of that, or that she was very good at any of it, but if it came down to it, she could take care of herself now. That was not something she could have said only a few short years ago.

Yet in Brome, the Captains treated her as a precious piece of blown glass that might shatter at the smallest tremor. She spent most of her time cloistered away in her cavern abode with little interaction with others she didn't already know. Granted, when she did speak to strangers in town, they often responded with a mixture of dread and distrust. It was clear many of them would never accept her as a true member of the rebellion.

It was good to get away from all that. Nonetheless, it had proven difficult to maintain the eagerness she'd felt when they'd left Brome three weeks ago. How could she when there was absolutely nothing for her to do on this ship but wait?

The door to the cabins opened. Nyona stepped out onto the deck, tucking her hair under a band meant to keep her short curls somewhat contained against the wind. "Good morning," she said cheerfully. Now that she knew the Conclave did not have Tovi, her mood was much improved. She still worried for her child, to be sure, but the knowledge that the Xeydeyans had taken Tovi by mistake tempered her worry.

"Good morning."

"Anything new?" she asked as she sat on the bench next to Alia.

"No. It's another day at sea."

"You know what I mean."

"Still, nothing new." Alia had grown weary of Nyona's pestering on this front nearly as much as she'd tired of the journey overall. The power of the ocean absorbed and disrupted the energy of Ability, and Alia's Sempiternal status had not altered that expected outcome. Her Ability would remain useless to her until she came near land again, and Nyona's repeated inquiries would not change the plodding nature of their voyage.

"It will be soon, I'm sure of it."

"We're not even to the midpoint," Alia reminded her. "There's still lots of ocean to go. Weeks, even, at this rate. And when it does return, I can't look for her until Hasso gets a better idea of where she might be. It's hard enough reaching someone in Corinas when I don't know where they are. We're talking now about a completely foreign land."

"I know." She leaned forward and rested her forearms on her legs. "I hate all this waiting. I wish there were some way you could reach out now to make sure she's safe. Mathis, too."

"You and I are in complete agreement on that." While Alia remained confident the Xeydeyans would not harm Tovi—mostly because Kelda and Ciara and the others were so confident of it as well—she hated not knowing for certain. As for Mathis, she held no comfort at all that he still lived. She'd searched for him to no avail while she was still in Corinas, and the Conclave still maintained that strange shield she dared not cross. Yet she knew in her heart the Masters would have no reason to keep him alive after they'd mined his brain for information.

A door slammed behind them, causing both her and Nyona to jump. "My goodness," said Mila, the ship's wealthy owner. "Sorry about that. Let go a little too early." She squinted and shielded her eyes from the sunlight while her loose-fitting trousers and long-sleeved shirt fluttered in the wind. "It looks to be a glorious day. Not a cloud in sight."

"That is so," Alia agreed. Their host seemed to relish travel for the sake of it. They were purportedly on their way to Xeydeya to spend a few months in her third, or possibly fourth, home; maintaining so many residences had to involve a lot of travel, and who would go through all that effort if not for pleasure?

"Is Hasso up?"

"Yes. I saw him down in the galley earlier, though I think he's since returned to his cabin."

"Such a hard worker, that one. He's always planning his next steps before he even knows what they are." Mila waved a greeting at a group of sailors near the stern.

"I suppose," Alia said. She'd call it scheming instead of planning, but the woman's general point wasn't wrong. "You've known him a long time, right?"

"Oh, yes. Years."

"Did he recruit you into..." she looked around to make sure no sailors hovered nearby. "The rebellion, or did you meet him after?"

Mila looked at her askance. "It must be a morning for questions! I have so many myself, actually. For example, why would a sweet young woman such as yourself, *Althea*, and you, *Naomi*, wish to embark on foreign travel with a person of Hasso's...reputation? It must be quite the story, but alas, Hasso has kept your purpose under wraps, the scoundrel. I would love to hear it."

"Oh, there isn't much to tell, I'm afraid," Alia said with a small, forced laugh.

Mila smirked and lifted her chin. "I'm quite certain that is not so. Well—perhaps another day we shall have that chat. We still have many weeks of travel left to us, after all. Oh! I must go speak to the Shipmaster. Have a pleasant rest of your morning."

Alia smiled as Mila trotted toward the bow where the Shipmaster had appeared from the bridge, though it felt more a grimace. This trip could not end soon enough. It had been obvious from the moment they'd stepped onboard that Mila didn't buy their cover story or their false names.

"What do you think she knows?" Nyona muttered.

"I have no idea. More than she lets on, that's for certain. It would have been nice if the Captains had given us more information about who'd be taking us to Xeydeya."

"Or Hasso, for that matter. He never says anything about anything."

Alia rolled her eyes and nodded in agreement. "Let's go talk to him. Maybe he doesn't realize how persistent she's been. It will only get worse."

"We'd be wasting our time. He will not tell us anything he hasn't already."

"It's not like we have anything else to do today," she said with a flick of her hand.

Nyona stretched her arms up into the air. "Do what you want, but I'm staying out here. It is far too nice to be cooped up inside arguing with Hasso."

"All right. Wish me luck, then."

Alia pulled open the door to the cabins and walked up a flight of stairs. Four tiny rooms, built on top of some kind of storage space, housed Mila and her guests. Hasso's was at the far end of the short, narrow hallway.

She knocked on his door. "Yes?" came the response from inside.

"It's Al—Althea." No one else was within earshot, but it didn't hurt to be cautious.

"Come in."

Hasso's cabin was a twin of her own. The door barely cleared the chest bolted to the floor at the foot of the bed. A small writing desk and chair were similarly fixed against the opposite wall underneath a round window. Hasso sat at the desk, dressed in an uncharacteristically bright blue overcoat. If it weren't for his long, black braid draped down his back, she could almost believe he were someone else based on his clothing alone. They were all playing roles.

"What do you want?" he asked without lifting his head from whatever he was doing.

"It's Mila. She acts like she knows who Nyona and I really are. Does she?"

"Not from me."

"From the Captains?"

"I doubt it."

"Why?"

He shrugged in that infuriating way he did when he was holding something back. Before the ocean had swallowed up her Ability, she'd been tempted more than once to perform a truth assessment on him, as it had been clear from the start he knew more about their mission than she or Nyona. Although doing so without his permission would have been a betrayal of his trust—so far as that existed, anyway—a part of her wished now she'd let go some of her scruples before the opportunity had passed.

He turned his head to look at her. "Is that it?"

"You should know she will keep asking about it. You should talk to her to reinforce our story. Maybe she'll listen to you and leave us alone."

He grunted. "Maybe. Have you regained your use of Ability?" he asked.

"Why does everyone seem to think that will happen so soon? The ocean fully disrupted my use after what—three days or so? No one should expect a change until we're about that far from Xeydeya. We've weeks to go until then."

Unlike when she had had an implant, her Ability still thrummed under the surface of her consciousness, and she could access it without issue. The problem came when she tried to cast it away from her to accomplish anything useful. It felt like she imagined it would to have two perfectly good legs yet be unable to walk.

Hasso stared out the window. "I thought you might be different."

"You shouldn't have," she said, feeling more than a bit defensive. "Ability is Ability, and the ocean is the ocean. Once we get closer to Xeydeya, things will return to normal, and I'll be able to reach out to Kelda or Ciara to tell them of our progress."

"Hmm. I suppose we shall see." He raised his eyebrows. "Did you want something else?"

She flipped her hands out before her, palms up. "What about Mila?"

"What about her?"

Typical. "If you won't talk to her, what should we do if her inquiries persist? We can't keep putting her off."

"I would suggest you stick to your cover stories."

"She won't believe them."

"That should not trouble you. She can believe, or not believe, what she wants. We're not paying her to know the truth."

His cavalier attitude set her even more on edge. "What if she's working for the Conclave?"

He threw his head back with a sharp bark of laughter, which was more disturbing than anything she'd ever heard come from his mouth. "She is no agent of the Conclave. I can assure you of that."

"How can you be so certain?"

The corners of his lips turned up in a slight smile. "I just am. Now, if you would please excuse me, I would like to return to what I was doing."

She shook her head and turned to leave. Nyona had been right. Talking to Hasso was always a waste of time.

14

MASTER GERSEMI

EIGHT WHITE-ROBED ADEPTS SAT IN THE TOWER'S TOPMOST floor on red-cushioned chairs spaced apart at the points of a compass. They sat in silence, eyes closed, spinning a critical web of Ability. A young Master appeared to be dozing in the far corner. Gersemi frowned at her dereliction of duty as she scanned the Adepts for the one she sought. "Where is Adept Kora?"

The Master jumped up from her chair. "Headmaster!" she exclaimed, causing several of the Adepts' eyes to flutter open for a moment. "I was not expecting you this morning."

"Clearly. I imagine once Master Charla hears of your need for additional rest, she will assign you to a duty less...taxing," she said. That vacuous woman seemed to discipline no one, but the proper ordering of the Conclave required this one to believe she might.

"I apologize, Headmaster, most sincerely, I—"

Gersemi held up her hand to forestall whatever excuse the woman was about to spin. "Adept Kora?" she asked, annoyed at having to repeat herself.

"She should arrive any moment now, Headmaster, with the next shift."

"I shall wait, then." It would have been far easier to have the girl come down to her floor, but that would have raised more questions from others than she cared to address. She inspected the Adepts, all members of the Second and Third Initiates, once more. "I presume the situation remains the same? No one has attempted contact?"

"No, Headmaster. We would have reported such a thing to you immediately." The woman's tone bordered on insubordination, yet she spoke truth: Gersemi's question had been rhetorical.

Ever since so many of their Adepts disappeared, a contingent of Adepts had maintained a shield over the Conclave every hour of every day. If the traitor was stupid enough to try a direct attack, her efforts would ricochet and, if they were lucky, incapacitate her. After Mathis had proved his heritage to all during that botched truth assessment, they had changed the shield to allow any effort to communicate with him to go through, with proper monitoring of the conversation, of course. Jeyne hoped to use any intelligence gained to assist her Guards as they made their way toward the mountains—the place where, based on the bit of information Adept Kora had pulled from Mathis's mind, they now believed the rebels hid.

Gersemi smiled at the memory of the satisfaction she'd felt when the nattering hens surrounding her had finally recognized why she'd been so insistent on his capture. No other Son of an Adept in recorded history had ever displayed such skill. Not only had he avoided giving up anything more than the barest hints of information about the rebellion, he'd somehow glimpsed some of Adept Kora's own truths, as well. No one had yet found an explanation for how he had managed this.

The others might now know Mathis for a Son, but she still kept to herself the true reason for his strength. When she first saw him, she thought for certain someone would recognize him as her own. He was tall, like she was, with the same emerald-green eyes, the same cut of jaw, and the same color of hair as when she was young. But no one had.

Leyta, as the Principal Master of Generation, should have

known the truth. That she had not, and still did not, was another indication of how untrustworthy the lineage records were due to incompetence, sabotage, or both. Why she bothered keeping them at all at this point was beyond Gersemi. Once Mathis embraced his destiny—something that might take time after so many years of rebel indoctrination—the records would become much simpler.

Thoughts of the rebellion returned the reason for her visit this morning to the forefront of her mind. "How much longer?"

"My apologies, Headmaster, they seem to be running late. I'm certain she will be here soon, but if you prefer, I would be happy to have someone escort her to your office when she arrives?"

She clenched her jaw. She'd already waited longer than she wished to, but she didn't want to waste even more time by leaving, nor waste the effort she'd already spent climbing all the way up here. The nagging suspicion that had plagued her since the middle of the night had reached a crescendo and required immediate resolution. "I will wait a little more."

Last night, she'd woken up hours before dawn. Unable to get back to sleep, she'd read through the most recent intelligence reports again. Most were pure dreck, the product of Masters eager to report any claim, no matter how ridiculous, concerning their missing Adepts. Time and time again, these claims had proven false, so she paid them little mind anymore. One report, based on information from a former member of the Order of Extirs, the Conclave's long-ago disbanded company of assassins, was so thinly sourced it spoke only of whispers and innuendo. She'd tossed it to the side, annoyed she'd wasted her time with it.

She'd turned next to the report of Mathis's capture, which she must have read a hundred times by now. Those who had taken him had been most fortunate the injuries they'd inflicted upon him had not been serious. Otherwise, the Masters who'd overseen his capture would have met the same fate as the Guard who'd wielded the knife that had sliced into the side of Mathis's throat.

As she skimmed over the description of his injury and the follow-up report from Adept Kora, she noticed something new—

something that made her wonder about the Adept born outside the Conclave and her association with Mathis. Something that set off a cascade of thoughts that led to a conclusion she couldn't dismiss out of hand.

Could there be some truth to that Extir's report, after all?

The replacement Adepts arrived at last. They filed into the room, one by one, their eyes widening when they noticed Gersemi. They acknowledged her presence by bowing their heads as they passed. "Adept Kora," Gersemi announced when the red-haired girl crossed the threshold. "I require your service."

"Of...of course, Headmaster." The girl glanced about at her companions, but they ignored her as they flowed around her with bowed heads.

"I will not keep her long," Gersemi told the supervising Master. "Maintain the circle with an existing placement until she returns."

"Certainly, Headmaster."

Gersemi led the Adept down the hallway until she felt confident no one could eavesdrop through conventional means. "I wish to speak to you about Mathis."

Inexplicably, tears welled in the young teenager's eyes. "I apologize, Headmaster. The failure was entirely my own. I was incautious, and never have I encountered such a thing before, and he took me by such surprise, and I didn't realize what was happening until it was too late—"

"No, no, no," she said to stop the girl's blubbering. "I'm not talking about your truth assessment of him. I want to discuss the first time you encountered him, back on the ship. You told Master Kati you thought he recognized you then, did you not?"

"Yes," she said, wiping at her eyes.

"Why did you think so?"

The girl's face was flushed and blotchy, a characteristic unbecoming of an Adept, and her eyes darted back and forth from Gersemi to the wall. "I...I gave Master Jeyne a complete report when I accounted for my unauthorized use of Ability, Headmaster."

Gersemi's ire rose in part due to the Adept's recalcitrance and the rest due to Jeyne's failure to bring a disciplinary report involving Mathis to her personal attention. "Give your report again to me," she ordered in a tone that brooked no disobedience.

Adept Kora's face drained of the color it had amassed from her tears. "Yes, Headmaster. When we encountered the customs ship—well, false customs ship, I suppose—we—all us Adepts, I mean—were in our cabin below decks. I heard the boarders insist on searching the hold where we hid. Soon after, I felt a strange, weak Ability nearby. I thought it might be one of our missing Adepts, injured on the customs ship, perhaps. So I opened myself up to it. It all happened so fast, which was why I failed to ask first for permission to use my Ability.

"Before I knew what was happening, his presence surrounded me, desperate but almost...joyful? And so, so relieved to have found me. That is why I thought he recognized me. I demanded he identify himself, and his presence fled. Right after that, though, the rebels came into the cabin, and I could tell he had been the one to reach out to me. I notified Master Kati, and she took care of the rest."

Gersemi's stomach sank at her words. "The young girl you saw in his mind during the truth assessment—you sensed he cared for her deeply, did you not?"

"Yes, Headmaster," the Adept replied, bobbing her head up and down like an errant spring toy. "He panicked when I extracted those images, and that's when he..." She swallowed, leaving the rest unsaid.

"Do you think it might have been her he sought on the ship that day?"

Adept Kora's brows furrowed. "Now that you mention it, the emotional signals were similar. But that doesn't make any sense. The girl I saw during the truth assessment was no one I've ever met. Why would he think she would be amongst Adepts?"

The pebble of suspicion in Gersemi's mind had become a boulder. Adept Kora wouldn't know about this child who had somehow found her way to the rebellion. And if Mathis had been looking for her that day, and desperate in doing so, then that meant she must no longer be with the other rebels. And if she was no longer with them…

Gersemi waved her hand, distracted by her churning thoughts. "Thank you for your time, Adept Kora. Return to your duties."

"It is my pleasure to serve, Headmaster."

Alone once more, Gersemi remained frozen in the hallway. Her head swirled with frustration and increasing anger. Why had no one considered this possibility before? Why hadn't *she*? It had all been a ruse, the Xeydeyans' cessation of trade and its recall of its most prominent merchants. Their smug envoy had set this up months ago. Kalisfena Tatyn had proved Gersemi for a fool.

Her cheeks warmed as the heels of her shoes clacked against the floor. She would have words with Jeyne. Not sharing the details of Adept Kora's disciplinary report would be inexcusable in the ordinary course, let alone when it showed they'd wasted months chasing the wrong trail. And Jeyne's complete derogation of her agent's credibility…what else had that agent communicated that Jeyne had dismissed outright? What other warnings had they ignored?

If her missing Adepts were an ocean away, it would explain why no one had detected any Ability whatsoever from them, no matter how hard they tried. She'd always been skeptical of the theory that the rebels had performed mass implants; there weren't enough devices in all of Corinas to block so many Adepts' Ability.

Her instincts told her she was correct in this. Before she called an emergency meeting of her Directorate, however, she first needed to confirm one other thing.

∼

Darkened, rough-hewn stone reflected the passing of the ages in this part of the Conclave. At the bottom of fifty-three steep, wide steps, massive wooden doors opened to the Ritual Hall. No one was inside at this time of day, as she expected. Gersemi hurried down the sloped aisle past rows of curved, dark wood benches. When she'd been young, the crush of bodies packed in each row had made Ritual unbearable at times. Today, their dwindling number of Adepts left most rows empty.

Along the back of the platform, just inside the simple door that led to the venerated chambers of Seclusion, Gersemi manipulated a tiny lock using an intricate pattern known only to the most senior members of the Directorate. A hidden panel to the right clicked open.

She waited for the glow lamp to sense her presence. When it did not, she waved her arm in front of her until the lamp sprung to life. The other lamps proved more reliable as she passed, guiding her steps upon ancient stones that dated to Corinas's founding. As she descended farther into the earth, the surrounding air warmed. Moisture sprouted at her brow and her robe weighed against her as she carefully navigated the final slippery steps.

At the end of a stone path, two eunuchs—tall, pale, and far more muscular than any eunuch should ever be—stood before a silver door. Augmented by Ability, they'd been trained since birth for this singularly important role. "Headmaster," they murmured in a single voice, staring straight ahead with cloudy, unseeing eyes.

"Open the door," she commanded.

In the middle of a small, dark cavern, a pillar of crystallized stone the width of a large tree protruded from the earth, its jagged point nearly reaching the ceiling. A dull, red glow emanated from within its uneven surface, pulsing brighter in regular intervals like a heartbeat. In Gersemi's imagination, the pulses quickened as she approached.

A twinge of guilt crossed her mind. Leyta had reported weeks ago that the Provenance was sound, and although the woman had not been reliable of late, there had been no obvious signs that her assessment had been wrong. Still, the Headmaster's first duty, as it had been since the Founding of the Conclave, was to protect the Provenance. She should have come sooner.

How the Provenance had come to be was lost to time, but without it, Adepts, and by proxy, the Conclave, would not exist. Nearly everyone—including the Conclave's own residents, Adept and Master alike—believed Ability came from within. Yet without the Provenance, what Ability an Adept possessed would be as useful to her as wings to a worm.

The rough surface of the Provenance scraped against her skin as she rested the palms of her hands against it. She breathed in and out, slowly and with presence, like she used to do as an Adept when preparing to use Ability. After a few moments, warmth flowed into her hands. A remnant of inaccessible Ability within her, the tiny amount all Masters retained, stirred in response.

I know you, the Provenance seemed to whisper.

A sense of powerful acceptance enveloped her. She gasped as Ability coursed through her, and she leaned into the stone, reveling in the exquisite reminder of a time lost to her. As always, it ended almost as soon as it began. She pulled away her trembling fingers and pressed them to her lips in a gesture of gratitude.

Leyta had been correct. The Provenance was whole. And if the Provenance was whole, then Gersemi's intuition was correct. Blaming the rebels for their missing Adepts had been nothing but a waste of time.

A new plan to recover her Adepts began to form as she retraced her steps back to the surface. Her Directorate might not like what she had in mind, yet she was confident they would go along with it. They, and the very future of the Conclave, had no other choice.

15

MATHIS

GRUNTS OF EXERTION ACCOMPANIED THE DULL CLANGING OF
weapons in a pleasingly familiar way. The trainees' breath coalesced
in the brisk air, their cheeks pink from cold and exertion. As this
inexperienced group of Guard recruits hammered away at each
other with the unfailing vigor common to the young, their
commanding officer shouted her displeasure at their efforts.

Mathis hadn't held a weapon in months. He had no doubt his
own skills had diminished in that time, and he itched to join their
practice. A quiet snicker followed the thought. His captors might
have allowed him certain freedoms—far more than anyone with
sense would give to a rebel prisoner—but they'd never allow him
access to a weapon, no matter how dull. The Masters would not
have held on to power for as long as they had if they were that
stupid.

Granted, their decisions, at least when it came to him, didn't
always make the most sense. A month had passed since they'd tried
to extract information from him with a truth assessment. Given
that they hadn't gotten much of anything out of him then, he'd
expected further assaults against his mind to follow. Instead,
various Masters had come and gone, asking him about this and

that, and they'd done nothing but sigh and glare when he refused to answer. No torture. No further assessments. Just the same unanswered questions, over and over.

They must be leery about a repeat of what happened the last time. They needn't have worried. He had no idea how he'd glimpsed into that Adept's memories, and he doubted he'd manage to do it again.

Master Jeyne, the one with a Guardswoman's mannerisms, was his most frequent inquisitor. Her questions covered the same themes with each visit: how many fighters did the rebellion have? Where were they located? How did they recruit Guards away from the Conclave? Sometimes, a shorter woman with proper mannerisms named Master Beryl came with her. She tended to ask specific questions about towns and cities under the rebellion's sway, though it was easy to ignore her questions as he honestly did not know the answers.

Both women were part of the Conclave's Directorate, which only added to the mystery of his circumstances. Why would the heads of the Conclave waste their time questioning him when they could send an Adept or two and be done with it?

A blunt training sword skittered across the ground. A tall young man with white-blond hair ran over to grab it, breathing heavily. As he stood up, his eyes met Mathis's. "Sir," he said brusquely with a quick nod of his head before he dashed back to his companions.

Mathis shook his head at the absurdity of a Guard recruit calling him "Sir," though it happened all the time these days. All the regular folk of the Conclave—the Guards, the servants—treated him as if he were an honored guest. He lodged in a large room, walked around unescorted, had no apparent duties, and members of the Directorate and even the Headmaster visited him occasionally. Such perks were not the markings of a prisoner.

Whatever these people had been told about him, it certainly hadn't been the truth. He was still working out how he might turn that to his advantage. Someone had to know where they were keeping Tovi.

Someone coughed behind him. A short man dressed in a long black jacket with a silver emblem embroidered on the chest stood with his hands clasped before him. A red tattoo covered one of his hands, marking him as a servant of the Conclave. "Your pardon, Sir. The Headmaster has requested your presence."

Such false courtesy, and so unnecessary. Mathis eased up from the railing to his full height so that he towered over the eunuch. "Requested?" he said with a raised eyebrow.

"Yes, Sir." His collegial expression remained unchanged. "If you would come with me?"

Mathis nodded and gestured for him to lead the way. It might be physically impossible to lose one's sense of humor with one's testicles, but all the eunuchs he'd encountered in this place still lacked it entirely. He couldn't blame them; he imagined he'd feel much the same way in their shoes.

As they left the training grounds, Mathis couldn't help but wonder at the purpose for this summons. It had been several weeks since he'd faced the Headmaster. Perhaps this time he'd figure out a way to get her to explain why he still lived, or at least learn something to help the rebellion once he escaped.

Minutes passed in idle thought before he realized he didn't know where the eunuch was taking him. He'd expected to return to his own rooms, but he instead found himself in a part of the Conclave far grander than anyplace he'd been before. Tapestries depicting various landscapes hung along the walls, lighted from above by elongated, delicate glow lamps that reflected against the silver-tiled ceiling. A deep crimson runner protected the white marble floor. Doors alternated on both sides of the passage. Maybe Tovi was behind one.

The eunuch paused at the bottom of a curved staircase with elegant, iron balustrades. "After you, Sir."

"Where are we going?"

"As I said, Sir: The Headmaster has requested your presence.

Shall we proceed?" The eunuch held out his hand toward the stairs as if he were merely being polite.

Mathis snorted softly. His escort was safe from him. He'd do nothing to jeopardize the chance of finding Tovi, and it wasn't as if he'd worked out a satisfactory escape plan even if he had found the girl. Supposing they got out of the Conclave grounds undetected, they'd still be stuck on an island, and the Masters hadn't left him with any of his money or gear.

They continued up several flights of stairs. At the third and final landing, the eunuch touched his arm. "To the left, Sir."

This corridor lacked carpeting, and their quick footsteps echoed against the bare marble. Unlike the lower floor, narrow windows periodically punctured the stonework on both sides. He caught glimpses of both Corval and the strait separating the city from the rest of Corinas, yet their pace was such that he could not place where he was in relation to the rest of the complex.

They turned a corner. At the end of a short passage, two eunuchs with long blond hair tied at the napes of their necks and with uniforms incorporating far more silver than his escort's flanked carved wooden doors. They glared in unison at Mathis and his short companion alike.

"This is Mathis," his escort announced. "I have brought him to see Headmaster Gersemi."

"We know who he is, Enece," dismissed the left one, his frown not dissipating as he spoke. "We'll take it from here. Return to… whatever it is you do that passes your time." He yanked on one of the large silver door handles and slipped inside.

Without another word, Enece bowed and retreated the way they'd come. Several awkward minutes passed as the second eunuch stared straight ahead. Alone in this strange place, Mathis fretted over who might be beyond those doors. The Headmaster, and who else? Might there be an Adept, ready to pluck from his mind everything he knew of the rebellion?

Or someone worse?

Don't be stupid, he chided himself. *They could kill you anywhere, and they're not going to make a mess in the Headmaster's fancy quarters.* His reasoned logic did nothing to calm the sudden agitation of his nerves.

Right as he was starting to rethink his earlier commitment not to make a break for it, the door opened anew. "You may enter," the returning eunuch said in a sour voice of disapproval. He held the door open wide with his arm and leaned back against it, as if to avoid even the possibility of coming into contact with Mathis. Unlike all the other servants, this one must know his true identity.

Mathis stepped inside, uncertain of what—and who—to expect at this unusual audience. He quickly scanned the room. In an alcove illuminated by two silver glow lamps, the Headmaster sat behind a large desk so clean he doubted it ever saw any actual work. She appeared to be the only person in the room, but he doubted that was so. They would never leave him, a rebel traitor, alone with the most powerful woman in all of Corinas. There must be others hiding somewhere—probably behind those thick drapes hanging along the sides of four large windows. He could use that round paperweight on her desk as a weapon if it came down to it, or even better, that poker near the massive, unlit hearth.

"Mathis. I am glad to see you today," the Headmaster said in a friendly voice that carried no sincerity. "Please, sit," she said, gesturing to the chairs on the other side of her desk.

If he moved quickly enough, he certainly could overpower her —a win in his book, even if it meant he didn't make it out of the room alive. He eyed that paperweight again, wondering how hard he'd have to hit her head. The thought of killing someone in this fashion filled him with unease, yet he'd be doing it for the good of the rebellion, and all of Corinas.

His murderous fantasy quickly passed. Even if he succeeded, they'd just install a new Headmaster who would be certain to take swift retaliation against the rebellion. The win, as significant as it might be, would be temporary, while the blowback would be fierce. No. Restraint, for now.

He pulled back a chair and angled it so he faced the windows more than the door. She didn't seem to notice his precaution. "I apologize I have not been able to visit with you for a while," she said. "I've been busy with matters of state."

"What do you want?"

"How direct you are! Is this how you speak to your Captains?"

"You're not my Captain."

She smiled. "I find your candor refreshing. So. I shall be similarly direct. I wanted to speak with you today about your role."

"I already told you people a hundred times. I'm a fighter. That's it."

"No, no—not your role with the rebellion. Your role here, with the Conclave."

He smirked. "Pretty obvious that role is 'prisoner.'"

"It pains me to hear you say that."

"Why? Sure, you might let me wander around here and there, but I'm not free to leave. Am I free to leave?" he challenged.

She bobbed her head from side to side, her lips pulled back in a pained expression. "It is as it must be, for now. Nevertheless. You are a Son of an Adept. The Conclave is your home, not your prison."

His stomach twisted at the matter-of-fact way she described his unwanted heritage. "Never."

"I understand you feel that way now. How could you not? They took you from us when you were but an innocent child, and they told you so many lies for far too long. But you...you are special to us, Mathis. You are meant for something far greater than anything the rebellion could ever offer you."

"Freedom? Autonomy?" he snapped, all concerns of hidden attackers forgotten. "Allowed to be responsible for my own life, my own future? There is nothing greater than that."

The Headmaster tilted her head, examining him. "Oh, my dear man. They certainly have pulled the wool over your eyes. Think. When did your Captains ever grant you true freedom? True autonomy?" She shook her head. "To them, you are—as you say— a fighter. That is all. I imagine you have spent your life following their orders, no matter what you might prefer. Did they ever allow you to decline their commands? I think not."

Her words hit upon an uncomfortable truth. He'd long lost count of the number of times they'd sent him off on some mission against his will, or the number of times he'd had no choice but to follow the leadership of those unworthy of that power. But that was the way of things, and no one had forced him to remain. At any time, he could have gone off to make a life for himself somewhere else, doing...something. "Orders are orders," he said gruffly. "Your commanders here would expect the same."

"That is so." She folded her hands together and leaned forward. "Which brings me to the reason why I brought you here today. I want to offer you an opportunity you would never have with the rebellion. If what you most desire is autonomy and responsibility for your future, I suspect you will agree to my proposal. Still, you are free to decline it."

"I don't need to hear it; the answer is no." He wanted no part in whatever she was scheming. "If there's nothing else..." He pushed himself up from the chair.

"How would you like the command of your own Guard unit?"

Mathis paused, his arms half-bent, trying to digest her nonsensical question. "What?"

"I am offering you the command of a Guard unit."

He sank back into his seat. "That's not possible."

She chuckled. "I am the Headmaster of the Conclave. I can make anything possible."

He kept his expression impassive as he worked over her words in his mind. Men could fight, support logistics, and sometimes act as advisors is they were lucky, but they were never in command. Ever.

"I see I have piqued your interest, have I not? I know it is most unusual, and doubly so given your past affiliation with the rebels. But the truth of the matter is, we are short on individuals with leadership potential right now. I understand you've been spending a lot of time at the training grounds, yes? I'm sure you've noticed we have a great number of new recruits, and we don't have enough commanders here to supervise them all. So, I would like you to take one on. It would be a Lieutenancy, at the start, with the possibility of the usual advancement if you do well, which I'm certain will be the case. One day, you could even make Captain."

He blinked several times. "This…this is the stupidest thing I've ever heard."

"Nonsense! We know you are a talented fighter. I'm certain you'll be able to teach our recruits a thing or two," she said with a small smile.

"A command isn't only about fighting."

"Would you follow someone who could not? Still, your capabilities in combat are not the only reason I am offering you a command. It is clear to me you possess the innate traits of leadership. One cannot learn how to be a leader; one either is, or is not. You are the former, and I do not wish to waste your talents."

His mind whirled. As a child, he'd dreamed of having a command one day, as all boys were wont to do until they learned better. When he'd joined the rebellion, he'd hoped they would be different, but they, too, adhered to traditional roles. That they did so infuriated him, given that his younger sister Sonya had moved up the ranks despite her quick temper and rash behavior. Had she not died because of her utter lack of sense, she'd probably be a Captain by now. And Mathis would still be a fighter. Or, at best, a bodyguard to a couple of Adepts.

The Headmaster was not wrong. The rebels would never offer him this.

What are you even thinking? Only a fool would believe this woman's lies. There was no way the Masters would allow him any say over their own Guard.

*Even so…*Nothing of his experience here had been to his expectation. Fires, he was still alive!

*Still…*This must be an attempt to turn his loyalty. They must think him spineless; he would never, ever do something that could harm his friends. Training Conclave Guards, who might one day fight against them, would do just that.

Then again... He didn't have to train them well. And spending more time around fighters would allow him to refresh his own rusty skills and gain intelligence the rebellion might use against the Conclave later on. Plus, he might get access to other areas of the complex—and perhaps even outside of it. No Guard unit could properly train in what he'd seen of the Conclave's small training grounds. And if he gained the trust of those in his command, he could use them to help locate Tovi—and then finally, finally get out of this place.

"I can tell you have much to think on. Please, take as much time as you need to decide."

He smiled, and it wasn't entirely faked. "No need. I've decided."

16

ALIA

WHAT HAD BEEN MERELY DOTS OF LIGHT AGAINST A SMUDGE of shadow along the horizon only hours ago had materialized as individual structures built amidst green hills. The buildings were stranger than any Alia had ever seen, with squared-off corners and of a gray-and-blue color that reflected sunlight almost like metal. They crowded together and jutted impossibly high into the air. Shorter versions of the same lined the docks, clean and gleaming. She saw nothing like the dilapidated shacks she expected that offered temporary comfort to sailors or warehoused goods in transit.

So, this is Xeydeya. After weeks at sea, they'd reached their destination. Xeydeya's capital and primary port city, Amrava, was not at all what she expected, either. The country was important to Corinas on account of its natural resources, but back home, it wasn't thought of as being particularly sophisticated beyond its capacity for trade. Yet as they approached the crowded docks, packed with ships bearing the green-and-black livery of Xeydeya in addition to many she didn't recognize, she realized her understanding of this place—likely nothing more than the product of the Conclave's inflated view of its own superiority—was incorrect.

Alia stood up straight and exhaled as anxiety warred with anticipation inside her chest. She could not wait to get off this damned ship. Even now, with land so tantalizingly close, her Ability remained unusable. When they'd left Corinas, the ocean had interfered with her use of Ability in fits and spurts before disrupting it completely. She'd expected the reverse process to occur as they neared Xeydeya, but it had not. Nyona fretted about this almost as much as Alia, but she was certain that once Alia's feet were back on solid ground, everything would return to normal. Alia wished she could be as certain as her friend. *I guess I'll find out soon enough.*

Nyona, dressed in the same style of loose trousers, long shirt, and belted jacket Mila swore was appropriate in Xeydeya, joined her at the railing. "We should be docking soon."

"I hope so. What do you make of those buildings? I've never seen anything like them."

"Me, neither. They're so close together. I wonder what they're made of?"

"Steel and glass," Hasso said from behind them.

Alia's jaw dropped slightly, the shock of his pronouncement overwhelming the irritation she might have otherwise felt at him sneaking up unannounced. "*Fires.* That is glass? How did they make it so smooth? How did they keep the glass from shattering? And all that steel—even those squatty ones must have cost a fortune. How in the world could they ever afford it?"

"Ask Mila."

She wrinkled her nose. Not having to deal with the ship-owner and her prying questions anymore was another reason she couldn't wait to disembark. "I don't need to know that badly. I just can't believe I've never heard of this before. Our own merchants come here, do they not? And people like Mila."

The corner of his mouth twitched, though his pale blue eyes remained impassive. "The Conclave wants its citizens to believe that Corinas is the most advanced society in the world because it has Adepts. They have the means to make sure word that this is not exactly the case does not spread."

A horn from somewhere in the harbor sounded a sharp pattern, then repeated it, interrupting their conversation. "Commence docking!" shouted the Shipmaster. "Berth forty-three!" She rushed to get out of the way of the sailors scurrying to follow the Shipmaster's commands. The ship slowed as it approached an open berth tucked between two Xeydeyan giants with masts three times the height of their own and massive, cream-colored sails that could envelope an entire building. How easy it must have been to hide someone as small as Tovi in a vessel like that!

Their ship thudded into the dock, causing Alia to fall sideways into Nyona. She blushed as she regained her footing, as no one else seemed so unbalanced. Hasso had remained near the railing with his arms crossed against his body, and neither the Shipmaster nor Mila stood near anything that could have provided them with support even if they'd wanted it.

Mila caught Alia's glance, and to her chagrin, appeared to take it for an invitation to join them. "Good morning to you both. Welcome to Amrava. Are you ready to disembark?"

"Yes," replied Nyona. "I'm looking forward to walking on land again."

"Althea," Mila said, looking to Alia, "do be careful when you take your first steps out there. After so much time out at sea, your balance likely will be compromised." She smiled. "Some people fall flat on their faces."

"Thanks for the warning," Alia said, annoyed at the insinuation—likely accurate as it was—that she wouldn't stay upright.

"Can I ask you a question?" Nyona asked Mila, which only annoyed Alia further. The sooner they got away from her, the better. She shot Nyona a glare, but Nyona had turned to gesture at the cityscape. "Those glass buildings. They must have been incredibly expensive. Do you know how they built so many?"

"It's all relative. In Corinas, where we lack our own steel and those who know how to work it, creating buildings like these would be beyond impractical. Here, where steel is plentiful, they've developed methods for its use we can only imagine. We've tried for as long as I can remember to get them to share their techniques, but while they are free in trading their materials, the Xeydeyans have so far rebuffed our entreaties for practical knowledge. The same goes for glass. Someday, someone might get them to change their minds, but as it is now, you won't see buildings like this anywhere else."

Nyona shook her head. "Can you imagine someone trying to build something so tall of stone? Or even wood?"

Alia snorted. "The Conclave's towers are the tallest buildings I've ever seen before today, and those are still minuscule compared to these."

Mila raised her eyebrows. "So, you've been to Corval, have you, Althea?"

Alia pursed her lips. It was one thing for Mila to suspect Alia wasn't who she claimed to be, but another thing entirely for Alia to drop hints suggesting her true background. "A long time ago. It is the capital, after all," she said with a small shrug. "It looks like we're about ready to go. I will check in with Hasso." She felt a moment of guilt for leaving Nyona alone with Mila, but it was short-lived. Nyona could hold her own.

"See that woman over there?" Hasso said as she joined him at the railing.

"Which one?"

"The tall one with the braided hair."

"That doesn't help." Braids seemed to be a common hairstyle here; for once, Hasso's own long, black braid would blend right in.

He gestured with a slender hand. "The one in the blue jacket who's coming our way. That's our escort. She's a member of the Xeydeyan government." The woman he referred to wore pants that flowed around her ankles, similar to those Alia wore, except that the merchant's long, blue jacket, belted at the waist with a silver buckle, appeared far finer than Alia's shorter version. Her dark hair was piled atop her head in a wide, braided stack several inches tall.

As she navigated through the crowd toward them, she carried herself with a grace in sharp contrast to the bombastic activity of the sailors and dock workers around her.

A sharp intake of breath parted Alia's lips. "I know her!"

Hasso turned toward her, his brow furrowed. "How? From the Conclave?"

She dropped her voice to a near-whisper. "No. I saw her when Mathis and Lieutenant Elcy met with her in Valen a few months ago. Through his eyes," she clarified, when it became obvious her words had only further confused him. "Mathis said she was helping fund the rebellion. Is she going to help us find Tovi?"

His expression softened. "I'm told that's the plan."

Two dock workers shoved a gangplank toward their ship. Mila was the first one off, with Nyona close behind her. As they shook hands with the Xeydeyan envoy, several thick bracelets made of a gray metal protruded from below the sleeves of her jacket. Light glinted from the additional jewelry on each of her fingers.

"Let's go," Hasso said.

Anticipation welled anew as she followed him toward the gangplank, yet all thoughts of testing her Ability fled upon her first steps on the dock. The movement caused such a wave of nausea that she felt the color drain from her face, and she focused on her emergent desire to avoid throwing up in front of everyone.

"Oh, my. Is everything all right, my dear?" the envoy said, concern etched in the small lines around her eyes.

"Yes," Alia lied, swallowing. She held a hand out toward Nyona for support.

"You poor thing. It must be quite disconcerting for you right now. Let us walk. Moving will help you adjust, you'll see."

Alia acquiesced, not wanting to risk opening her mouth again. Nyona looked at her expectantly, but Alia shook her head, setting off another wave of nausea. Until her mind and stomach came into accord, there would be no chance of using her Ability.

Mila introduced their party. "Kalisfena Tatyn, you know Hasso. Our other friends here are Naomi and Althea."

"Althea?"

"That's what she said," Hasso responded dryly.

The merchant laughed, a lilting, flirtatious sound. "Hasso, you have not changed one bit," she said. "Well—Althea and Naomi—I am pleased to make your acquaintance, no matter what you are called. You may call me Kalisfena. We are friends now, you see, and friends never insist on formalities."

Alia glanced toward Hasso, but he paid her no mind. As someone who'd been helping the rebellion all along, it would not be surprising if Kalisfena knew their true identities, but still, it would have been nice if Hasso had told them what to expect—and how much information might be safe to divulge. It would be naïve to assume there weren't people here in Xeydeya interested in currying the Masters' favor. Alia's capture would mean more to them than a thousand Mathises.

Leaving the docks behind, they turned onto a straight, wide street. Instead of dirt or cobbles or even wooden slats, this street consisted of a smooth, gray substance with elevated platforms on either side that looked to be of the same material. Carts and horses moved down the middle of the street while people, mostly Xeydeyan, walked along the raised sides, safe from traffic. Tall and elegant to a person, Alia felt small and ungainly in comparison, and her slowly recovering balance didn't help.

The street became more crowded the farther they traveled into the city. Street noise drowned out Mila and Kalisfena's conversation even though they walked only a few paces ahead of her. At one corner, what seemed to be an endless flow of carts forced them to wait before crossing the road. Feeling a little better, Alia decided to test her Ability before they moved again. She gathered a tiny thread from within and tried to cast it toward Nyona.

Nothing happened.

It took a moment for her to recognize her failure. She was on land, and nowhere near water. *You're still disoriented*, she reassured herself. *Try again*. She did.

Then again, and again, and again.

She stepped into the street, mindlessly following the others. A dull sense of shock somehow kept sheer panic at bay. Something was wrong—terribly, terribly wrong. Might it be all the steel in this city? After all, implants, the devices meant to block an Adept's use of her Ability, were made of the same metal. But implants required insertion into one's skin to have an effect, and having one did not feel the same as this. Then, she'd not been able to gather up her Ability at all. Now, it was like it had been on the ocean— she could access it and try to use it, but her efforts accomplished nothing.

"What is that?" Nyona exclaimed, pointing toward one of the impossibly tall buildings across the way.

Kalisfena followed her gesture, shading her eyes against the sun. Two black spots moved as if suspended along the top portion of one building. "Ah. It is nothing to be worried about. They are the window washers. It is an important job in a city such as this, you see. They keep our towers as clean as the day they were built."

"Those are *people?* How do they get up there?"

"It is a system of ropes and pulleys. They are quite safe, you can rest assured. It has been many, many years since we've had an accident. But we have found that nothing quite replaces the human hand in this task, you see. Now. Come along. Our destination isn't much farther."

"Can you believe that?" Nyona said to Alia as they continued to walk.

"No." There were many things today she could not quite believe.

Nyona leaned in closer and lowered her voice. "How are you feeling? Are you able to test anything yet?"

Alia kept her gaze straight ahead. "I think it's best to wait."

Nyona nodded, accepting her lie without question. Although an Adept relied primarily on her Ability to find one's truth, she also learned to read outward signs suggestive of falsity. In Nyona's case, that skill must have diminished with disuse, or she'd not developed it very much to begin with.

Kalisfena finally paused before an opaque panel set in the middle of a tall building indistinguishable from those surrounding it. The panel opened, creating a doorway in the glass. Alia quickly followed behind the envoy, uncertain how long the entry would remain open. After their entire party was inside, the panel closed with a pleasant *swish*. It was then that she noticed the attendant who had his hand on a lever of some sort that must control the door, and she felt a little foolish.

The building's foyer extended upwards into a vacant expanse that must have accounted for at least three floors. This ground floor also was almost absurdly empty, with only a raised desk near the entrance, behind which the attendant had retreated; a few seating areas devoid of people; and scattered vertical panels of varying solid colors in a display she presumed was meant to be artistic. Perhaps a society that could build into the clouds cared little for the efficient use of space.

At the far end of the foyer, a second attendant stood before four sets of metal panels, each with a vertical seam running down the middle. The attendant stood up straighter and adjusted her blue jacket. "Good morning, Kalisfena Tatyn." Her eyes darted toward Alia and her companions. "Are these all your guests?"

"Yes. Please take us to the forty-second floor."

The woman bobbed her head. "Right away, Kalisfena Tatyn." She pressed a small button recessed in the wall.

Kalisfena turned to Alia and Nyona. "I presume you have not been on a lift before?"

"I—don't believe so, no," responded Nyona. Alia agreed with a quick shake of her head. She had no idea what a "lift" was.

"I must give you a little warning, then. It can feel strange at times, you see, even to those used to such transport. You might not notice it as much, though, as you are still adjusting from being at sea." She smiled as if she shared with them a special secret, her teeth bright against her amber skin in this light. "You are still adjusting, yes? You do not yet feel as you should?"

"No," Alia answered quite honestly. Even if her stomach had

settled, the fact that she couldn't use her Ability left her bereft of normalcy.

The second metal panel from the left split in half, each side disappearing into hidden recesses in the walls. The attendant held her hand against one side and gestured toward a tiny room that didn't seem it would fit more than ten people. She followed the others inside the small space. Kalisfena, Mila, and Hasso then turned around almost as one, startling her.

Hasso twirled his finger in the air. "We go out the same way we came in."

Alia followed his gesture, her face aflame. By this point, all of her preconceived notions of Xeydeya had fallen away. Despite lacking Adepts of their own, this country was far more sophisticated than she'd grown up to believe. Why hadn't Hasso mentioned any of this? She'd assumed he'd been here before; the Captains wouldn't have assigned him to this mission, otherwise. Yet during their entire trip, he'd not said anything about Amrava that would have prepared her for any of this, leaving her to fumble about as if she were an uneducated bumpkin.

The panels closed. A jolt and a sudden surge upward made Alia's stomach turn. She held her hand to her lips in what she hoped appeared a casual gesture as she resisted, once again, the urge to vomit. Their movement lasted far longer than seemed possible, then stopped with another, yet smaller, bounce. Once the panels opened, she wasted no time exiting, breathing a sigh of relief.

Kalisfena patted her on her shoulder. "You will grow used to how things are here in time, I can assure you."

As if I will stay here any longer than I must, she thought to herself as she followed Kalisfena down a brightly lit corridor.

"Here we are." Kalisfena pulled a metal key from her pocket and inserted it into the lock. Alia frowned at that; in a place such as this, she would have expected locks like those the wealthy in Corinas used, the ones embedded with some Ability that allowed even non-Adepts to operate them without a physical key. Kalisfena opened the door, gesturing for Alia and Nyona to enter.

"Alia! Mother!"

So surprised to hear her true name, it took Alia a moment to identify the blur of motion zooming toward them. "T—Tovi?" she stammered, as Nyona cried out and dropped to her knees to embrace the child they'd come here to find.

17

MASTER GERSEMI

For the first time in a very long time, Gersemi could breathe without a nagging stitch of worry. Soon, her stolen Adepts would be home, and the rebel threat would be extinguished at the same time. The citizenry would embrace the return of order that only the Conclave could provide, and she could focus on rebuilding their power so no one—foreign or domestic—dared challenge the Conclave ever again.

Mathis was at the center of her plans, as he should be. No one could deny her that now. They'd seen his exceptional qualities with their own eyes—first during his truth assessment, and now as the first male officer in more than five generations. Her incredulous Directorate might have only allowed him command over a unit of male neophytes, yet those boys had progressed faster in three weeks under his tutelage than they had under more seasoned commanders.

Gersemi perked up at a shift in the conversation. "They should have had their pet respond right away, instead of sending a message by courier and risking the possibility that we would not receive it in time," Charla groused from the far end of the table. "Or at the very least, they should have had their courier bring their message to a Tribunal closer to the mountains. We've already wasted precious time. Why should we sit around and wait even longer before moving on Xeydeya?"

"Master Charla has a point," Gersemi said. Their message had been quite clear, and the rebels should have responded immediately if they wished to avoid certain destruction. *We have found you, traitors*, her Adepts had transmitted toward the area of the mountains known for the kind of cliffs and valleys Adept Kora had seen in Mathis's mind. *Your mountains are no longer a refuge. Guards are en route with orders to destroy everyone and everything they find—unless you do exactly as we demand.* The message had reached three or four people in the rebels' ambit capable of receiving it; while that wasn't many, it was more than enough to inform the rebel leadership of their options.

Jeyne, sitting to her immediate left, shook her head. "We have wasted nothing. Had Alia—"

"Do not speak that name," Gersemi snapped. How many times must she remind them?

"Apologies, Headmaster," said Jeyne, though she seemed far from chagrined. "I meant to say, even had *the traitor* immediately sent the same response as the courier, we wouldn't have pulled back the units we'd already dispatched toward this new 'Brome' of theirs. Our people need to be in place in case their delegation does not appear, or if the talks over their surrender fail. Plus, we've needed this time to conscript the necessary ships for transport. We almost have enough now, I think, to carry our Guards, plus those we anticipate will return to us."

"I still think it is a mistake to allow them the opportunity to negotiate," Charla complained. "We've given them our terms. What more do they deserve?" Others in the room nodded their agreement.

"It brings me no pleasure, but everyone here understands the reality we face," Gersemi said, now annoyed she'd opened the door for Charla to re-argue a settled decision. "We lack the resources to fight on two fronts, especially when the more important foe is an ocean away. We need more bodies. They must know this, as well; half our Guard has defected to them, after all."

Charla leaned back in her chair and folded her arms across her chest as if she were a petulant child. "A gallows is what we should give the whole lot of them," she muttered.

Beryl, sitting to Gersemi's right, grimaced at the comment. "I dislike the idea of giving them control over even a minor township, let alone the possibility of more through negotiations. But Headmaster Gersemi speaks true: this is our only option, as we've all agreed."

"I wouldn't say we've *all* agreed," said Leyta from a seat toward the middle of the table. "Some of us merely acquiesced."

"If you disagree with the plan, Master Leyta, you may voice your dissent in the proper fashion," Gersemi said coldly. The woman's continued sulking after the necessary cleanup in Generation had grown tiresome. What was done, was done, and she would not indulge further insubordination. "Is that what you wish to do?"

Leyta pursed her lips together for far too long before she shook her head.

Jeyne coughed into her hand, shattering the uncomfortable silence that had developed after Gersemi's challenge. "In any event, while delayed, the rebels' message appears to be true. Some of our wayward Guards have already appeared at the designated ports."

"Have you dispatched orders?" asked Gersemi.

"I sent a brief update, but the original orders I sent weeks ago still stand. We will make sure those who return are re-educated before we disperse them under the leadership of those whose loyalty has never been in question."

"How long until we have enough?"

Jeyne shrugged. "It depends. I'm sure many Guards will not return until after our negotiations are complete, but we don't need them all to launch an attack on Xeydeya. I estimate we will be ready in about four to six weeks."

"That is much too long. Can't you supplement with our new recruits?"

"I've dispatched those who've received the minimal essential training to the port cities, but they won't make up for the need for fully trained Guards. And those who have recently shown up from the southern cities aren't anywhere near ready to fight."

"And the situation in the west remains unchanged?" Gersemi asked Beryl.

She nodded. "Unfortunately. We cannot cede any authority, however minor, that far from Corval. In fact, once we're at full force again, we should add more resources to the area to ensure those living there remember what it means to be a loyal citizen."

"I agree. You're certain there will be no trouble in the southeast?"

"Yes. The rebels' retreat into the mountains lost them quite a lot of influence down there. Allowing a few select individuals— those who had no involvement in the rebels' leadership structure, of course, and only after proper Adept screening—to deal with the day-to-day governance in a few towns will not risk a return to chaos."

Gersemi nodded. "All right. So, to answer your question, Master Charla, we will wait a little longer. However, my patience grows thin. If their delegation fails to arrive in the next week or so, we will convene to reevaluate our position." She placed her hands flat on the table before her. "Is there anything else?"

"No, Headmaster Gersemi," Beryl replied.

"Then you are all dismissed. Master Jeyne, it would please me if you joined me for lunch."

Jeyne raised one eyebrow slightly. "Certainly, Headmaster."

The others filtered out of the room, nodding to Gersemi as they passed. Even Leyta managed to show the proper respect despite her sulking. "Come," she said to Jeyne. "Let us eat in my solarium so we can enjoy today's sun. It has been far too gloomy of late."

"That sounds nice, Headmaster Gersemi."

"Please—we're alone now."

Jeyne inclined her head in acknowledgement, yet Gersemi didn't expect her to drop all formalities. Her Principal Master of Security was no Leyta.

In a well-protected space in the corner of Gersemi's private garden stood a tiny solarium with precious smooth-glass panes interlocked with ribbons of steel. Some other Headmaster had installed it before she was born; its construction was an extravagance Gersemi could never justify herself. However, she was not one to turn down its comforts on the rare sunny days when the briskness of autumn evolved into the chill of winter.

Their lunch waited for them on a wrought-iron table centered underneath the glass ceiling. Glow lamps emitted additional warmth, though they would not be necessary for much longer as the sun was almost overhead. Gersemi sat down in one of the two matching chairs with thick blue and green seat cushions, and Jeyne took the other. "So, tell me," she said as she reached for a ceramic cup of fragrant, warmed wine. "Why did none of your agents provide us with advance notice that a rebel courier was en route?"

Jeyne stroked the arm of her robe, scattering the light that reflected off its silver ornamentation. "I'm not working with a full cadre of agents, as you know."

"Hmm. I am starting to think it is more of an issue of competence."

The younger Master frowned. "The agents available to me are more than competent, but they're spread too thin. That courier could have taken any number of routes from the mountains, and a single rider will never attract much attention, anyway. It's also possible someone did learn of it and sent their own message that hasn't yet arrived. We're stymied by the lack of Adepts in the field."

"You seem to fall back on that excuse quite a bit of late."

A few drops of wine splashed out of Jeyne's cup as she plunked it down on the table. "It's not an excuse. It is a reality. My people don't have regular access to an Adept, and you've declined to adopt my alternative."

Gersemi wrinkled her nose and took another long drink. Jeyne's proposal had been nonsense. Even if they had enough eunuchs to distribute throughout the country while maintaining sufficient service at home—which they did not—it would only waste more important resources. She would not make Adepts spend their efforts and time reaching out to people who, more likely than not, would never have anything worthy to report. Not even the Tribunals and unaffiliated Masters out in the field had much to say during their regularly scheduled communications.

Besides, eunuchs could not handle such responsibility. They were as they were because they lacked the capacity to be anything else. Only a very few could function outside a Master's direct supervision, and they'd already deployed those with Guard units on critical missions. Jeyne's suggestion was useless, and there was no reason to take her bait to discuss it yet again.

Gersemi set down her cup. "Have you heard anything else from that other agent of yours?"

"Which one?"

"The one whose reports of Xeydeyan involvement you dismissed out-of-hand," she said, daring Jeyne to break eye contact. To her credit, she did not.

"No. There wasn't much to go on in the first place, and she's passed along poor intelligence in the past."

"Why do you even keep a channel open, then?"

"We have so few agents left in Xeydeya as it is. I will take what I can get."

"Does she retain any of her other skills?"

Jeyne shook her head. "Not that I'm aware of."

"That's unfortunate." *What I wouldn't give for a competent Extir or two right now.* She'd been newly a Master when the Conclave had officially disbanded its order of assassins. A small group of them had continued on in secret for a time, but even that effort had ended after they'd begun to act independently. By the time she'd risen to Headmaster, the Conclave had exiled or executed all remaining Extirs. It would be too much to hope that in all that time, any who still lived would retain their deathly arts.

"Please, eat," Gersemi said, gesturing toward their plates of warmed grain, fruit, and cheese. "There is no need to dwell on what cannot be undone. I invited you to discuss other matters."

Jeyne nibbled on a piece of cheese, an edge of suspicion in her eyes. "What other matters?"

"If the rebels fail to arrive or do not treat in good faith, are you prepared to move forward?"

"Yes, though it would make rescuing our Adepts that much more difficult. And if they're entrenched up there, it could take months to finish the job, especially with winter coming on. I don't think they mean to engage in a fight, though. We're offering them something they'd never be able to achieve on their own. They'd be fools to reject us."

"I think you are granting them far more logic than they deserve. After all, they didn't even see fit to have the traitor inform us of their decision right away."

"I presume it was because she didn't want to risk revealing the method she's been using to hide from us all this time."

"What point is there in that? We know where she is now."

"Maybe she's trying to protect the child? She must be using the same technique."

"Again, to what end? When we find our Adepts, we will find her." She sipped her wine to chase down a bit of cheese. "How much longer until your units are able to act?"

"About three weeks, depending on weather conditions. Our people will need to take greater caution as they approach as we don't yet know the full extent of their defenses. I'm assuming they are robust, given that they've managed to remain hidden for so long."

Gersemi allowed the flavors of cinnamon and cloves in the wine to linger over her tongue. "It is strange, isn't it, the position we find ourselves in? It is the natural right of the Conclave to govern Corinas. The rebellion is nothing more than a collection of disgruntled individuals who refuse to accept their lot in life—yet here we are, preparing to cede to them power to which they have no right."

"I do not disagree, Headmaster. It was why I first opposed your plan." Jeyne furrowed her brow. "But it *was* your plan, and I now agree it is our best—and only—option. Are you having second thoughts?"

"No, no," she responded quickly, not wanting to leave any impression of doubt in her subordinate's mind. "I am simply musing on the absurdity of the situation. Though I suppose it is but one more change in circumstances we will adjust to, in time."

"That it is," Jeyne said, nodding. "That it is."

"Speaking of," Gersemi said as if she'd just thought of it, "I am pleased to hear of Mathis's progress."

Jeyne lifted her dark eyebrows. "In this, Headmaster, I remain unpersuaded. He may be a Son, and a powerful one at that, but he's spent most of his life with people who have no respect for that role. We will continue to keep a close eye on him until I am convinced his loyalties have shifted—if they ever do."

"They will, Jeyne. I have no doubt about that. The rebellion offered him nothing but a life of lies and deceit; here, in his rightful home, he has the opportunity to rise as far as his capabilities will take him, among people who can appreciate his unique qualities." Gersemi smiled and reached for a piece of fruit. Jeyne would come around to her way of thinking. She always did.

18

MATHIS

"Again," he barked.

The boys launched into another repetition of the drill, a variation of the lunge-and-twist he'd taught them yesterday. Primarily an evasive maneuver, it left open the opportunity for a counterattack. Paired with other techniques, it could make for a dirty, unexpected move, but if they ever fought against the Conclave someday, they'd need to know tricks like these.

Grunts of exertion carried across the practice yard. All those under his command had received little formal training before being assigned to his unit. He recognized the Masters had meant this as an insult, yet working with these boys suited him fine. It would be far easier to turn such youngsters to his side than those more seasoned. He'd already identified several who'd given hints here and there suggesting he might persuade them to fight for the rebellion, and he was already well on his way to convincing three or four, as well. If nothing else, they'd help him find Tovi, and then he could get out of this place.

One of those recruits, who claimed to be seventeen despite his rounded cheeks and complete lack of facial hair, swept his leg behind the ankle of his sparring partner, sending him sprawling. "Zevon!" he yelled. "What was that?"

He grinned as he kept the other boy pinned to the ground with his wooden training sword, revealing a gap in his front teeth. "I was trying to win, Lieutenant."

"That wasn't part of the drill." Mathis lifted his chin toward another recruit he'd identified as promising, a tall, slender lad with nearly white hair. He responded in kind, then began moving closer to Zevon.

"Sorry, Lieutenant," Zevon said in a decidedly unapologetic tone, oblivious to the taller boy creeping up to him from behind. "I saw an opening, so I took it."

"Great," Mathis replied in a monotone. "So, what would you do next?"

"Kill him?" The boy under his sword yelped. "I mean, if this wasn't a drill," he clarified.

"Is that so? You left yourself awfully exposed."

Zevon looked over his shoulder just as the tip of the taller recruit's training sword scraped against his neck. "Fires, Silar," Zevon complained, to scoffs of laughter from the other boys. Silar smirked as he retreated to his original position.

"Overconfidence can be as bad as incompetence, if not worse," Mathis said. "Overconfidence might get you a temporary gain over an opponent, but if you aren't one hundred percent aware of what else is going on around you, you'll end up losing, no matter how good a fighter you are." A few nods suggested he'd made some sense. He was still getting used to having this kind of authority. "All right. Let's try it again, and this time, don't try to add something fancy, Zevon."

"Yes, Lieutenant."

The drill continued. Mathis shouted pointers and reprimands, and occasionally praise to the few who deserved it. They weren't a bad lot, though he didn't pretend they were anywhere near fighting capacity. From what he'd seen, the Conclave didn't turn down any willing recruit, no matter how dismal the prospect, probably because they'd lost so many Guards to the rebellion. No one said as much—the Conclave would never admit to such a weakness—but the truth was plain.

Of all the boys in his unit, Silar showed the most promise. The son of an itinerant artist, he'd come to the Conclave seeking a better life than what his mother could provide. He moved with purpose and took every critique to heart. Rarely did he make the same mistake twice, though he still made plenty in the first instance. Then there was Zevon, whose raw talent Mathis hoped to mold into some semblance of order. He was a boy desperately trying to act the man, and ripe for a mentor's influence.

"That's enough for today," Mathis called out as the hour drew to a close. "We'll continue where we left off tomorrow." Out of the corner of his eye, he spied his shadow, the shorter-than-normal eunuch named Enece, who rarely spoke to him despite observing every training session. He was there to make sure he toed the line, Mathis was certain, though he'd never interfered with his unorthodox style. The Headmaster might have given Mathis a command in a clumsy attempt to sway him to her side, but Enece's constant presence proved she didn't trust him.

As she shouldn't.

At the railing surrounding the small practice yard, the boys dropped their wooden swords into a barrel and wiped at their faces and necks with grayish rags. Mathis edged closer to where they'd gathered. While he could not leave the Conclave's complex, the members of his unit could, so long as they always returned before nightfall. Not everyone used their free time this way, and certainly not every day, but enough did that their idle chatter after training sessions often revealed news of the outside world. As limited as it might be, they were his only real sources of information.

"I heard they were already here," Silar said, running his hands through his sweat-dampened hair.

"No, no, no. That was just a courier. I saw her when she left," Zevon bragged.

"Liar. You did not."

"I did too!"

"Sure, sure," Silar said, nudging the boy next to him and rolling his eyes.

Zevon scowled. "You weren't there. You can't say what I did or didn't see."

Mathis stepped in before Zevon's temper turned physical. "What are you all going on about?"

"Zevon claims he saw a rebel courier leave the Conclave earlier today."

He kept his face a perfect mask of nonchalance and avoided looking in the direction of the eunuch, though he was too far away to hear their conversation, anyway. None of these boys knew his true identity—they all thought he was just some old Guardsman and accepted his command as a quirk of the Conclave without understanding its exceptional nature. "Oh, really? They just let a rebel walk out the gates, you say?" he said wryly, and the other boys chortled.

"They did," Zevon huffed. "I had gone into town after lunch, and when I came back I noticed a horse tied up just outside the front gate, which was passing strange. Then this tall, blonde woman in dusty brown clothes and a long braid down her back came charging out, hopped on the horse, and took off. I thought maybe she was a thief or something, but the Gate Guards didn't do anything. I asked them who she was, and they told me. You all can go pound fire for all I care."

"What did she look like?"

"Was she by herself?"

"Did they say if the rebels really are surrendering?"

Mathis held out his hand to stop the barrage of questions the other boys fired toward Zevon, their earlier skepticism apparently forgotten. "Wait a second." He pointed to the one who'd asked the last question, Mateo, certain he'd misheard. "What did you say?"

"About the rebels?"

"Yes, yes," Mathis said, his impatience growing.

"That they're surrendering?"

"Where did you hear such a thing?"

Mateo glanced toward his companions, clearly discomfited by being singled out. "Just around, Lieutenant. Everyone's talking about it."

Silar nodded. "It's all over town that the rebels are giving up."

Mathis's stomach turned. It couldn't be true. The rebels would *never* surrender to the Conclave, especially not now when they had the upper hand. The Conclave lacked martial might, lacked the support of the citizenry—and now, even lacked Adepts out in the field, as he'd learned from the boys. Instead of kowtowing to the Masters, the Captains would be pushing their advantage. "Did the Gate Guards say anything else?"

Zevon shrugged in that way young men did when they thought the answer mattered little. "Some envoys apparently are coming here to discuss the terms of the rebellion's surrender. I guess they were supposed to be here already, and the Masters are hopping mad they aren't."

Mathis was no child, to be taken in by such ridiculous rumors, and he didn't want to entertain further discussion amongst his unit. He'd never get any of them to flip to his side if they thought that side would soon not exist. "Well, whatever is going on is no concern of yours. Now, off with you, before I decide that your time would be better spent on more drills." The words were barely out of his mouth before the boys scattered.

Ruminating on whether this distressing news could be true, he set off for his own quarters near the barracks housing his unit. The Masters had—begrudgingly, he presumed—allowed him to move from his original room somewhere on the other side of the Conclave. Officers always lived near the barracks, and that wasn't something they could deviate from and still expect anyone to accept his commission.

Even so, they kept him separate from all the other officers, claiming some issue of female propriety that made no sense at all. The arrangement suited him just fine. It was hard enough to play the dutiful Lieutenant all the time in front of his unit; maintaining the act amongst the other commanders would be beyond difficult. He'd thought maybe they'd put him over here to make it easier for the Masters, or even the Headmaster, to continue their questioning of him about the rebellion, but not a one of them had visited him since his move. Not that he minded.

Once in his room, Mathis pulled off his dusty boots. Footsteps passed by his door—those of the eunuch, he presumed, on the way to his own quarters right next door. Eunuchs didn't serve the Conclave's Guard like they did Masters and Adepts, but they'd passed Enece's assignment off as a necessary exception, given Mathis's separation from the other officers.

The footsteps backtracked, followed by a knock on his door.

Mathis sighed. He was in no mood to speak to Enece right now. To his surprise, though, it was not the eunuch he found when he opened the door, but Zevon, still clothed in his dirty practice gear. "Oh. It's you," he said.

The boy glanced to the side. "Sorry to bother you, Lieutenant. Do you have a few minutes?"

"Sure. What's on your mind?"

Enece passed behind him with a polite nod toward Mathis. "I wanted to talk about tomorrow's drill schedule," Zevon said.

Mathis frowned at the strange request. The schedule tomorrow was the same as it was every day. He then noticed the boy's wide-open eyes, seemingly trying to tell him something. "Oh, uh—of course. Come on in." He poked his head beyond the doorframe to make sure the eunuch hadn't lingered, then pulled the door closed.

"Sorry, Lieutenant. You said I should only tell you, and no one else, if I heard something about a missing Adept, so I didn't want to say anything out in the hall."

"Shh," Mathis hissed, paranoia that Enece might overhear overwhelming his excitement at possible news of Tovi. He'd spent the good part of his first three evenings here making sure there wasn't a peephole drilled through the thick stone wall separating their rooms, but he might have missed something. "I am planning to use some of that equipment on that old exercise path tomorrow," he said in a loud voice. "Let's go out there now, so you can help me teach the skills we'll be working on."

To his credit, Zevon caught on quickly to his nonsense. "Certainly, Lieutenant. Happy to help."

After Mathis laced up his boots once again, he and the boy hurried back outside. Past the main training grounds, various arrangements of steps and railings dotted an old stone path. No one really used them anymore, and this time of day, so close to the evening meal, they were the only people on the path. There was no sign the eunuch had followed them, either.

"So. Tell me what you heard," Mathis said, striving to keep the eagerness from his tone.

Zevon kicked at a loose stone, causing it to tumble ahead of them on the path. "It was when I was talking to the Gate Guards about the rebel envoys. They were saying how surprised they were that the Masters were willing to negotiate terms of surrender at all instead of executing them all for their crimes."

"Yes, that is surprising," Mathis said in a deadpan. "It's one reason you shouldn't put too much stock in what they told you about that courier. They probably led you on as a lark."

"I thought about that, Lieutenant, but what they said made sense given what I've been hearing in town. But that's not what I wanted to tell you. They went on to say that the reason the Masters were probably willing to talk to the rebels was because of 'the missing Adepts,' they said. I didn't know what they were talking about, so I asked, and they said, 'That's why all those Adepts came back and are cloistered away in the towers now. The rebels picked off a bunch of them before the Masters got wise to it.'"

Mathis glanced toward the Conclave's yellow-and-amber stone towers. A feat of construction rising eight or nine stories each, they were far taller than any other building in Corval, or, for that matter, anywhere he'd been in Corinas. "So all their Adepts are up there, now?"

"That's what they said. And from the sounds of it, a lot of

Adepts—dozens, maybe—got nicked, too. The Masters are trying to keep it on the hush-hush."

Mathis frowned. The Captains had once hoped to gather up more Adepts for the rebellion's use, but those efforts ended not long after the failed rescue attempt of Alia's friend. They'd been too busy trying to rebuild the rebellion itself, and even in Brome, he'd heard nothing suggesting the Captains intended to return to their old plan. None of what the Gate Guards had said made any sense.

Except for the towers. He could believe the Masters would keep an Adept they didn't want found all the way up there. Could Tovi see him now, he wondered, if she were to look out one of those tiny windows? Was she waiting, wondering why he wasn't doing more to find her and take her home?

His shoulders sagged with guilt. For weeks, he'd been playing at commander instead of focusing on rescuing Tovi. Sure, he'd cultivated relationships with recruits like Zevon and Silar in the hopes they would eventually help—Zevon would not have brought him this information otherwise. Yet a report was one thing. Finding Tovi and extricating her from the Masters' grip was something else. How could he use them for that? "Have you ever been over there?"

"Over where?"

"Near the towers."

The boy shook his head. "No, Lieutenant. They would never let the likes of me anywhere near that part of the complex."

Nor the likes of me, Mathis thought. *Or especially* me. Yet he had to find a way, somehow, for him or his boys to get to those towers. He would not let Tovi down.

19

ALIA

SEVERAL YOUNG GIRLS GIGGLED AS THEY LEANED THEIR foreheads against the floor-to-ceiling windows and allowed their arms to float up in the air. Alia shook her head at their antics. Those glass panels did not seem in any way capable of preventing her from falling to her death if she were to crash into one accidentally, so she kept her distance. She didn't care how long the Xeydeyans had been building with the material; in her opinion, glass could never provide the same security as stone.

All over the city, buildings of the same metal-and-glass construction rose into the sky. When they'd arrived in Amrava a few weeks ago, the sight of so many tightly packed towers had mesmerized her, and she'd wondered how they could have ever afforded it. She'd come to learn that such structures were common throughout Xeydeya, and wooden or stone buildings, such as those prevalent back home, were only for the poor and rural. Amrava was neither of those things.

"We should sit down," Nyona said. "It's about time."

Alia nodded and turned away from the view. "All right."

Many of the others had already taken their seats around small tables set throughout the room. They chatted with each other as if there were nothing at all unusual about their circumstances. Perhaps, to these girls, there really wasn't. They might wear loose pants and belted jackets of varying colors instead of identical white robes, but someone else still controlled every aspect of their lives.

She and Nyona selected their usual table near the back, leaving a chair open between them for Tovi. The child was on the other side of the room, gesticulating to her new friends during what Alia imagined was some wild tale of her time with the rebellion. The Adepts—if they could still be called such—were fascinated with Tovi, and she was happy to indulge their curiosity. Alia suspected the feeling was mutual. Tovi had lived most of her life with little exposure to children her age, let alone those who shared—or *had* shared—Ability.

At the thought, Alia tried once more to use her own Ability, though she no longer felt much angst at her inevitable failure. That she continued to try at all came more from stubbornness than any true expectation of success. Still, she told no one of her attempts— not Tovi, not Nyona, and especially not their hosts. Given their extreme disdain for the power, it was better that the Xeydeyans believed she was like all the rest, with no sense of it whatsoever. Kalisfena no longer even asked her about it, so she must have done a decent enough job hiding the truth.

The reaction to losing what had once been a constant presence varied amongst the forty Adepts in the room. One older girl had been rather matter-of-fact about it, noting she would have lost her Ability in a few years' time anyway, though she harbored some guilt about not passing it on to a new Adept. Tovi herself had confessed she didn't miss her Ability at all. *No one asks me to do anything scary anymore,* she'd said. *All they ask me to do is learn.* Yet there were those who mourned the loss, like Tovi's young friend Khyana. She'd been one of the first Adepts to come to Amrava, yet Alia had spied her wiping away silent tears on a number of occasions.

Still, not a one, not even Khyana, had asked to join Alia when she returned to Corinas. That was a puzzle she'd yet to unravel. At first, she'd attributed their recalcitrance to their warped perspective of her. To them, she was the hated Sempiternal who'd abandoned her rightful home to join the rebellion. As the days went by, however, and their reaction had thawed—mostly due to Tovi vouching for her—the situation remained the same. These girls genuinely seemed to *like* it here, despite the circumstances.

Nyona caught Tovi's attention. She came to sit between them, although Alia imagined she'd rather sit with her friends. Her initial excitement at their arrival had faded, probably in part because Nyona had nearly smothered her with attention and rarely let her out of her sight even now. The precaution was unnecessary; the Xeydeyans had demonstrated they did not mean to harm any of these girls, and they allowed no one to leave the building, anyway. Tovi was safer in here than she'd been in Brome, or anywhere within the Conclave's domain, really.

Chatter diminished as their instructors walked to the front of the room. They all wore the same flowing clothing as Alia herself, though it was better designed for taller people such as them. Most of the women followed Kalisfena's example by piling their braids on top of their heads, though some pinned them in intricate loops that must be a nightmare to untangle at the end of the day.

Kalisfena surveyed the room. "Good morning, everyone."

"Good morning," Alia responded in unison with the others. It felt almost like she were an Adept back at the Conclave, taking part in the morning Ritual. Did the Xeydeyans appreciate the similarities? If they did, they probably would dispense with all this. She doubted they'd want to emulate the Masters in any way.

"Today, we will focus on mathematics. I am pleased so many of you have progressed beyond the basic concepts. However, because others are still struggling with simple figures, we will break into different groups today so you can all get the attention you require." Her unctuous smile belied the condescension in her words. "Rest assured, there is no shame in finding this subject matter difficult. You see, your life until now has left you ill-prepared to receive this knowledge. Together, we will work through this, as our goal is for each one of you to become productive members of society."

Alia glanced around the other tables as Kalisfena continued to detail the day's lessons. The other Adepts, including Tovi, hung on Kalisfena's every word. It reminded Alia of the idolatry Adepts heaped upon the Headmaster of the Conclave, and she didn't understand how that could be. Kalisfena was a member of the Xeydeyan government, but she wasn't the head of it as far as Alia knew. Even so, that these girls would act this way toward the person responsible for their abduction, no matter her position and how well she treated them now, was more than passing strange.

Then again, nothing about this situation made much sense. Kalisfena had led Alia and her companions straight to this building upon their arrival, making no attempt to hide the location of the Adepts. Nor had the Xeydeyans ever intended to use the Adepts' Ability, which everyone had assumed was the reason they'd scooped up so many and brought them here. Instead, Kalisfena claimed they'd done so to give these Adepts a chance for a better life. *It is good you are out of Corinas*, she liked to say, *away from the taint of Ability and those who only mean to use you for ill purpose.*

At least they could go home now without worrying about what to do with all these Adepts. As soon as Hasso completed whatever other business he had in the city, he, Nyona, and Alia would take Tovi back to Brome and leave behind all the rest. These Adepts were the Xeydeyans' problem now, as far as she was concerned.

She suppressed a sigh. She'd wasted time coming here, and would waste more time returning, all because Kalisfena and her peers hadn't kept their allies in Corinas appraised of their plans—including that they were well aware Ability did not work in Xeydeya. That was time she could have spent back home trying to find Mathis, who needed her help. Or Marta, of whom the Xeydeyans denied any knowledge.

Alia stared out the window. Between the two buildings across the street, she thought she spied the tiniest sliver of ocean. She missed being outside, and the brush of fresh air against her cheeks. The Xeydeyans refused to let any of them leave the building—for their safety, they claimed—and Hasso told her to play along for the sake of comity. As the days dragged on, though, she was becoming less and less willing to keep up this friendly charade. No matter what the Xeydeyans might think, she was not a child in need of a caretaker, nor a victim in need of saving.

Kalisfena eventually finished her introductory remarks and left the Adepts to the supervision of the others. Nyona followed Tovi over to where the more advanced students congregated. Alia yawned as she waited for others to join her table, already bored. Taking part in these lessons was another thing she did at Hasso's request. It wasn't as if she could really learn all that much in a few short weeks, so she didn't bother trying.

It seemed hours had passed before Kalisfena returned to the room. Alia glanced toward her, anticipating the announcement of a sorely needed break. The envoy's cheeks were flushed, as if she'd rushed to get there, and her eyes darted around the room until they locked on Alia's own. "Alia, my dear. Will you please come with me?"

"Sure." From where she sat at a different table, Nyona raised her eyebrows in question, to which Alia responded with a small shrug. No matter the reason for a break, she would take it. She followed Kalisfena out into the corridor.

"My apologies for pulling you away from your lessons. But, you see, I have received some disturbing news from Corinas."

"What about?"

"I don't mean to be mysterious, you see, but I prefer to speak to you and Hasso at the same time. He's to meet us in my office." The material of her pants made a *swish swish* sound as she hastened toward the lift. "I would have asked Nyona to join us as well, but I did not wish to disturb Tovi's work. She has such a brilliant mind."

"She always seemed rather smart."

"Yes, but now that she is freed from Ability, she can explore her true capability. You could do the same if only you applied yourself. I have seen the look in your eyes. You need to let go of your memories of Ability and embrace a better life."

Alia didn't bother responding to what had become a repeated refrain. Kalisfena had made it clear she wanted Tovi and Alia to remain in Xeydeya with the other Adepts. *Ability corrupts,* she'd said with a look of disgust. *Here, you can be truly free. Why would you ever wish to return to Corinas?* Hasso's failure to make it clear they would leave Xeydeya, and soon, didn't help the situation. He claimed he didn't want to offend Kalisfena and risk her cutting off funding to the rebellion, but it seemed to Alia that prolonging the inevitable would only make things worse.

Once in the lift, Kalisfena kept her eyes forward while she fidgeted with the rings on one of her hands with her thumb. Alia stood beside her and tried to adopt a nonchalant posture despite burning with curiosity as to what news the envoy had to share. They ascended in silence before the lift came to a halt at the top floor, which was reserved for Kalisfena and her personal staff. Alia had been up here only a handful of times.

The doors slid open, and they stepped out into a quiet, open area flanked by rows of squared beige columns. Before a partial wall of the same color, a young man sat at a large desk facing the lift. "Good morning, Kalisfena Tatyn. You have some new messages." He handed her a stack of small papers.

"Thank you," she said, flipping through the pages. "Has Hasso arrived?"

"Yes, Kalisfena Tatyn. He is waiting in your office."

A series of abstract paintings hung along the passage to the left, each one containing its own collection of complementary hues. The first one was reds, the second greens, and the third yellows, each with a tiny plaque identifying the same artist. Kalisfena owned this entire building, Alia had learned, one of the tallest in the city, and she seemed to have put art everywhere within it. Some of it was local, but most were by artists from countries Alia had never heard of. Kalisfena claimed to have personally selected them all during her worldly travels.

Kalisfena's office was an expansive, light-filled suite with glass walls and an unobstructed view of the dark-blue ocean. Hasso looked up from where he sat in a wide, squared, green-cushioned chair with high arms. He wore his usual close-fitting black garments, having given up adhering to the local fashion soon after their arrival. "Kalisfena. Alia," he said as he started to push himself out of the chair.

"Sit, sit," Kalisfena said, waving him back into his seat. "Thank you for coming. I know you were attending to business elsewhere today, but this couldn't wait." She sat down across from Hasso in one of the four matching chairs while Alia took the one next to him.

"I'd finished what needed to be done. Unless what you're about to tell me changes things."

Alia glanced between them, annoyed that Hasso had kept Kalisfena appraised of his activities while refusing to do the same for her. Stuck in lessons all day, she'd seen little of him of late, and he'd kept quiet about his comings and goings. On the rare occasions when she'd had the opportunity to ask him what he was up to and when they might return home, his responses were vague and unsatisfying.

"I'm afraid it does," Kalisfena said. "You see, I have learned that the Conclave and the rebellion have agreed to treat."

Hasso frowned and folded his hands together under his chin, resting his index fingers on his lips. "What?" Alia asked, certain she'd misunderstood. The Conclave and the rebellion...negotiating? That would never happen.

"The Conclave has finally realized we have their Adepts. They have offered the rebellion a seat at the table of governance of Corinas if they assist the Masters in returning these poor creatures to Corinas. So, you see, this unfortunate development places me in a bit of a predicament. I simply will not allow you to take these Adepts back to Corinas. I did not think that was your intent in coming here, but I am no longer certain." Her tone was friendly, yet there was an unmistakable hint of threat not far under the surface.

"You know the reason why we came, Kalisfena Tatyn, and that reason remains true," Hasso said calmly, reverting to her formal name. "We are content to leave the Adepts in your care."

She looked down at her hands and rotated one of her many silver rings. "It displeases me that I had to learn of this distressing news from someone else, Hasso."

"My sources reported nothing of this, and it's not like she can communicate with anyone in Corinas," he said, jutting his thumb in Alia's direction. "If I'd heard of this, I would have told you, as it would have been as much a surprise to me."

Alia nodded in agreement. "The Masters would never offer such a thing, and the Captains would never agree to it, either. We want the Conclave's power destroyed, not shared."

"Do you? Sempiternals are not welcome in Corinas, yet you have repeatedly indicated your desire to return. Are you the key to the rebellion's treachery? What else have you been hiding from us?"

"I know nothing about any of this," Alia protested, hoping a general disclaimer would suffice. What she hid from Kalisfena, she hid from everyone—yet even so, it had nothing to do with this ridiculous rumor.

"I can assure you, Kalisfena Tatyn, that Alia is not in some secret league with the Captains. But let's take a step back and calm ourselves. I doubt the veracity of this report. It seems specially designed to disrupt our alliance. Who sold you such a tale, and why would you believe it?"

Kalisfena shook her head, her lips pressed together. "This did not come from a single source, which is why I am surprised you did not know of it, Hasso—if, indeed, you truly did not know."

"I said—"

She cut him off with a wave of her hand, all traces of friendliness gone from her voice. "I do not care. My sources, unconnected from one another, are credible, and all have reported the same thing. Your leadership means to betray us, despite everything we've done for them and everything we've agreed to do." Her knuckles tightened as she gripped the arms of her chair. "So, you see, herein lies my problem. If your Captains have cast away our arrangement, what am I to do with you?"

20

MASTER GERSEMI

GERSEMI SURVEYED THE TRAINING GROUNDS, MAKING SURE to keep out of sight of those practicing below. Instead of her usual public robes, with their expanse of silver embroidery that would betray her slightest movement, she wore a plain robe of dark gray, the sort she wore when she was alone in her chambers without the expectation of visitors. Over that, she wore a brown cloak that had once been Mathis's. They were of a height, and it was the only one she had on hand similarly unadorned as her robe. She'd received a few strange looks from some of the Masters she'd passed on her way here, but she cared little for their opinion. She was the Headmaster, and she could do as she pleased, including wearing the laundered clothing of her son.

He has such control over those under his command, she thought as she watched Mathis with his charges. *They follow his every order without question.* At the conclusion of one exercise, Mathis ruffled one of the boys' hair, who ducked away, laughing as he smoothed his white-blond hair back down. Yet the moment of levity was brief, and the boy returned to his formation quickly and with no prompting. *They respect him—as they should.*

The results Mathis had achieved with this unit in such a short time were beyond impressive. Even Jeyne no longer suggested he was not worthy of his Lieutenancy. Frankly, he'd proven he should be at an even higher rank. Gersemi could make it so, but it would be better if the idea came from someone else in the Directorate. Soon enough, every one of them would be in a rush to give Mathis the respect and position that was his due without her having to say a word.

She smiled at the thought. They were so alike, he and she. She'd come into power at a young age as well, and there were those —not many, of course—who'd doubted her capability. Most had quickly learned the error of their ways, and she hadn't long suffered resistance from those who did not.

A gust of cold wind caused her cloak to flutter off to the side. Mathis glanced up in her direction, and she quickly pressed her back against the wall as to remain concealed. Almost immediately, she recognized the ridiculousness of her response. Here she was, the most powerful woman in all the world, hiding like some mid-Initiate Adept. Why did it matter whether Mathis learned of her observations? Anyone would feel privileged to gain her attention, no matter the reason for it.

Still, she pulled the cloak tighter to her body and remained where she was. There was no reason to distract him from his duties, and she did not want their first conversation since he'd become a Lieutenant to take place in the presence of others. Besides, she didn't want Enece, who skulked around the corner, to suspect there was anything more to her visit than idle curiosity concerning the Guards' first male commander in generations.

Almost as if she'd used Ability to connect with the eunuch, he appeared. "My pardon, Headmaster Gersemi," he whispered. "Master Jeyne has requested a meeting. She is waiting in the Directorate's Room. She said it is urgent."

Gersemi frowned slightly. Jeyne wouldn't call a meeting of the Directorate on her own unless she had news of great import. "Are the others on the way?"

"No, Headmaster. She said she wished to speak only to you."

Annoyance replaced her apprehension. If Jeyne wasn't asking to meet with all the others, then what she had to say couldn't be as urgent as she claimed. Still, she would go along with it, for now. Jeyne was critical to her plans for Mathis, and little courtesies such as this were the things that would help secure her support. "All right. I am pleased to see your reports of Mathis are accurate, Enece. Continue the good work."

"Thank you, Headmaster," he said, bowing deeply.

Gersemi headed toward the stairs, more than satisfied by what she'd seen that morning. She wasn't stupid or naïve; she'd always known there was a chance Mathis's acceptance of this position had not been true. If that had been so, she had hoped that once he began acting the part of the commander, he'd realize how much more he could achieve here in his rightful home. Her fear had been that, despite that truth, he would nonetheless reject the Conclave—and her—on account of the rebellion's many lies.

Everything in Enece's reports, and in those of others, had bolstered her hope and refuted her fear. Still, it was one thing to read about his transformation, and another thing to see it herself. Mathis had truly accepted his home. It was as obvious to her as it would be to anyone with eyes and ears.

It took Gersemi some time to return to the area of the complex where she normally spent her days, and as she walked, she wondered what it was Jeyne wanted to tell her. Her Principal Master of Security had been waiting for reports to come in from the field, so Gersemi assumed she finally had some news. *It had better be good.* The rebellion's delegation still had not arrived to discuss the terms of their surrender, and while they purportedly were close, her patience had grown thin. She'd already waited longer than anyone of right mind should have, and only because Jeyne's Guards near the mountains were not yet ready to strike.

Gersemi entered the Directorate's Room without preamble. Jeyne's chair squealed against the stone as she scooted it back to stand. "Headmaster," she said with a slight incline of her head. "Thank you for coming. I have most urgent news."

"Yes, that is why I am here." She tossed her cloak over the back of one of the empty chairs and stood behind it. While she had been willing to grant Jeyne this meeting, she didn't wish to suggest she would remain any longer than necessary.

"I appreciate it. As you know, I've been waiting for—"

Gersemi sliced the flat of her hand through the air. "Spare me the backstory. I need not hear it again. Tell me what it is you wish for me to know now."

"We've confirmed the child is in Amrava. We've also confirmed the traitor is there, too."

Gersemi gripped the back of the chair. *Fires!* She pressed her lips together and breathed deeply in and out through her nose. "For how long?" she asked after the initial wave of fury had passed.

"About a month. My agent dispatched a message within a few days of their arrival, though I only received it today."

"How did they capture her when we could not?"

"I don't think they did," Jeyne said defensively. "She arrived on a boat owned by someone known to have connections with the rebellion, and they disembarked publicly and freely. And..." Jeyne grimaced. "You will not like this."

Gersemi glared. "I don't like any of this."

"She entered the city in the company of Kalisfena Tatyn."

Rage flooded Gersemi's mind, causing her vision to narrow and blur at the edges. "That *bitch!*" she said aloud. Of course the traitor would align herself with that duplicitous envoy. Of course! Gersemi stewed in her anger, stoking it with the memories of every perceived insult Kalisfena Tatyn had ever thrown her way.

Jeyne blinked rapidly several times. "I confess I'm uncertain what we should do with this information."

"Is it not obvious?" Gersemi snapped. "The rebellion and the Xeydeyans are aligned. They had no intention of treating with us."

"Maybe."

"*Maybe?* How could it be otherwise?"

"Our truth assessment of the courier revealed no falsehoods. You are right to be suspicious, but maybe the traitor betrayed the rebellion, as well. It is in her nature, after all. Maybe Kalisfena Tatyn offered her a better arrangement."

"Maybe, maybe, maybe," she chided. "That the courier believed her message was true does not mean the rebellion's leadership meant it. You know better than that."

"Headmaster—"

"I am done waiting. We must accept the most likely scenario as the truth and proceed accordingly. Heed well your orders: First, I want you to send all of your available coastal units to Amrava. Put them on your fastest vessels and have them depart right away. I want a detachment en route before daylight tomorrow."

"Headmaster, we're not ready to—"

"I've had quite enough of your protests, Master Jeyne," Gersemi said, using the formal address to emphasize her displeasure. "You've had more than enough time to prepare for this."

Jeyne's cheeks flushed. "We don't have enough people yet, not if we want to recover our Adepts safely and ensure that Xeydeya will never consider such treachery again. And far too many of the Guards I have in that location are those who've returned from the rebellion under the terms of our agreement. They've said the right words and done the right things, but no one's performed truth assessments yet. I can't guarantee their loyalty."

"Every day we wait is another day our Adepts must endure unspeakable danger. We don't know what has already happened to them. We don't even know if they still *live*." Her voice shook from her anger. "Send who and what you have. Your commanders will keep the returned in line, and I don't care how many of them we lose so long as we take back our Adepts."

"I appreciate the urgency, Headmaster Gersemi, believe me. I still must register that I think this is a mistake. If we send *all* our true Guards in the port cities, we'd be leaving ourselves open to even more treachery if this is in fact all part of a rebel plot."

"Send in a few Guards from elsewhere, then. I don't see why this is so difficult for you to understand."

"I have no more to send!" Jeyne snapped, raising her voice.

"Everyone we have that is at all competent is either in the ports or waiting near the mountains."

"What about all the new recruits I see around here? There must be at least one unit capable of maintaining basic order in a city."

"In the face of a rebel attack? No one here is ready for that kind of duty."

"Why not?"

Jeyne threw her hands up in the air. "Because building skill and discipline takes time. What would you have me do? Our lack of Guards was the only reason we agreed to treat with the rebels in the first place."

Gersemi swallowed a bitter laugh. It had been her idea to negotiate a resolution with the rebellion, as she'd been certain the Conclave had no other choice in the matter. How very wrong she'd been. "I'm sure you, the Principal Master of Security, will find a way to make it work. That is your job, isn't it," she said in a low voice, her threat unmistakable.

Jeyne scowled. "Yes, it is."

"Excellent," she said magnanimously. "Now, for the second part of your orders: Send word to the units twiddling their thumbs near the mountains that they are to proceed. There is no reason to hold off on attacking Brome now that we know the rebels have played us false."

"We do not know that for certain. All we know is that the traitor is in Xeydeya. We have good reason to believe she was not taken there against her will, but that is the extent of our intelligence. I was also thinking of sending some of those I have in the mountains to the coasts to address your first orders."

"You will need to think of something else, then. I expect those units to move on Brome as soon as practical."

Jeyne folded her hands before her. "These are significant departures to our agreed-upon plan, Headmaster Gersemi. I suggest we convene a meeting of the full Directorate to discuss all our options before we take irreversible actions."

Gersemi narrowed her eyes. "You could have requested a Directorate meeting to begin with, Master Jeyne, but you chose to bring his information to me alone, and I, as the Headmaster of the Conclave, have the right to act as I see fit. While I try to seek consensus in our decisions, as it makes my life easier to not have to deal with your petty squabbles, I always have the final word. No meeting is necessary. Do as I am ordering you to do. Now."

Two spots of color remained high on Jeyne's cheeks, but she jerked her head in a brief nod. "I will do as you command, Master Gersemi, but I want it to be clear I am doing so under protest."

"I don't much care. Just get it done."

21

MATHIS

UP AHEAD, ZEVON DROPPED TO THE GROUND AND frantically waved his hand behind his lower back. Mathis and the others hid behind some tall shrubbery. A group of Guards passed in front of where they squatted, chatting and oblivious. After a few moments, Zevon gestured forward, and they all moved ahead at a low crouch.

At Silar's suggestion, they'd timed their departure for when the Gate Guards changed shifts. He'd noticed it took the replacements a few minutes to settle into their routine, and they likely would pay even less attention than usual to those passing into the city. The Guards at this side gate were also not nearly as conscientious as those who manned the front gate, as other Guards were the only ones who ever used it. Still, Mathis had told the boys to act as though their lives depended on getting out of the Conclave without being seen. For him, that was likely true.

If the Gate Guards challenged him, he had an excuse ready. *This is only a training mission,* he'd say. *All recruits need to learn how to gather information sight unseen, and they can't do that in here.* At that point, unless the Headmaster had given them specific instructions he was never to leave these walls, not even with his unit, he figured he'd be able to convince them it was perfectly appropriate to accompany his boys into the city for an afternoon training exercise.

Zevon held up a fist as they approached the gate, which was wide enough to accommodate a cart of supplies. When something to the left momentarily distracted the new Gate Guards, he moved through the gate and disappeared to the right. They quickly followed him, though not so fast as to draw the Guards' attention their way. To Mathis's great surprise, it worked, and they melded into the throng of citizens who passed by on the street with no one the wiser.

The urge to run as far and as fast as he could hit him like a punch to the gut. The boys would think it was part of the exercise, and wouldn't pursue. He'd get down to the docks, and he'd find a boat to take him to the mainland before anyone realized his true intentions.

As quickly as it came, the feeling subsided. If Tovi were with him, he would not hesitate. Instead, he continued to stroll with the others, wondering all the while if he'd ever figure out a way to gain access to the towers where the Masters had to be hiding the girl.

He followed the boys for several blocks to a small park. Zevon jumped up on a bench and let out a whoop. "We made it!" he yelped. Several passers-by looked over at them with alarm, and at Mathis's glare, Zevon returned to the ground.

Silar grinned. "I thought for sure those Gate Guards would see us."

"I did, too," Mathis admitted. "That they didn't is a reflection of your efforts. Zevon, you didn't hesitate to drop out of the line of sight when those Guards were close, and the rest of you responded immediately to his lead. Those are skills that will keep you all alive out in the field. Though none of that will matter if you later draw attention to yourself for no reason," he finished wryly.

"Sorry, Lieutenant," Zevon said, though his grin diminished his sincerity.

Mathis shook his head with a smile. These five were those with whom he'd developed a particular camaraderie—those he hoped to enlist in his efforts to find Tovi, and eventually, turn against the Conclave. For now, though, he meant to use them to gather intelligence. Since his capture, summer had passed into autumn, and now, even the first few weeks of winter had gone by. What had he missed in all that time?

He could not trust what little information he'd heard of the rebellion inside the Conclave—especially not that stupid rumor concerning their supposed surrender. The biases of the Masters and their underlings colored all news within those walls. He needed to find out what *real* people were saying.

"All right," he announced. "It's time for the next part of the exercise. Use the skills we've practiced to learn as much as you can about the rebellion. Meet back here in two hours. Got it?"

"Are you going back inside?" Silar asked.

"No. I'll be doing the same as you, so don't think you can get away with making stuff up to try to impress me," he joked.

"Not a chance, Lieutenant." Silar lifted the collar of his black coat and blew into his hands. "Let's get moving, boys. It's too cold to stand around doing nothing, and two hours isn't much time."

Mathis waited until they'd dispersed before he set off on his own. He wasn't entirely certain of the direction to take; he hadn't been in Corval for years, and he had spent little time there in any case. Nothing looked as he recalled, and he quickly got lost. When he finally regained his bearings and located the narrow building he sought in what had once been one of the dingier parts of town, he was dismayed to find it freshly painted, with glow lanterns set in sconces to either side of a sign proclaiming the name of a restaurant.

In case the decor was a front for the safe house, he went inside. Small, round tables packed with diners filled what he remembered as a dark, inhospitable space. Music came from somewhere in the back, almost imperceptible over murmured conversation and the clatter of utensils.

"Good afternoon," said a young man in a short blue coat who stood behind a pedestal. "Are you here for lunch? I'm afraid there will be a bit of a wait for a table, but I might be able to fit you in at the bar, if you didn't mind sitting there."

"Uh, no. I was just passing by. Is Cinta working here? Short woman with long blonde hair?"

"I'm sorry, but no one of that description works here. Might she have worked for the last establishment? We only opened a month ago."

"Ah...I'm sure that was it. Well, thanks anyway," Mathis said before he ducked back outside. *That's that*, he thought. *Next.*

None of the three other safe houses he checked produced any better results. One was now a shop for upper-class women, while the other two no longer existed at all: all he found was an abandoned, burned-out shell at one location and an empty space in the block between buildings at the other. Although he'd known the Masters had spent the last few years purging what remained of the rebellion from the capital, he'd hoped to find some sign of his former contacts. They would have known better than anyone what was really going on.

Disheartened, he allowed the flow of pedestrian traffic to carry him down the street. There might be other safe houses in the city, and he wished he had some idea of where they might be. The rebellion considered safe-house locations to be amongst the most sensitive of information, however, and those outside the command structure only learned of those they needed when they needed them. He'd only known of the others because he'd used them during his sister's last, failed mission.

For not the first time, he couldn't help but reflect on the fact that it had been the Conclave, not the rebels, who'd finally given him the one thing he'd always wanted: the chance to lead. He'd watched his sister fail time and time again yet rise in the ranks of command, and he'd seen the same thing happen with others. Women always seemed to get the benefit of the doubt, no matter how many mistakes they made. For all that the rebellion wanted to change the governance of Corinas, changing the underlying social order wasn't part of their plan.

What you have now isn't real, you know. The Headmaster had her own agenda for giving him a command that had nothing to do with his capabilities, and she'd take it away in an instant if that outcome better served her interests.

And once he left this place with Tovi, he'd return to being simply Mathis, a fighter in the rebellion, and under someone else's command. His Lieutenancy would become nothing but a fond memory of the strange time he'd spent as a prisoner of the Conclave.

But for now—now, to these boys, he was their commander, and he loved every minute. It would be a failure of leadership if he returned to them today without *some* new information of his own.

The street he was on emptied into a large market square. Buildings of red and yellow stone surrounded the square on three sides, with arches cut into them to allow passage through to other streets. Inside, permanent stalls ran the length of the square in rows, with tiny alleyways behind them. Now that it was winter, heavy canvas enveloped most of the stalls, leaving only a small space open for entry at the front. The color of the canvas informed shoppers generally what lay within—green for local foodstuffs, yellow for crafts, blue for foreign goods, and so on—with small signs hanging from the canvas providing further information. At the middle, a smooth stone tower rose above it all, with clock faces on each side. He didn't have much time before he had to be back at the park.

Despite the enclosed stalls, the cacophony of trade carried into the square, making it difficult to focus in on individual conversations. He was out of practice, and it wasn't as if he'd had special training in intelligence work. At first, he could only make out mundanities about matters that didn't concern him. One snippet of a conversation might have been about the rebellion, but the speakers turned a corner crowded with shoppers and he wasn't able to follow.

Mathis meandered down the row of stalls, then stepped inside one for a vegetable merchant and pretended to browse. A woman and man, bundled up in heavy coats, sorted through a basket of gourds next to him. "Soon enough, things will return to normal, don't you think?" she said as she balanced a dark-green squash in her hand. "The rebellion is on its last legs, after all."

"We can only hope," the man with her responded. "I am tired of all this fighting. Did I tell you what happened to my cousins?"

"I don't think so."

"Oh, you'd remember if I had. It was horrible. The rebels attacked their village outside Napimir. They killed half the people who lived there and then destroyed everything."

"Fires! Are your cousins all right?"

"Yes and no. They weren't there at the time, but they lost everything they had. They ended up having to move in with our grandmother down in Aldham. It's been awful. They have nothing of their own, and I don't think they've found employment, either."

"That's terrible. People can't keep living in fear like this. I'm glad the Masters are finally doing something about it."

Another customer forced her way in front of Mathis and began haranguing the proprietor about the quality of some turnips, making it impossible for him to continue listening in on the couple's conversation. Their story was far too similar to those he'd heard in Valen. What they blamed on the rebellion had to be the work of the Conclave. How could anyone think the rebellion would ever harm the citizens of Corinas—the very people it wanted to save?

As he continued his way through the market on his way back to the park, he heard even more disturbing rumors. The rebels were fading, running away, or agreeing to put down their arms. They'd lost their Adepts and had nothing more to gain from fighting, so they'd given up. The Conclave's Guard had attacked them in the mountains, and they'd fled in disarray. They had finally seen the error of their ways and were coming back into the fold with the Masters' forgiveness. None of it made any sense, but *something* must have changed to cause so much chatter.

What he didn't hear, however, was anything suggesting the Conclave had lost more of its own Adepts to the rebellion. As he'd suspected, the Gate Guards had been playing with Zevon when they'd sold him that tale.

By the time he arrived at the park, all five boys had already gathered near the same bench from which they'd departed earlier. "Early, huh? I hope that's not because you all gave up."

"Of course not, Lieutenant," said Silar. "We just didn't want to be late returning from our first mission."

Mathis couldn't help but smile a bit. "Not a bad habit to have." He pointed to Mateo, the oldest of the group. "Report. What did you learn?"

"Nothing specific, Lieutenant," the boy responded, scratching at the slight shadow of hair at his jawline. "There's a rumor going around about the rebellion pulling back, but I heard so many versions of it that I can't say which might be true. Maybe none of them are."

"Did anyone else hear anything about the rebels disengaging?"

All the other boys nodded at the same time. "I heard some merchants talking about it inside a tavern," Zevon said. Before Mathis could ask him what he had been doing in a tavern in the middle of the afternoon, the boy continued. "They were saying how they'd had to change their shipping routes because their regular port in the north had been 'overrun' with rebel Guards who'd come back to our side. They were complaining about how the Conclave had conscripted their ships, too, and filled them full of Guards before sending them out to sea, and how they couldn't afford more losses."

That was new, yet it aligned with some of what he'd heard himself. He didn't like to think that those who'd only recently joined the rebellion were already switching back, nor that the Conclave might be transporting them away. Were they coming to Corval, or was the Conclave trying to position them closer to Brome? "What about you?" he asked, pointing to Silar. "What did you learn?"

"That Zevon was right."

Zevon sat up straighter and grinned as he turned to look at everyone. "Aren't I always?" he said to groans from the others.

"All right, all right," Mathis said. "Let's not get ahead of ourselves. Silar, what do you mean?"

"It sounds like it really was a rebel courier he saw a few weeks back. I stopped by that big provisioner's shop down the street from the front entrance to the Conclave—you know, the one with the animal carvings all around the door? Anyway, one of the workers there is an old friend of mine. He said the courier went there to get supplies before she left town."

Mathis squinted. "How did he know she was a rebel courier? That's not something anyone with sense would announce."

"He said she was with another woman, and he overheard them talking about it. No one pays attention to stock boys."

"Did you ask him what they looked like?"

"Yes. He said the courier was tallish with long blonde hair braided down her back, just like Zevon described. The other one was shorter and kind of stocky, with curly black hair. He said he noticed her first because she had a big lock of white hair in the front."

Mathis's heart skipped a beat. Cinta, the rebel agent who'd once operated out of the safe house that was now a fancy restaurant, matched that description. If it really had been her, then the story of a rebel courier who'd brought news of the rebellion's surrender had suddenly become very real. "What did your friend overhear?"

"Not a lot. He heard the courier say that 'the message' had been delivered, and something about emissaries being on the way to meet the Headmaster. The other one promised to see her safely out of the city and back to some place called Brome."

A chill swept through Mathis. No one would know that name unless they really were of the rebellion. Between everything he'd heard in the streets, to what Zevon and Mateo had reported, and now this…If the rebels were giving up, where did that leave him?

22

ALIA

Nyona held out her arm in front of Alia's chest, halting her forward movement. A retort died on her lips as a carriage she hadn't noticed rumbled past them. "Thanks," she said, belatedly grateful for the second set of eyes.

"It reminds me of walking with Tovi," Nyona said with a laugh.

Alia managed a smile in response, though Nyona had already started to cross the street. She walked as if they had somewhere to go.

Granted, meandering through Amrava with no apparent purpose was better than being cooped up inside. Three weeks ago, when Kalisfena's minions escorted her to her quarters after the confrontation over what she and Hasso knew—or didn't know—about the rebellion's supposed plans to treat with the Conclave, Alia expected never to leave again. Yet the very next day, Nyona had arrived at her door, ecstatic to deliver news that one of their handlers had given them permission to go outside for the first time since their arrival. Whether this was due to a miscommunication or Kalisfena's change of heart, Alia had jumped at the chance to breathe fresh air. Since then, she and Nyona had gone out at least ten times, and they even had a small purse of coins to spend as they so desired.

In the first week of their excursions, she didn't see Kalisfena or Hasso once. Hasso was prone to disappearances, so she figured he was off somewhere trying to learn the source of the rumor that had so upset Kalisfena. As for Kalisfena herself, upon inquiry, one of Alia's instructors noted she was busy with important business, but would reveal nothing more specific than that.

In the second week, Hasso returned. As usual, he'd not told them much about what he'd been up to beyond a vague indication he was trying to deal with the problem at hand. When Nyona had suggested they leave for Corinas right then, before Kalisfena changed her mind and retaliated against them or Tovi for whatever she thought was going on with the rebellion, he claimed there was no way for them to leave without her knowledge and permission.

It wasn't until late in the third week that she spied Kalisfena again as she passed by the room where Alia had her lessons. Alia asked to speak to her, on grounds that she wanted to better understand her and Nyona's changed circumstances, but the instructor she'd asked said there was no need. The woman asserted their walks outside were part of the curriculum, as exposure to the city was the best way to familiarize themselves with daily life in Amrava—and while she and Nyona were ready for that next step, the other Adepts, the children, needed more by way of education before they would be ready to venture outside.

The premise made little sense, but she was not in a position to argue against their logic. So, she decided she might as well absorb all she could of Amrava while she was still there. Hopefully, it would not be for much longer.

"I can't believe how warm it is," Nyona said when they paused at the next intersection. "Fires, it's supposed to be winter! If we were in Brome, we'd be bundled up in the thickest furs we could find by now."

Alia glanced around at the few other people who also waited at the corner, but none of them, Xeydeyans all, seemed to notice

Nyona's use of a curse word that obliquely referenced Ability. "Once we're back home, you'll wish it were more like this," Alia said as she squinted up at the nearly cloudless sky that served as a backdrop to the upper stories of the aptly named skyscrapers. Even in the shadow of those giants, the air that wafted up her blousy pant legs held not even the barest hint of a chill.

Nyona nodded, then pointed to the right. "We haven't been down there, have we?"

"I don't think so, but everything looks the same to me." The street Nyona referred to was much like every other, with skyscrapers, numerous shops, and a steady stream of people. A woman in the crowd with long, curly blonde hair caught Alia's attention. In a city where the locals all had brown and black hair, visitors with lighter-colored locks stuck out.

The woman glanced toward them for the briefest of moments before continuing on her way. Alia gasped. *Impossible.*

"What? What is it?" Nyona asked, turning her head this way and that.

Alia shook her head and pulled her hand away from her mouth. She had to be mistaken. "I'm sorry. I didn't mean to startle you."

"Well you did, so what was it?"

"I saw a woman up there, and for a second, I thought it was Marta."

"What?" Nyona lifted her chin, straining to see ahead. "Where?"

"Don't worry about it; I'm certain it was nothing but wishful thinking."

"What if it wasn't? Which way did she go?"

"To the right." The woman's long blonde hair made her easy to spot as she moved with the flow of pedestrian traffic. "Do you see?"

Nyona peered down the street. "I do! Oh—and she just went into that housewares shop. Perfect. Let's go."

Alia followed her, feeling more than a little foolish. Even if

Marta were in Amrava by choice, that wasn't the sort of place she'd be likely to visit. They were chasing a stranger, though she supposed there was no harm in making sure. It wasn't as if they had anything better to do.

The door to the shop slid open automatically as they moved toward it. A soft, pleasant bell chimed. Inside, solid-backed shelves displayed a collection of white plates and bowls with intricate designs of different colors painted along their rims, all of which seemed far too delicate for actual use. A young Xeydeyan woman at the counter near the far wall turned their way. No one else was in the store.

"Where did she go?" Nyona murmured.

"I don't know. Are you sure she came in here?"

"I thought so," Nyona said glumly.

The young woman approached. "Welcome," she said with a generous nod of her head, revealing the jeweled pins that held her braided black hair in a circlet. "May I help you find something in particular today?"

"Uh—no, thank you," Alia said. "We were just looking."

"Ah. You are from the south, yes? These items up here would not be to your liking, I would think. Please, follow me, and I will show you something more to your favor."

Not wanting to be rude—they had barged into her shop, after all—Alia nodded in acquiescence, then shrugged to Nyona as the shopkeeper led them to the back corner of the store. They'd look at whatever wares the woman wanted them to see, pretend to struggle over the purchasing decision, then leave empty-handed with false promises of a return visit.

"I think you'll find what you're looking for in here," the shop-keeper said more loudly than seemed necessary. She pulled back a blue velvet curtain hanging against the wall, revealing a dimly lit stockroom.

Nyona poked her head in and looked around with some confusion, then yelped with delight. "It *is* you!" she cried.

Marta emerged from the shadows. "Shh!" she hissed. "I'm glad to see you, too, but we must keep quiet," she said as she gave each of them a quick hug in turn.

Alia squeezed her tightly, shocked and elated. "I can't believe it's really you. How are you here?"

"I'll explain everything when we're someplace where we can talk more freely. Here—take this." She handed Alia a bowl of thick pottery, the kind common in Corinas, glazed in a vibrant purple color. "Eloi will package this for you at the counter. Don't worry; you won't have to pay for it, but it will help make it look like you came in here for a legitimate reason in case someone followed you."

"What is going on?" Alia asked, startled by the urgency in Marta's voice and the prospect that someone might have been following them, unnoticed.

"It's a distraction," she said matter-of-factly. "I will leave first so we aren't seen together. When you're done here, go back to Third Avenue. Follow that for about five minutes, then take a left on Forty-sixth street. You'll see me again there."

"Wait." Alia grabbed her arm. "What if we get lost?"

"You know how the grid works, don't you?"

"Yes," said Nyona. "Don't worry; we will find you. Forty-sixth and Third. Got it."

The door chimed. "I'll be with you in a moment," Eloi called out to the three Xeydeyan woman who had come into the store. They all appeared to be true shoppers, yet Alia could not help but wonder if they were really Kalisfena's agents.

"See you soon," Marta whispered. She lifted a small paper bag stamped with the name of the store. "My purchase," she said with a little smile.

"I hope you enjoy it," Eloi said, her voice carrying beyond their little group. She maintained her genial smile as she reached for Alia's bowl. "I think you will enjoy your selection, as well. Let me wrap it up for you." She prattled on about the sort of inconsequential topics one discussed with strangers while Marta left the store. To Alia's relief, the newcomers also ignored Nyona and her as they browsed the dishes near the windows.

Back outside in the bustle of people, Alia waited until they rounded the corner before she said anything to Nyona. "What in fires is going on?"

"I have no idea." She shifted her shoulders toward Alia to avoid a group walking in the opposite direction. "I've never known her to act so mysteriously. Have you?"

"Well, yes, and so have you. Sarabie?"

"Oh. That's right." No more needed to be said of the time when Marta had conspired with the rebellion to get her friend, Sarabie, out of the Conclave. Although their efforts had failed, Marta had tricked the Masters for months as to where her loyalty lay. It did not seem so strange, then, to find her here in Xeydeya, safe and sound. She was more resourceful than any of them gave her credit for.

They hurried down the street, block after block. Alia half-expected someone to jump out and grab them along the way. The street numbers ticked up and up, and in less than the five minutes Marta had estimated, they reached Forty-sixth. "Left, she said?"

"Right."

"Right?"

"No, sorry—I mean you are correct," Nyona said. She jutted her thumb to the left. "This way." Alia rolled her eyes and followed.

Marta stood outside a building indistinguishable from the one they'd been in before, other than that it might have been a few stories shorter. It was hard to tell from the street. She nodded in the briefest of acknowledgments before walking inside.

They found her waiting in a small foyer that was otherwise unoccupied except for a chair, a half-dead plant, and a middle-aged man with a short, grayish-brown beard who stood before a single set of lift doors. He glared at Alia and Nyona. "They with you?" he asked Marta, using a gruff mannerism that reminded Alia somewhat of Mathis when he was in a mood. The thought of her other missing friend made her smile; if Marta was safe, there might still be hope for Mathis, no matter how great the odds.

"Yes," Marta replied.

He nodded once and pushed the round button that called the lift. The doors opened. After the three women entered, Marta pressed the button for the seventh floor. The doors *swished* together, and the lift began its upward climb.

Nyona rounded on the former Master. "We've heard nothing of you since you were captured. How did you get here? Did the Xeydeyans bring you? Have you been here all along? Why haven't you gotten word to Tovi? She's been worried sick about you! We all have."

Marta held out her hands. "Please, I will explain everything. I have been here for many months, I think as long as Tovi, though we came on different ships. The Xeydeyans thought I was you," she said, looking at Alia.

"Me?"

"Yes. They thought you were the one traveling with Tovi back when they took us both. Apparently, some messages had crossed about your description, and they didn't realize their mistake until we arrived here and someone finally figured it out. Once they did, they had no use for me and they let me go. I stayed so I could try to get to Tovi, and, well…things kind of escalated from there."

Alia furrowed her brow. "Wait—are you suggesting they meant to abduct me as well as Tovi?"

"I'm not suggesting it—that absolutely was their intention."

As Alia tried to process Marta's allegation, the elevator doors slid open. They walked down a short hallway with dark hardwood floors and white doors staggered along both sides, each bearing a sequential number. Marta stopped before the one marked as seventy-four. "Here we are." She pulled out a key from her pocket and unlocked the door.

Light filtered into a sparsely furnished room through beige shades covering the windows. A Xeydeyan woman, sitting in a green chair made of some sort of smooth material, watched them with interest. Her braids were short and flat against her head, her fingers bore only two rings, and she wore no bracelets at all, unlike the over-the-top displays of wealth so many of the local women favored. "Good afternoon."

"Alia and Nyona, this is Lora Stretyn. She's been helping me, and she wants to help you, too."

"I am pleased to meet you finally. We have been waiting for the right time to make our introduction."

Alia wasn't interested in exchanging inane pleasantries with someone whose agenda was unclear. "Do you have a ship that can take us home? That's the only help we need right now."

"Kalisfena Tatyn is allowing you to leave? That is a surprising development, seeing as how they went through so much trouble to bring you here."

Alia exchanged a quick glance with Nyona. "I don't know anything about that, but it's been clear since the day we arrived that we would one day leave with Tovi." She assumed Marta would have told her all about the child.

Lora Stretyn examined a long fingernail. "Yet you are still here, are you not?"

"Well, yes, but that's only because of some stupid rumor about the rebellion treating with the Conclave. She fears we are part of some scheme to betray her."

She looked up with a small smile. "Now that would be rich! So, are you? In on some scheme?"

"Of course not."

"Then why did you come here in the company of Mila and Hasso? They are known schemers, after all."

"You know them?" she asked carefully. Marta might have mentioned Hasso, certainly, but she wouldn't know Mila's name. Alia herself hadn't seen the ship-owner since the day they'd arrived.

"Oh, we go back some years," Lora Stretyn replied. "They are not all that they seem, you know."

"I imagine I could say the same about you."

"Alia, please—"

"It's all right, Marta. She is right to be suspicious. Unfortunately, her suspicion is misdirected."

"Is it? She says you want to help us, yet I've heard nothing but accusations and riddles." Alia's ire grew as she spoke. "Can you get us home or not? As I said, that's the only help we need."

"You don't understand," Marta interjected. "There's no home for you to go back to."

Nyona gasped. "Did something happen to Brome?"

"No—not that we've heard, anyway. What I mean is that even if Lora Stretyn took you back to Corinas, you'd have nowhere to go—at least, nowhere safe. The Captains didn't send you here to find Tovi. They sent you here knowing Kalisfena Tatyn would not let you leave, nor Tovi, nor any of the other Adepts they've found. If you returned, your life would be in danger."

"What?" Now Marta was the one making no sense whatsoever.

"The Captains—Levina, Jana, and all the rest of them—arranged for it all. Once they realized they'd never have enough Adepts of their own to fight against the Conclave, they decided the better course was to rid Corinas of Adepts entirely. Including—I daresay, especially—you."

23

MATHIS

MATHIS TOSSED THE DAMP RAG HE'D USED TO CLEAN HIS boots over to the pile of dirty clothes in the corner of his room. He sighed, searching for something else to do. Maybe he'd finally read one of those books sitting on the shelf above his desk. That might be a way to kill at least a few hours.

He hoped his unit, sequestered in their barracks, were keeping themselves entertained without getting into trouble. With the cancelation of all public training for the foreseeable future—likely so the rebels wouldn't see how few fighters they had—they'd have plenty of energy to burn.

News of the rebel delegation's imminent arrival had spread like an oil fire yesterday, proving the truth of the rumors he'd heard in the city last week. Who had come to treat on the rebellion's behalf? It would be far too much to hope for Captain Levina or Captain Jana. They might actually tell him what they hoped to accomplish with this gambit. They'd also understand that everything he'd done here had been for Tovi, and he was confident they'd make her release a priority of their negotiations.

Or maybe they did not know he was here, and that was why he was once again being treated as a prisoner. He'd tried to leave shortly after he'd returned from the empty training grounds that morning, but had found the inside latch of his door disabled. Enece had responded to his pounding on the door with profuse apologies, claiming it was necessary to remain in his quarters for his own safety, Mathis must understand.

He idly flipped though one of the books. It was about the Conclave, as were all the others. Mathis had ignored them in his time here, uninterested in reading the Masters' propaganda. Today, however, he needed something, anything to distract him. He sat down, propped his feet up on his desk, and started to read.

He'd just finished a particularly unbelievable tale about the so-called First Adept when the latch clicked. For a moment, he considered trying to overpower the eunuch when he opened the door, but quickly discarded the idea. He'd make no rash moves for now. With a sigh, he set the book aside and folded his hands together over his chest. "What do you want?" he called out.

The door opened. "That is a rather rude way to greet some-one," Headmaster Gersemi said with a hint of amusement. Her gray robe, with its ornate silver designs, sparkled in the light. Enece hovered behind her like a stubby shadow.

Mathis scrambled to get his feet on the ground. He'd seen the Headmaster a few times from a distance in the last few months, but this was the first time she'd spoken to him since she'd offered him his command. "I thought it was him."

"I didn't imagine you were expecting me. Enece, you may leave us. Return to your duties."

"Are you quite certain, Headmaster? I am happy to wait here, in case you have need of me."

"If I had need of you, I would have said so," she said icily. "Go. And do not hover nearby. I will know if you attempt to listen."

He bowed deeply from the waist as he backed away from the door. "Yes, Headmaster. My apologies."

She closed the door and turned to face Mathis with a smile. "Now we can speak in peace."

He wondered at her confidence in remaining alone with him.

Maybe her attitude came with the territory of being the most powerful woman in all of Corinas. Or maybe it was because she knew, as well as he did, that if he harmed her—relegating himself to certain death in the process—the Masters would only pick another Headmaster, and the Conclave would continue as it always had.

He hoped it wasn't because she sensed, somehow, that his feelings toward her had become more...complicated. He couldn't deny the enjoyment he'd felt in his current existence as a commander, and she was responsible for giving him that opportunity. Some days, he had to remind himself that he still hated her for everything she stood for and everything she'd done.

Her presence unnerved him. "Why are you here?" he asked, hoping to end this audience quickly.

"Did you enjoy your time in the city the other day?"

He repeated what he'd told the Gate Guards. "It was a training session for my unit."

She nodded. "So I heard. What, precisely, were you hoping to teach your boys in the streets of Corval?"

"Intelligence gathering."

"Were you successful?"

"Yes."

"I can understand the lure of the city. It has been a very long time since I've been outside these walls, myself." She trailed a long finger along the table and then flicked away the resultant dust. "There is much to learn out there, if one knows how to listen. What did your boys learn?"

"That the rebellion means to treat with the Conclave." There was no harm in admitting that, given that the rebels had arrived.

"Hmm. And after learning this, you returned?"

"Yes."

"That pleases me. It demonstrates you are beginning to understand that this is your true home."

"My actions aren't for you."

"Not entirely, this I know. But all the same, you would not

have come back through that gate if some part of you did not relish your new life." She sat in the vacant chair and arranged her robe as if she were preparing for an audience. "I understand you believe we have Nyona's child here."

That damned eunuch must have overheard him asking his boys if they'd seen or heard of an Adept matching Tovi's description. Well, it would do no good denying it now; maybe he'd get lucky, and she'd admit to something that would help him locate the child. "Yes."

"You care a great deal for the girl, do you not? I wish you had asked me about her earlier, if this was what you suspected, as I could have put your mind at ease. We do not have her."

He snorted. "Sure. All right, then."

"Why would I mislead you? Besides, if she were here, I would see no reason to keep you from her. You are a Son of an Adept. There is no impropriety in it."

"I don't know why you do much of anything," he answered quite honestly.

"Why are you so certain she is here? Did you watch our Guards steal her away with your own eyes?"

He hadn't. When Tovi disappeared, he'd been off chasing rumors about one of the Conclave's own missing Adepts. Alia had been the one to tell him of Tovi's capture, and she would never mislead him.

"Of course you did not," the Headmaster said, "because nothing of the sort happened. I will not deny that we want her; she is an Adept, and she should be surrounded by those who understand her skills and needs. Fortunately, if all goes well in our meetings with the rebel delegation, she will finally come home."

"Are you suggesting the rebellion has offered her in trade?" He was aghast at the possibility—not only because it would amount to a complete betrayal, but also because it would mean that Tovi had made her way back to Brome, and he had remained at the Conclave for months for no reason. Not even his command could ever make up for all that wasted time.

"No, but they will if they wish for our talks to be fruitful. This is not widely known, but Nyona's child is not the only Adept who has gone missing. As a condition of their surrender, the rebellion must agree to help us recover them all."

He didn't want to believe her, yet Zevon had heard the Gate Guards making a similar claim of missing Adepts weeks ago. When Mathis had heard nothing more to that effect in Corval, he'd ruled it out as a possible truth, and now he wondered if he'd been too hasty in doing so. The Conclave had ways of making sure that unwanted rumors did not percolate amongst the populace. "Where is she, then, if not here?"

"Our missing Adepts, including her, are all in Xeydeya. The Xeydeyans have always taken far too great an interest in our Adepts. I should have known it was because they coveted them."

Mathis took a breath and let it out slowly. Pieces of the puzzle fell into place, though the remaining gaps seemed even larger than before. According to Lieutenant Elcy, Xeydeya had aligned with the rebellion for years. That meant—if any of this were true—the rebels probably had the ability to negotiate with Xeydeya for the Adepts' return. But why would they ever agree to do so? A major goal of the rebellion was to reduce the Conclave's power, and keeping a bunch of Adepts an ocean away could only help that effort.

"I can see you are giving this careful thought, as you should. You'll see the proof of what I am telling you soon enough when the child returns with the others, and the rebellion no longer exists. But please, rest assured your position here is safe no matter what happens. You've demonstrated your clear talent for leadership. In fact, I have it on good authority you are up for a promotion," she said, reaching forward to rest her hand on his knee. "Do not be surprised if one day you are elevated to a Captaincy. Nothing will constrain your greatness here."

Her familiarity raised the hair on the back of his neck, and he jerked his leg away from her. This needed to stop. She could try all she wanted to bribe him, but a Captaincy was an unenforceable promise. The other Masters would never agree to it.

She gave him a sad smile. "Oh, Mathis, my dear. You still do not understand how special you are, do you? Of course, how could you? Not even the others know, not yet. Maybe I should have told you before. I have been waiting, watching, to see for myself if you were as I expected. And oh—you have been so much more. You are everything I could have hoped for. So, it is past time you knew the truth. Then, you will understand why you are as you are."

Her rambling turned his stomach. "I'm sure I don't need to know whatever it is you want to tell me."

"Perhaps." She leaned forward again, though she didn't touch him this time. "I think it will help you appreciate why you belong with us, and why you will rise to a greatness here, in your true home, you could have never attained with the rebellion."

"Say what you want to say, then," he said with a shrug, as if he hadn't a care in the world. Nothing she could say to him mattered.

Looking back, he could only laugh at how wrong he'd been.

24

MASTER GERSEMI

GERSEMI FELT AS IF HER HEART WOULD BURST. *HE KNOWS. He knows!*

It must have come as a shock, as it would for anyone, for Mathis to learn he was the child of the Headmaster of the Conclave. Yet he'd accepted it without denial, as she'd hoped he might. He must have recognized, deep down, he was different—special. The privileges she'd bestowed upon him were nothing she'd ever grant to any other Son. Only her Son was worthy of such opportunity.

My Son. When the words had left her lips, words she'd never before said out loud, they had gone forth with a delicious vibration. Soon enough, she would repeat those words to everyone, and the world would know Mathis for who he was, and for who he was meant to be.

Her overall exhilaration made it more difficult than it should have been not to fidget in her seat, though few would notice if she did. Today, the only people in the Public Room besides a few members of the Directorate were two-dozen Guards and about half as many servants whose efforts to arrange a small table of refreshments echoed strangely. Most of the food likely would go to waste; there were only two rebels coming, after all.

That the rebel delegation was so small had come as a surprise. Gersemi had taken it as an insult at first, until someone suggested they might have kept their entourage to a handful of people to avoid detection as they traveled to Corval. She begrudgingly conceded the point, as no one had noticed them along the way. At the end of the day, it was no matter, so long as the people they sent had sufficient authority to negotiate on the rebellion's behalf.

Having only two guests did give her a convenient excuse for not inviting everyone in the Directorate to attend this first meeting. She had not been able to keep Leyta away, unfortunately. The Principal Master of Generation had insisted on her right to attend, arguing that the focus of the negotiations should be on the return of their Adepts as soon as possible lest any of the older ones pass into the time when they otherwise would be in Seclusion. Gersemi doubted any of those missing were anywhere near the time of losing their Ability, but it wasn't worth arguing the point. At least Leyta sat in the chair farthest away from her, so she'd be spared the woman's prattle.

To her immediate left, Jeyne sat rigidly upright as she observed the servants making their final preparations. She, too, was someone Gersemi wished she could do without today. The Principal Master of Security had been in a furor since she'd acted on Gersemi's orders to begin simultaneous attacks on Amrava and Brome. Ships had already left for the Xeydeyan shore, and more would depart in the coming days. Jeyne would have preferred to wait to send anyone at all until they'd completed their negotiations with the rebellion, yet it was long past time for action. The rebels could help finish the job.

As for Brome, the rebels were lucky the winter snows had stymied the Conclave's efforts to launch a strike against their mountain outpost. Last week, after finally learning the delegation was near, Jeyne had ordered those Guards to stand down.

A eunuch in a crisp black uniform hurried toward the dais and bowed. "Headmaster; Masters. Your guests have arrived."

A stir of anticipation spread amongst her companions. "Send them in," Gersemi ordered with a wave of her hand.

The servant bowed once more, then retreated past the Guards who stood at attention near the entrance to the Public Room. More Guards flanked both sides of the dais. If the rebels exhibited any ill intent, they would not be long for this world.

"I wonder who it will be," said Beryl, leaning forward to direct her conversation past Gersemi and toward Jeyne. "Do you think it will be one of their Captains we've heard so much about?"

"Perhaps," said Jeyne, "though I doubt they'd send someone at the top of our most wanted list. They aren't that stupid."

"I'm not sure your conclusion as to their intelligence is sound," Gersemi murmured. "They are rebelling against their rightful government, after all."

Beryl leaned back in her chair, but not before Gersemi noticed her slight eye roll. The Principal Master of Governance usually did not cause her much difficulty; whatever had gotten into Leyta and Jeyne had better not be spreading to the rest. The Directorate needed to appear to the rebels as a united front if any of this was to work.

The double doors to the Public Room opened. Three women who moved and dressed as those accustomed to fighting entered the room first. They carried no weapons, yet they spread themselves out as if they expected a fight at any moment.

Two figures in plain brown robes, one tall and one short, came next. *The emissaries.* They didn't look like much. The lanky one, with reddish-brown hair, freckled cheeks, and an angular jaw, couldn't have been much more than thirty years old. She tripped on her hem as she walked forward, as if she were unused to wearing formal attire. The second one seemed more comfortable in her garb, though she was much older, with her gray hair gathered into a small, neat bun at the back of her head. Something about her was vaguely familiar.

After a moment, Gersemi had a jolt of recognition. *Was that—Kelda?* She'd never considered the rebels might send her, despite the choice being obvious in hindsight. The former Master knew the Conclave. She knew Masters. And she knew Gersemi, having grown up in the same Initiate so very long ago.

The pair reached the dais. Neither bowed or showed any other display of respect. "Good day," Kelda said. "I am Kelda, and with me is Lieutenant Elcy. We are here on behalf of the rebellion to discuss the terms of our cooperation."

"Your surrender, you mean," Gersemi corrected.

"If it were that, we all know these talks would not be taking place. You most certainly would not be offering us any control in exchange for our assistance. So, I think 'cooperation' has a nice ring to it, does it not?"

"We expected the rebellion to send some of its Captains as its representatives," she said, pivoting away from Kelda's cavalier words, which, unfortunately, were true. "Instead, what we have is a mere Lieutenant and a disgraced former Master. What authority could you possibly have to negotiate with us?"

"I and Lieutenant Elcy—who is a Sixth-degree Lieutenant, by the way—have full authority to reach an agreement with the Conclave. Our Captains are out in the field, ready to act once our talks conclude."

"I see," Gersemi said, brushing at her sleeve in a gesture of disdain. In other words, their Captains had not come in case these negotiations fell apart. If it came to that, Kelda and this Lieutenant must have agreed to sacrifice themselves for their ridiculous cause instead of those who were actually in charge. *Fools.*

"I might recognize some of those with you, but perhaps you could do us the favor of introductions? You yourself are looking well, Headmaster Gersemi."

"I wish I could say the same of you. It appears life on the run has been most difficult."

Kelda grinned. "Oh, I wouldn't call it that. I suspect I have spent most of my life far more at ease than you have, especially of late."

Gersemi returned a thin smile, not willing to give Kelda any satisfaction in her veiled insult. "With me today are four members of my Directorate. This is Master Jeyne, Principal Master of Security. And to my right is Master Beryl, Principal Master of Governance. The two of them will handle the bulk of our discussions. We also have with us Master Leyta, Principal Master of Generation, and at the other end, Master Ryna, Principal Master of Finance, both of whom have indirect interests in these talks."

"We are pleased to make your acquaintance, or re-acquaintance, as the case may be. Shall we begin, then? There's no time like the present."

"A moment, please." Gersemi nodded to Enece, who stood near the side door. He ducked inside her private foyer and returned with Adept Kora, her vivid red hair pulled back into a neat, formal arrangement. Gersemi was pleased she'd had the foresight to select her for this task. As one of their strongest Adepts, she could overcome any blocking Kelda might try. She was probably the one who'd taught Mathis how to resist a truth assessment; she'd always loved nothing more than to teach.

Adept Kora walked up the steps to the dais. She stood with grace, resplendent in her pristine white robe. *She holds herself well,* Gersemi mused. *One day, she will make a fine Master.*

"What is the meaning of this?" Kelda demanded as her companion, who'd remained remarkably silent for a purported Sixth-degree Lieutenant, scowled.

"We cannot begin our discussions until we assess the sincerity of your motivations," Gersemi said. "You understand, of course, having once spent your life among us." She lifted her arm to displace Jeyne's hand, which had bumped against hers.

"We did not agree to this. In fact, the communications we received from Master Jeyne assured us our negotiations would not be conditioned upon a truth assessment."

"Headmaster, if I may—" Jeyne began.

"No, you may not," Gersemi replied, keeping her face a mask of civility while she seethed internally at Jeyne's presumptuousness. "I fear there must have been some miscommunication. We could never agree to such a thing."

"How can this be a good-faith negotiation if you've read our minds?"

"How can we know that *you* will negotiate in good faith without a truth assessment, when you've done nothing since you left us but seek our ruin?" Gersemi snapped.

Kelda folded her arms over her chest. "That is not true, Gersemi, and you know it."

A shocked silence descended over the public use of her name without her honorific. Not even the members of her Directorate would dare do so in mixed company. That this...this frumpy old *traitor* would do so caused her blood to boil.

"I think it would be best if we dispensed with a truth assessment for now, Headmaster," Leyta announced. Before Gersemi could reprimand Leyta for speaking out of turn, the others joined in with their assent.

"We are here to treat in good faith," said Beryl. "Let us not begin on the wrong foot by insisting on something we do not absolutely need."

Jeyne threw the last stone. "Also, I did tell them we would not require it. I would not have us go back on my word."

Gersemi held back the fury she longed to unleash. It would not do for these people, nor her own Guards and servants, to see her lose her temper. She folded her hands together on her lap, gripping her hands so tightly that her knuckles whitened. "Well, then. We seem to have a consensus. For now. As willing members of the rebellion, you already have quite a hill to climb when it comes to gaining our trust."

"I think that feeling is mutual," Kelda said, patting a wisp of her hair back into place. "Which is why I feel obligated to inform you that if your Adept—such a dear child, I'm sure—tries to perform a truth assessment on me or Lieutenant Elcy without our consent, I will know of it immediately, and these talks will end."

"That will not happen," Jeyne quickly assured her, despite it being obvious Kelda was bluffing. As a former holder of Ability, she might notice a surreptitious attempt to learn her own truth, but she couldn't possibly detect what transpired in the mind of her Lieutenant.

"As I said: it appears we have a consensus. Thank you, Adept Kora, for your time, but we will not need your services today, after all."

The Adept inclined her head. "It is my privilege, Headmaster."

"If you are now sufficiently satisfied," Gersemi said to the rebels, her voice thick with sarcasm, "then we may proceed."

"We have one more question first," the Lieutenant said, having finally found her voice. "The answer will calibrate our position in these negotiations."

She waved her hand in the air. "Ask and be done with it, then."

"Does Mathis live?"

Hearing his name, even from a rebel's lips, made her heart leap. "You know of him?"

"His safety is of great importance to us. So, if he lives, we will be more inclined to view your proposals positively. If he does not..."

Gersemi beamed. "He lives, though I'm afraid he no longer considers himself one of you. In fact, he is a Lieutenant himself now, in command of his own unit of the Conclave's Guard, and he has accepted the Conclave as his true home. Did you know? That he is a Son? I'm certain you did, Kelda. You seem to know a great deal."

Kelda raised her eyebrows. "You made him a Lieutenant? Son or not, I find that very hard to believe. Nor can I believe he would turn from what he's known his entire life."

"He recognizes his exceptional nature," Gersemi said. *Soon, everyone will know why.*

The Lieutenant frowned. "Kelda is right. I think we need to have some proof of what you claim. Can we see him?"

"I see no harm in that," Gersemi said. She beckoned to Enece, who had returned to his post in front of the side door.

"Yes, Headmaster?"

"Please fetch Mathis and bring him here immediately."

"At once, Headmaster." He bowed deeply before scurrying away.

Gersemi returned her attention to her skeptical guests. "While we wait for Mathis to arrive, why don't we enjoy some refreshments? Food always brings people together. And is that not what we are trying to accomplish here today? A coming together of sorts?" Now that she would soon be able to show off her Son, she was feeling rather magnanimous.

At the table, silver trays held round slices of crusty bread and various types of cheeses ranging from a nutty, hard yellow to a soft, mild cheese with a white-coated rind. Small and sweet purple and green fruit, a recent gift from a merchant in Corval who'd found a new trading route, filled matching bowls. Instead of wine, however, Gersemi had opted to serve a light, sweet tea.

As they nibbled on the various offerings, the rebels listened, but did not take part in, the Masters' idle chit-chat, the sort about the weather and other unimportant topics. Gersemi herself participated very little, wondering all the while what was taking Enece so long and trying to ignore the tiny knot of worry that perhaps, for all her bravado, Mathis would refuse to come.

She whirled about when the side door opened again. Mathis entered the room, and oh, the wait had been worth it. She made a mental note to reward Enece for his initiative. Instead of the worn training garb Mathis had been in earlier, he now wore the full, formal regalia of a Lieutenant of the Guard, in crisp black with silver emblems. He smiled ever-so-slightly.

"Mathis!" the rebel Lieutenant exclaimed. She took two steps toward him before Jeyne moved into her path.

"You do not need to be near him to see he is well."

"But—"

Kelda pulled on the back of her companion's robe. "It is all right, Lieutenant Elcy. Master Jeyne is correct; we can see he's well from here," she said rather glumly for someone who claimed to care so much for his wellbeing. "It's true, then?" she asked Mathis. "You have accepted a Lieutenancy from the Conclave?"

Mathis looked down for a moment at his polished black boots, then focused his gaze directly on Kelda. "Yes." His voice carried through the room with strength and with no hint of regret.

Gersemi's heart filled with joy. She crossed over to join him and then turned to face the others, resisting the urge to take his arm. "As you can see, we have told you the truth. Mathis is prospering with the opportunities we—and not the rebellion—have provided. He is settled now in his new home, back where he belongs." She beamed as she stood next to him, drinking in the crestfallen looks on the rebels' faces. *My Son!*

ALIA TRACED HER FINGER OVER THE RAISED LETTERS ON THE label of a bottle of wine. It purported to come from a country she'd never heard of, though her education in geography was not particularly sound. To the Conclave, Corinas was the center of everything—the most important, most influential, and most prosperous country in the world.

No wonder they never let Adepts leave their shores. The truth of things would decimate half the Masters' teachings, if not more.

"That one is a particularly lovely specimen, if you enjoy fresh, younger wines," the wine merchant said in that false, friendly manner people used when they were trying to sell you something. "It has been in the bottle for less than one year."

"Hmm. I'm not sure that's for me," she bluffed. She knew nothing about wine.

"Were you looking for anything in particular?"

"Not really. You have such a large selection; it's hard to take it all in."

"Ah, yes, thank you." The merchant, an older woman with bright blue eyes, beamed at Alia's faint praise. "I've spent most of my life curating the collection you see before you. Not these exact bottles," she said with a light laugh. "But the vineyards and the winemakers. All the best wines in all the world are here in my shop."

"Hmm, I can see that," Alia lied. She might not be able to perform a truth assessment on the merchant—not that she ever would for something as trivial as this—but the woman exuded the sort of confidence one has when convinced of one's truth. It would be no harm to go along with it.

"Well, then, I'll leave you to your browsing. Please let me know if you have any questions."

"Thank you." Alia let out a little sigh of relief as the woman moved away. Hopefully Marta would arrive soon, as she didn't know how long she'd be able to keep up this charade. The note that had arrived under her door that morning had not been precise as to the time.

This would be their first meeting since she'd learned of the rebellion's duplicity a week ago. Had it only been a week? It seemed an eternity, yet she still found it difficult to wrap her head around the extent of the Captains' betrayal. How long had they wanted to be rid of her? Before she'd even arrived in Brome? They'd looked her in the face and lied, repeatedly, without her noticing any of it. *So much for thinking you didn't need Ability for that.*

Hasso had, to her great surprise, admitted to the entire scheme. Maybe now that they were stuck in Xeydeya, keeping the truth from them didn't matter anymore. Or maybe, just maybe, he had the capacity for guilt somewhere deep inside of him.

Nyona had taken his confession particularly hard. How could she not? The people she'd come to trust had concocted an elaborate ruse to send away her child, and they'd allowed her to fret and worry for weeks and weeks that the worst had happened.

Alia herself had struggled with her own emotions since learning the truth. While she was well used to the Masters viewing her as being a mere tool to be discarded when she proved no longer useful, she hadn't realized Levina and Jana judged her the same. She thought that she'd finally found a real purpose amongst the rebellion. She thought she'd finally found her true home.

A soft bell chimed, the same sound it seemed every shop in Amrava used. In busier establishments, the repetitiveness of the sound must drive its employees mad. "Why hello there," the wine merchant said. "What can I do today for the friend of one of my best customers?"

Alia glanced over her shoulder to see Marta in the entrance, who lifted her chin in acknowledgment. "Greetings, Amycia Nelvyn. I have a need for something quite unique."

"I figured as much. Would you like to see my special collection?"

"Yes, I would. But I see you have another customer today. Might she be interested in viewing your special collection, as well?"

The wine merchant looked toward Alia, her eyebrows slightly raised. "But of course. Come, then. I shall take you both to see my special collection."

Down a narrow flight of stairs, below the street level, lay a place that reminded Alia more of home. Unlike the shop above, which had the usual floor-to-ceiling windows typical of Xeydeyan architecture and smooth walls that separated it from the neighboring establishments, this space relied on wood, and stone, and a dimness that hinted of secrets hidden around every corner.

"Please, take your time," the merchant said. "I will be upstairs if you need anything."

"Thank you, Amycia Nelvyn," Marta replied.

They passed by rows of wooden shelving with tiny compartments holding individual bottles of wine. There must have been thousands. "What was all that about?" Alia asked when she judged they'd moved far enough from the stairs.

"Amycia Nelvyn is a friend of Lora's. She lets us meet here, sometimes."

"Us?"

A few more steps answered Alia's question as the shelving ended to reveal a small, open space of stone and dark wooden beams. Lora Stretyn sat at a tall table drinking wine with an older man Alia did not know and, to her indignation, Mila and Hasso. "What are they doing here?" she blurted.

"Ah, you have arrived! Please, join us." Lora Stretyn pushed two delicate-looking cups of clear glass half-full with red wine toward the edge of the table. "You know Mila and Hasso, of course, and this here is Kieran," she said, gesturing to the older man who wore his gray-and-brown hair in a braid draped over his shoulder like Hasso's. "He's a longtime friend, as well."

"What is all this?" Alia demanded of Lora Stretyn. "I thought you didn't care for them. You called them schemers."

Lora Stretyn grinned. "Oh, that they are, though I do not judge them harshly for it. It was a necessary aspect of their past profession, and they've survived as long as they have because of it."

Past profession... A sense of foreboding settled over Alia. Mila, a former Extir? No wonder she'd been the one to transport them to Xeydeya, and why she'd been so curious about Alia's true identity. Kieran must be one, too, given his present company and the openness of their discussion.

Mila grinned as she poured herself some more wine. "You're quite the schemer yourself, *Alia*. I knew there was more to you than you let on. I'm glad my instincts weren't completely off, no thanks to this one," she said, nudging Hasso with her shoulder. "He kept your secret the whole time." He responded with a small shrug, as he often did as a substitution for opening his mouth.

"Are we certain we can trust this one?" Kieran asked of no one in particular. "She seems to be quite...comfortable...under the care of Kalisfena Tatyn."

Alia's anger flared. "Do you think I have much choice? You have some nerve to accuse me of that, especially when you're sitting next to someone who forced me into the situation."

"Now, now," Lora Stretyn said. "It is fair to say there might be an issue of trust on both sides, but we can leave that for now so long as we find a way to help each other."

"I don't need your help," Alia snapped. "I have no one who needs killing."

"Alia!" Marta admonished. "That's not what they're about. Anymore."

"Not usually, anyway," Mila said, nudging Hasso again. "The Xeydeyans have about as much use for Extirs as they do Adepts."

"You're not helping," he said quietly.

"I agree." Lora Stretyn scratched her cheek with a long fingernail. "Look, Alia. We invited you here today because we need to know what is going on—truly going on—with the rebellion."

"You've clearly learned plenty on your own. And I don't see how I could help you with that, anyway. I obviously know nothing of their true plans."

"You could try to speak to someone in Corinas with your Ability."

"Ability does not work here. Didn't Hasso tell you that?"

"For a regular Adept, yes. But not for a Sempiternal."

The casual way in which she threw out the term was unnerving, yet the lack of reaction from Hasso or Marta proved there was no point in denying it. "That doesn't matter. Believe me, I've tried to use it many, many times. Even Kalisfena Tatyn confirmed that being Sempiternal means nothing in Xeydeya."

Lora Stretyn folded her hands together. "She would say something like that. Yet you feel it then, do you not? Your Ability?"

"I…I'm not sure what you mean." She wasn't about to admit to it now, especially in front of strangers.

"Hmm. I will assume for the sake of discussion that you do, and your failures have been because you haven't tried the right things. That is where we can help you, if you will help us."

"I don't understand."

"Your friend is still alive."

The abrupt change in subject caused Alia further confusion. "What? Who?"

"That Son of an Adept you are so friendly with. Mathis? Is that right?" she asked Kieran, who nodded in response.

"Mathis?" Alia's mouth fell open. "Where did you hear this?"

"It came up in a report we received some time ago from one of our contacts in Corinas," Kieran said, his voice quiet and soothing, encouraging her to believe. "The Conclave did not execute him. In fact, quite the opposite has occurred—they seem to have great plans for him."

She told herself to remain skeptical, yet it was hard to ignore the incredible relief she felt at the possibility that Mathis might still be alive. "What do you mean, 'great plans'?"

"The Conclave made him a Lieutenant of their Guard. Our source thinks it is an attempt to win him to their side. And it appears to be working, as far as we can tell."

"What?" Her voice squeaked at the absurdity of it. "Never. Mathis hates the Conclave. It took him half his life to get over Hasso's involvement with his parents' death; he'll never forgive the Conclave for it."

"Oh, I forgot all about that," Mila said, smacking the flat of her hand against the table. "That was a nasty piece of business."

Hasso shook his head. "Again—not helping."

Kieran continued before Alia could react to the revelation that Mila knew something of Mathis's history. "In that same report, we received further confirmation that the rebellion intends to negotiate with the Conclave. They think they'll get to govern a portion of Corinas in exchange for helping the Masters retrieve their Adepts." He looked at Hasso. "I'm surprised you would align yourself with people so gullible. Perhaps that characteristic rubbed off on you after all this time, and that's why you did not see this coming."

"Circumstances change," Hasso muttered. "People change."

"I find all of this very hard to believe," Alia said. Mathis, alive and conspiring with the Conclave? The rebellion, surrendering and seeking the return of the missing Adepts to Corinas?

"I agree we must corroborate these reports before we decide on the best course of action," said Lora Stretyn with a nod. "That's where you come in, Alia. If you could reach someone in Corinas and find out what is really afoot..."

"I already told you—that's impossible."

"What if it were not? Hasso tells me that back in Corinas, you used Ability to communicate with Mathis. Wouldn't you like to speak to him again and confirm he is well? You could reach out to Marta's mother, too, and let her know she is safe. Or that other one we've heard so much about. Kelda, is it? Any of them could tell us far more about what's happening in Corinas than what our contacts can, and far quicker." She looked at Alia expectantly.

She threw her hands up in the air. "You are seeking something I cannot give." Reaching Mathis somewhere within the Conclave would be an arduous task even if she were in Corinas. And as for the others...Hasso was adamant Ciara had no knowledge of the Captains' perfidy, and for Marta's sake, she hoped that was true. He gave no such assurances when it came to Kelda. As much as it hurt her heart to think she might have been part of such a thing, there was no way the Captains would do any of this without her tacit acceptance. She had agreed with their plan to send Tovi on a mission away from Brome, after all, despite Nyona's protests. "I don't know what else to say to you people."

"What Kalisfena told you about Sempiternals is a lie. You *are* special here, and she knows it. If you are aware of your Ability, then we can help you find a way to use it." She leaned forward, her forearms resting on the table, and stared directly into Alia's eyes. "However, we won't risk ourselves on a lark. We will get you the information you need if it is worth our time. So stop being coy. Is it worth our time?"

Marta nodded her head toward Alia in a silent urging. Hasso also dipped his chin briefly in acquiescence. In that moment, Alia wanted nothing more than to reach for her Ability and quickly determine if she could trust any of these people. Instead, she'd have to rely on her own faulty intuition. How did normal people do this all the time?

But if what they told her was true…the first thing she'd do would be to perform truth assessments on the whole lot of them. Kalisfena, too. She grabbed one of Lora's proffered glasses of wine and swallowed its contents in a single gulp.

26

MATHIS

Zevon ran up to the gate. "It's all set, Lieutenant," he said, his voice quiet against the sounds of renewed activity in the training grounds. "She can meet us there at noon. She said that was the soonest she'd be able to get away."

Mathis blew into his hands to warm them as he watched his unit practice their sword technique against training dummies, and a cloud of condensation escaped through his fingers into the air. He regretted not going back to his quarters for his gloves. "She understands where?"

"I think so. I gave her the instructions Silar gave me."

"Good. Get in there, then. You're already late."

Zevon pulled on his own gloves and then fumbled with the frost-coated latch. Once inside, he grabbed a practice sword from the barrel and trotted over to Silar. The boys spoke briefly, then launched a joint attack against Silar's already ravaged dummy. Mathis made a mental note to get that one replaced soon, then laughed to himself. He didn't plan to be here long enough for that.

Several days had passed since the rebel delegation had arrived, and life in the Conclave had returned to relative normalcy despite the ongoing negotiations. No one in Mathis's ambit had any real

idea of how the talks had progressed, as few people were autho-
rized to go near the Public Room these days. He himself had been
nowhere near there since the Headmaster—he refused to consider
the use of that other word—had paraded him out like a trophy.
The look on Kelda's face when he'd claimed the Conclave as his
new home had nearly broken his heart.

I didn't have any other choice, he reminded himself. He'd hoped
Kelda could somehow sense something of his truth, though he
wasn't sure why he'd thought that might be possible. Like him, her
residual Ability only allowed for the receipt of communication
from an Adept. They were both essentially useless.

After he'd revealed himself to Kelda and Lieutenant Elcy, he'd
expected Alia to reach out to him. That she had not worried him;
he hated that she and Kelda might believe he had truly abandoned
the rebellion—abandoned Tovi. This farce had gone on too long.
Whatever else might be going on in the upper echelons of the
rebellion's leadership, he trusted Kelda, and while he'd not known
her long, he trusted Lieutenant Elcy, too. They needed to know
the truth.

He ordered another drill, and another. The next few hours
wore on as if they were days; each glance at the clock tower at the
edge of the training grounds left him disappointed. Not even part-
nering with Silar, who was nearly his height, to demonstrate moves
to the rest of his unit did enough to distract Mathis from the plodding passage of time.

Finally, the clock reached a quarter before noon. He clapped
his hands twice, and the motion stung his half-frozen palms. "It's
freezing out here. Early break for lunch. Silar, Zevon: a moment."

As most of his unit escaped toward their warm barracks, the
two boys he'd called out jogged over to him. Their cheeks were
flushed with exertion against the cold. "Are you ready?"

"Yes, Lieutenant," they said in unison.

"You remember the plan if things go south?"

"Yes, Lieutenant."

"Then let's go."

Years ago, Mathis had traveled through unused corridors and rooms to escape from the Conclave. While that had been in a different portion of the complex, he suspected such spaces were not unique in such an ancient structure. He'd conscripted Silar to find out if his instincts were correct. The boy was of a height and litheness that, when dressed all in black, he appeared from a distance much like the many eunuch servants running around. So long as no one looked for a tattooed hand or asked him questions, he would have a somewhat freer rein to move about the Conclave.

Like any good recruit, Silar hadn't hesitated in following his commanding officer's orders. Perhaps he thought it was all some elaborate training exercise, though he must have some sense this was not a normal assignment. Regardless, in no time at all, he'd found an abandoned subterranean corridor with offshoot passages leading both toward the training grounds and the Public Room.

Zevon had taken longer to complete his part of the plan. He, too, had asked Mathis no questions. With the rebel delegation in town, the Gate Guards were on heightened alert, so it was harder not only to get into the complex but also to get out. Zevon had come up with something last night—Mathis hadn't wanted to know the details—that got him past the Gate Guards and in a position to finish his task.

They reached the end of a dark passage and were met with options to go either to the left or right. To Mathis's relief, they'd encountered no one else. Silar had chosen well. "It's down there," the boy whispered, pointing to the right. "Around that corner."

"Zevon, you wait here," Mathis said. "If anyone comes, you know what to do."

"Will do, Lieutenant," the younger boy said before leaning against the wall as if he had nothing in the world to do. If someone approached, which Mathis didn't expect, he'd play the stupid, innocent boy who'd lost his way. His contorted wails of despondency would carry to warn Silar, who took up his own post right outside the designated room.

Mathis opened the door and stepped inside. Lieutenant Elcy

stood in the corner of the room, her fighting stance obvious despite her voluminous brown robe. Her posture relaxed slightly when she saw him. "Hello."

"Hello," he said. "Thank you for agreeing to meet me." The words sounded absurdly formal to his ears, but how, exactly, did you greet someone for the first time after you'd nearly gotten her killed?

"Don't be stupid." She crossed over and gave him a fast hug. "It is good your boy found me, and that you are well. I didn't think I'd ever see you again after what happened out at sea."

"Did the Shipmaster...?"

She shook her head. "Few of us made it back."

The guilt of his poor judgment rushed once more to the forefront of his mind. So many people died that day because of him. "I should have listened to you."

"Yes, you should have," she said with a sad smile. "But there's nothing to be done about it. It happened. This is now."

"I'm still sorry."

"As you should be. But more importantly, I presume that your request to meet with me means it's not true, what you said the other day? You're not really with them now, are you?"

"No, never," he said firmly. "But I couldn't really say anything else, not in front of all them."

"I am relieved to hear that. But it is true they gave you a Lieutenancy." She pointed to his training uniform. "Are there others here like you, other Sons, that are officers?"

"No. All the other officers are women."

She let out a low whistle. "They must really want you to stay for some reason, then."

He was fairly confident it was more an issue of *her* wanting him to stay versus *they*, but he didn't want to get into the Headmaster's delusions with the Lieutenant, not now. "I guess," he said. "I only agreed to it because I thought I could use it against the Conclave somehow, and I figured it would help me find Tovi and get her out of here. That's the only reason I'm still here. Have you bargained for her release yet?"

Her mouth fell open, and she lifted her fingers to her lips for a moment. "Wait—you think Tovi is here?"

Dread crept over him, causing the hairs on the back of his neck to rise. "She's not?" *Please don't be dead. Please.*

"No. The Conclave didn't take her. She and all the other Adepts are in Xeydeya. Alia is there now, too, looking for her," she explained in a rush. "I assumed you knew. It's all over Corval, about how the rebellion and the Conclave have both 'lost' Adepts. They've not kept you so isolated as all that, have they?"

He stared across the room at nothing. "I've only left the complex once, a few weeks ago, and they weren't thrilled about it, so I haven't been out since. I heard something about losing our Adepts, but I thought it was just another stupid rumor." He'd also discounted it because he'd been so certain Tovi was here. That she was not explained why none of his boys had heard a word of her this entire time. And if Alia was on a mission looking for her, that also explained why she'd not reached out to him; she had other things on her mind. "Zevon heard something about the rebels stealing the Conclave's Adepts, but I knew that wasn't true."

"I don't think the Masters exactly advertised their loss, for obvious reasons. And I'm guessing you must have been in town before their ships left for Xeydeya. Once that happened, the Conclave couldn't hide what was going on any longer."

"I did hear about the Conclave conscripting ships and filling them with Guards, but nothing about Xeydeya." He furrowed his brow. "Wait a minute. Are you saying the *Xeydeyans* took Tovi and the Conclave's Adepts?" He was no merchant, but he couldn't see how provoking a war with the Conclave would help their trade relations.

"Yes. That's why the Conclave is willing to treat with us. They have lost dozens of Adepts and they're panicking over it. They need our Guards to help them take back their Adepts and keep order here at home at the same time. Ships full of fighters left several weeks ago, and more will be on their way soon, depending on how these negotiations play out."

"Wait—so the Conclave's down a bunch of Adepts, and down a bunch of Guards, and the Captains want to help restore everything to them? Have the Captains lost their damned minds?"

Lieutenant Elcy raised one hand half-heartedly. "It's…complicated. A lot has happened since you've been here. The Conclave has lost much of its strength."

"All the more reason to take them out," he growled. "Not decide you want to become best friends. What's wrong with the rebellion? Is it true that we've lost?"

"No, but…like I said, it's complicated. People are tired. Tired of all the fighting, and all the running, and all the worry. If our negotiations go well, then we will get a chance to govern out in the open. Once we do, the people will see that our way is so much better than the Conclave's."

He snorted. "You think the Conclave will just let you govern in a way that's out of line with what they want? You'd better be doing some fast talking, then."

"Kelda is the one doing all the talking, and she's doing just fine."

"What have you agreed to so far?"

"Not much, other than some specific townships, mostly in the southeast, they'll give over to our administration. They're demanding we not involve our senior leadership, but I don't see how we can possibly agree to exclude the Captains from our future."

"It would be like them giving up their Directorate," he said, then raised his eyebrows. "Maybe that might be worth a trade."

She laughed. "That's not a half-bad idea. Still, it would never happen. Could you imagine not having someone like Captain Levina be part of what we imagine for Corinas?"

"Never." Memories filtered into his consciousness of the time he'd spent traveling all over Corinas with the Captain as they'd scooped up the remnants of a fractured rebellion and pointed them toward the safety and unity of Brome. Captain Levina had guided them through all of that. If not for her leadership, neither he, nor Alia, nor Tovi, nor Nyona, nor Kelda, nor anyone else in the rebellion would be alive today.

"Still, we're trying to figure out a way to make this work. We can't hide away in Brome forever. Sure, we can provoke a huge fight, and win much of it, yet the Conclave is *everywhere*. So long as they have even a single Adept left to their name, they will be able to influence the citizenry, and they still have many right here in this complex. What difference will it really make if we bring back the lot they've lost?"

Her argument made some sense, but it still didn't sit right with him. A thought popped into his mind. "How did Xeydeya take all these Adepts without us knowing about it? You said yourself they supported us. How come that one you met with—Kali-some-thing-or-other—didn't tell you? It seems she would have known if she was as high up in their government as you said."

"I don't know."

He shook his head, feeling more than a little helpless. Everything he'd believed true for the last four months had turned out to be a lie. "How is Alia supposed to get Tovi back all by herself?" Even if he left for Xeydeya this very minute, it would take him weeks and weeks to get there; no one in Corinas possessed the equivalent of a Xeydeyan merchant vessel, which traveled twice as fast as any other.

"Nyona and Hasso went with her."

Of course. Nothing would keep Nyona from defending her daughter—with her life, if need be. That Hasso accompanied her left him with mixed emotions; he still didn't trust him completely, but at least he knew his way around. And Mathis couldn't discount the ex-assassin's skills in finding out secrets others would prefer left buried. Hasso would likely find where Tovi was faster than anyone else, and when he did, he could keep her safe. "How long have they been there?"

"Oh, my—I'm not sure. They left soon after I arrived in

Brome, and I think the last time Kelda heard from Alia was before we got the offer from the Conclave, so, a couple of months?"

"They could already be on their way back, then. Have you heard?"

"No, but I wouldn't worry too much about that; their Ability won't work again until they get closer to home, anyway."

The door opened, setting Mathis's heartbeat racing. Silar poked his head inside. "Sorry to disturb, Lieutenant—but Zevon went back toward the entrance to this tunnel, and he says there's a disturbance outside. He doesn't know what it is, but he thinks we should head back."

"All right." He'd already heard all he came to hear—and more. "I'll send the boy around your way now and then," he told Lieutenant Elcy. "If you hear anything about Tovi or Alia—anything at all—tell him. Or tell him you want to meet again."

Lieutenant Elcy nodded. "It is time I left, anyway—Kelda will be looking for me if there's a problem." She embraced him once more, patting his back as she did so. "See you soon."

In the dark corridor, Zevon shifted back and forth on his feet as if he were about to flee any minute. Lieutenant Elcy had already disappeared around the corner. "You were supposed to stay at your post," Mathis chided the boy.

"I know Lieutenant, but it's good I left. Something big is happening. You can't hear it down here, but you will soon."

Mathis tried to imagine what possibly could be going on, but the first order of business was to get his boys safely back to where they belonged. "Is the way to the training grounds clear?"

"I think so. It sounds like whatever's going on is happening toward the front gate, but it's hard to tell for sure."

"Then let's be on our guard. Come on." As they hurried back the way they'd come, shouts carried into the corridor, growing louder and louder as they approached the surface. Zevon had spoken true. Something big was happening, indeed.

27

MASTER GERSEMI

Jeyne's leg banged into the table as she stood up, rattling their half-empty dishes. "What is the meaning of this?" she demanded.

Gersemi observed the woman who had interrupted their lunch with displeasure. A Captain should know better than to come barging in uninvited. If Jeyne did not punish her, Gersemi would be sure to. She had someone in mind to fill an open Captaincy.

"Headmaster. Master Jeyne. My sincere apologies. There is a disturbance outside the front gate."

"A disturbance? Go take care of it, then," Jeyne ordered. "Isn't that why we pay you?"

"It requires your attention, Master Jeyne. It is a very large crowd, larger than we've ever seen, and it's still growing. They are yelling about the ships in the harbor, and—"

"Ships?" Gersemi interrupted. It was far too soon for the fleet they'd sent to Xeydeya to have returned, and the Adepts on board would have heralded their arrival in any event. "Is it an attack?" If the rebels had been stringing out these discussions to lull her into complacency...

"No, Headmaster; they're our ships, though it sounds like

there's been a clash with some Xeydeyan merchants. There've been calls for medics. I've sent officers down to the docks to find out more and make sure there is no nearby threat, but we need to get this crowd under control in the meantime. If the citizens see you, Master Jeyne, and some of the other Masters, I'm certain they will calm."

"Go with her," Gersemi instructed Jeyne. "Find out what is going on and return immediately."

Jeyne turned her glare on Gersemi for the briefest of moments before she stalked out of the room, her robe snapping between her ankles with each rapid step. The Captain scurried after her.

Gersemi drank the rest of her wine, thinking. A hint of worry gnawed at her. She had expected a fight with the Xeydeyans; they would not give up the Adepts they'd stolen without one. That's why they'd needed the rebels' help, and the rebels' Guards. But it was much, much too soon for there to have been a battle, let alone one that resulted in the return of her own ships. By her calculations, in fact, the fastest of their ships would have only recently reached Xeydeya.

"Enece," she said to the eunuch who stood in the corner of the room, awaiting her commands. "Tell the others to meet me in the Directorate's Room. Ensure that Master Jeyne knows to join us there when she returns."

"Yes, Headmaster."

"Also, keep the delegation away from the Public Room. Tell them we are unavoidably delayed. Come up with something to keep them occupied."

"Yes, Headmaster."

"And find someone to clean this up. We're done with lunch for today."

"Yes, Headmaster."

By the time Gersemi reached the Directorate's Room, several members were milling about near the door. "What's going on out there?" Leyta asked. "It almost sounds like a riot."

Gersemi rolled her eyes. "It is not a riot, Master Leyta. Some of our citizens have found something to be agitated about, but there is nothing to fear. Master Jeyne is seeing to it."

"Then why did you call a meeting?"

She smiled thinly. "Let's wait for everyone to arrive, shall we?" She took her seat at the head of the table and adopted an expression of patient calm. Yet as the rest of the Directorate trickled in, a thread of anxiety tightened in her stomach. What was taking Jeyne so long? It shouldn't take more than a few minutes to assess the state of affairs and give the necessary orders to calm the crowd.

"All right," Leyta said, looking around the table. "We're all here now except for Jeyne. Can we begin? We're due to meet with the delegation soon. Did you inform them of the delay, or are they going to be twiddling their thumbs in the Public Room with a perfect view of whatever is going on outside?"

"Your concern for the comfort of the rebels is noted, Master Leyta," Gersemi said, her sarcasm plain. "Rest assured we've taken care of it."

Leyta glowered and pursed her lips, but said nothing more. *I must do something about that woman.* She couldn't change anything now, not when the rebels expected Leyta's presence during their talks. But once they were gone—hopefully very soon—there would be changes. This nonsense with Leyta had gone on far too long, and her antics were rubbing off on the others. Jeyne's attitude had grown worse over the past few weeks, and even that idiot Charla had dared to challenge Gersemi's decision to mount the assault on Xeydeya. Charla!

Her tolerance for such disrespect was rapidly coming to an end. She was the Headmaster, not any of them.

Jeyne walked into the room at last, shutting the door behind her. "We have a problem," she said without preamble.

"Is the crowd still out there?" Gersemi asked.

"No, we've dispersed them, but our citizens are quite distraught. From all reports, there are two or three of our ships in terrible condition in the harbor, and the few crew on board are telling a disastrous tale that is spreading fast."

"What are they saying?"

"That the Xeydeyan fleet was waiting for them somewhere in the middle of the ocean, closer to Corinas than Xeydeya. They attacked, and our side could not withstand the assault. The few in our docks right now are the only ones that got away."

"How many ships did we lose?" asked Beryl, her face pale.

"Three dozen, full of loyal Guards we could ill-afford to lose. Not only did we lose those meant to regain our Adepts, but our port cities are now unprotected, as well. There are rebel units nearby that could fill in the gaps, but they've received orders from their own commanders to stand down while our negotiations continue. If Xeydeya brings their assault to our shores, we will have few choices. I warned you, Headmaster, that we had launched this attack too soon. This is the proof."

"It was *not* too soon," Gersemi responded with some heat. "They clearly knew our plans. Why else would there be a fleet of Xeydeyan ships so close to our shores, ready for battle? Someone in your chain of command must be an agent of theirs, and you failed to notice."

Jeyne threw up her hands. "Oh, of course, blame me for your decisions. My commanders are loyal to the Conclave, far more than those Guards who defected to the rebellion and returned when they had no other choice. Any one of them could be an agent of Xeydeya. We had no way to screen them, as you refused to allow me use of any Adepts."

Gersemi felt her face flush at her subordinate's open insolence. "I did what was—"

Leyta spoke over her. "Not even we knew our ships had launched until after it happened," she said with a side-eyed glance toward Gersemi, who trembled with outrage at being cut off and ignored. "Nonetheless, the return of our Adepts must remain our top priority. That will be all the harder now. I agree with Jeyne, as I did from the beginning, that it was a mistake to send our ships before we had enough might to overwhelm any obstacle. The fact remains that we need more fighters, and more ships, and more commanders to lead them. The rebels have all that, and remain willing to give it to us if we accede to their remaining demands."

Beryl nodded. "We've already agreed to the turnover of several towns for their governance. Some others they've suggested are not ideal, but I think we can live with it, at least in the short term."

"They've not demanded much at all in the way of finances," said Ryna. "I see no reason why we can't give them what they need, under the circumstances."

"What about their Captains?" Charla asked from the end of the table. "How can we allow them to continue in their leadership roles, especially when we had...other plans for dealing with them?"

Beryl shrugged. "I don't think we have much of a choice. As the Principal Master of Governance, I am willing to accept this risk for the sake of security in our cities. We will make sure to watch them at all times, and if they prove a problem—well, we can deal with them."

"That takes care of their demands, then, doesn't it?" Jeyne said. "We could wrap things up this afternoon and begin preparations for a larger offensive."

Leyta half-smirked. "Don't forget: they also want Mathis."

Jeyne waved her hand in dismissal. "Let them have him. He may be a Son, but we've let those go before."

Gersemi had watched their conversation with growing indignation, and she could no longer remain silent. "I will not agree to let them take Mathis."

"If we agree to this, we can make another push for Xeydeya right away," Jeyne claimed. "If we wait much longer, I cannot predict our success. Even now I am uncertain."

Gersemi shook her head. "I will not allow it. Nor would I ever force him to return to a place he does not wish to be. This is his home now, as he said in his own words, and here he must remain."

Beryl furrowed her brow. "Surely he is not so important as to forego the full assistance of the rebellion in regaining our Adepts?"

Leyta, not missing a beat, piled on. "He's only one Son. We

have others, and our existing Adepts are far more important. Why are you insisting on something so trivial?"

"I need not explain myself to you," Gersemi said icily. "My decision is final. Mathis remains."

"Need to or not, I think you should. Agreeing to let Mathis go is the only thing keeping us from reaching an immediate deal to end the rebellion at this point."

"He is not just any Son," she snapped. The time had come to reveal to them the truth they'd all been too blind to see. "He is *my* Son."

A collective gasp rose from the Directorate. Leyta blinked several times. "I'm sorry. You are claiming Mathis as your own?"

Gersemi smiled, smug in the public confirmation of Leyta's failure in her duties—she was the one person who should have known. "Yes. Mathis is my Son. That is why he could push back so readily against our truth assessment and why he's performed so well in his command despite being a man. He is exceptional. None of you can deny that," she challenged. "I've spent years looking for him, and now that I've found him, I will not allow him to leave. He is a Progenitor Son, with far more strength than any other. He will secure the future of the Conclave."

"How could you possibly know all this?"

"I've known since not long after his birth. The amount of residual Ability in him was obvious even then. The Masters of Generation chose me to bear a child such as him. Not all those working in Generation were as incompetent as you, it would seem."

Leyta's cheeks reddened. "I will tell you now, I have looked at the records concerning Mathis, and they do *not* support your claim. He is not a Progenitor Son. He remains intact now only because he escaped from us so long ago."

"You mean the same records that show that the line of Sempiternals has been eradicated? The same records that failed to show a pattern of taint in Generation?"

Leyta narrowed her eyes. "That does not mean everything in the records is wrong."

"It certainly doesn't lend much credence to them. And you need not look to the records to see the truth of what I am telling you. You all sensed his residual Ability. No Son but a Progenitor could contain that much, and Mathis holds far more than any of those others you've got in Generation now."

"If you are so certain he is as you believe, then why didn't you send him to Generation when he first arrived? You knew of our difficulties. We could have been preparing him all this time, testing him, and if he truly had such capability despite what the records say, I could have used him in some of our recent ceremonies. Instead, you've let him play at command."

"It was not the right time." She wanted him to take part in Generation willingly, with the full understanding of who he was and what he was meant to be. He was almost there, and once he was, she'd turn him over to whomever she appointed to take Leyta's place.

"I am the Principal Master of Generation. I decide when it is the right time for a Progenitor's use. You should have told us of your suspicion from the very beginning."

"Maybe if you'd done your job properly, you would not need to rely on my Son to solve all your problems."

"Maybe if you'd not neglected your service to the Provenance, we'd not have these problems to begin with."

A tense quiet settled over the room. "The Provenance is whole," Gersemi said in a low voice. "As you well know. Do not attempt to blame your failures on that." She would not allow this woman to goad her into feeling guilty about tasking her duty to the Provenance to others. Whether Gersemi or someone else monitored the Provenance mattered little so long as it was done. And when she'd last visited herself, there'd been no hint of deterioration. Her service had been sound.

Leyta looked around at the members of the Directorate, ending with Gersemi. "In the past several years, you've made decision after decision that smack of little sense. You've ignored our counsel time and time again. And now we know you've withheld information—accurate or not—that apparently has been the primary motivator of your decisions. We can no longer tolerate functioning in this fashion." She pushed herself up from her chair and stood, her fingertips resting on the tabletop. "I believe it is time for new leadership," she said. "I call for a vote of no confidence."

Gersemi burst into laughter. Leyta had lost her damned mind. "You think now is the time to drag out a protocol unused for centuries? Now, when we are in the middle of a massive international conflict? I assume you think *you* should be Headmaster now, is that it?"

Leyta lifted her chin. "Is there a second?"

When no one responded right away, Gersemi snickered to herself. With this ridiculous display, the others would rid her of Leyta without Gersemi having to request it.

A chair screeched against the stone, and Gersemi's gaiety died immediately. "I will second," Jeyne said, standing at Leyta's side. "Master Leyta is right. I can't speak to whatever is going on in Generation, or with the Provenance, but your decisions in the area of Security have been irrational, and now, disastrous. Your choice to attack Xeydeya before we were ready has resulted not only in the deaths of hundreds of Guards we could not afford to waste, but has also made it that much more difficult for us to regain our missing Adepts. And now you are steadfastly refusing to accept the help we require all because of your obsession with Mathis. This is not how a Headmaster should act. You've placed your own desires over the Conclave and all of Corinas. I vote for no confidence."

"I vote for no confidence," Leyta declared, as if there'd been any doubt.

"I vote for no confidence," Beryl said quietly, though at least she had the decency to look down at the table as she did so.

"I vote for no confidence," said Charla, that ungrateful child who was only present in the room in the first place because of Gersemi's good graces.

One by one, the remaining six Masters of the Directorate voiced their votes. Not a one of them supported Gersemi.

"The Directorate has spoken," Leyta pronounced, her voice full of self-satisfaction. "Master Gersemi, the Directorate revokes your title and authority, effective immediately. You are no longer the Headmaster of the Conclave, nor, per the protocol, a member of the Directorate. Please leave."

Gersemi's cheeks burned with rage and embarrassment. For once, she had no ready retort.

28

ALIA

ALIA BREATHED IN THROUGH HER NOSE AND OUT THROUGH her mouth, over and over, in a slow, deliberate pattern. The pressure within her mind grew with each breath. She caught a thread of her Ability and slowly, slowly, wound it into a concentrated mass, unlike anything she'd done before. When she thought she might have enough—though she really had no idea—she overlaid it with her usual masking and cast it toward the lit candle on the table. Almost instantly, the flame extinguished with barely any trace of smoke.

Relief rushed through her, and she nearly clapped with delight. *It worked!*

The research Lora Stretyn had obtained from the archives of the local university was everything she'd promised it would be. Although these academic treatises were about a topic now verboten in this society, and thus not available to the public, she had the sort of connections who had access to the vaults where such things were kept. Hundreds of years old, they hadn't been well maintained, and the pages of a few had flaked away at the edges no matter how carefully Alia turned them. Fortunately, none of that detracted from the knowledge contained within them.

Given the Xeydeyans' current antagonism toward Ability, it was amazing these tomes still existed, especially given their focus on Sempiternals. While the collection included the work of several researchers, all of who used a single name to maintain anonymity, she presumed, one scholar was the most prolific. Besides detailing how a Sempiternal's use of Ability differed from that of a regular Adept's, that scholar, Lilla, had outlined a method of using Ability so beyond Alia's imagination she couldn't believe it would ever work.

She had never been happier to be wrong in all her life.

Amassing her Ability in this manner felt strange, and she wanted to make sure that what had happened the first time had not been a fluke or the result of a shift in the air. She lit the candle anew and leaned her back against the wall, pulling her legs into a folded position. With closed eyes, she began the breathing pattern anew.

The candle snuffed out once again at her command. She leaped up to relight it, and tried a third time, then a fourth. Each time, her confidence grew, and the effort to accomplish the task lessened. After the ninth iteration, however, she stopped herself, hearkening back to a warning within the scholar's work. She didn't want to waste her reclaimed Ability on something as mundane as an unneeded candle.

According to Lilla—whose conclusions she now accepted without question—the difference between a regular Adept and a Sempiternal all came down to their connection to something in Corinas itself, something deep within the earth Lilla referred to as the "Provenance." The scholar did not have a full understanding of it, but so long as a regular Adept remained physically in contact with the island nation, she could use Ability. That was why using Ability was so difficult, if not impossible, over water, and why all the other Adepts here in Amrava no longer sensed their Ability at all. They were simply too far away from Corinas and this…Provenance, whatever it was.

A Sempiternal's connection to this source was unique. Lilla

was frustratingly unclear on this point, writing as if she expected her readers to have knowledge of the subject well beyond Alia's understanding. From what she gathered after multiple readings, so long as she remained in Corinas, her store of Ability, which was much larger than that of a normal Adept, would constantly replenish, and she needn't fear burning out. Otherwise, some sort of protective mechanism prevented her from using her Ability in the usual manner so she would not inadvertently use too much of it. For once a Sempiternal burned away her Ability—something she hadn't realized was possible—then her Ability would never return, as if she were any other Adept.

Alia dismissed all that from her mind. Although she didn't know for certain how much stored Ability remained to her, she imagined it had to be more than sufficient to do what she needed to do. She'd agreed to find out what was happening in Corinas in exchange for access to this research, and in the glow of her success, she decided to give it a try now.

Of course, trying to communicate with someone in Corinas would be nothing like manipulating a candle a few feet away from her. She needed to give herself every advantage, which meant dropping her usual efforts to mask her use of Ability. If she were lucky, no one would be the wiser; no Adept would ever recognize a pattern of Ability such as this, not even if she sent it into the very walls of the Conclave itself.

Granted, if what Hasso's friend had reported about Mathis's changed loyalties were true, the Masters might learn of her intrusion even if she masked her use. For Mathis was, most assuredly, the best person for her to try to contact. They shared a unique bond, and if anyone could hear her using this peculiar method, it would be him. She had every confidence he remained committed to the rebellion—at least, for now. How he might feel about it after she told him of the Captains' duplicity, however...

Breathe in, breathe out. Breathe in, breathe out. Breathe in, breathe out.

She thrust a ball of Ability away from her with all her might. It traveled faster than she expected, faster than a thread of Ability ever could, and in the span of ten breaths she became aware of the yellow stone towers of the Conclave and its constant hum of Ability. To her great relief, the shield she'd encountered months ago was absent, and she searched further, uninhibited, until she found her target.

Mathis!

Alia? Confusion and excitement filtered toward her, along with a sense of true happiness that someone aligned with the Masters would never feel. *Is that really you? This is strange—*

I know. I can explain, but not right now. I don't know how long I can keep this up. I am so glad you are—

The door to her room slammed against the wall, scaring Alia half to death and severing her tenuous link with Mathis. Kalisfena charged inside wearing only a changing robe, her braids hanging loose. With a look of horror, her eyes scanned the room wildly until they found Alia on the floor.

"What are you doing?" she cried, before something at the far side of the room caught her attention. "Oh, no, no, no, you didn't, you haven't..." she babbled as she rushed over to the table where the ancient books lay open. She hurriedly flipped through the pages of one, sending tiny bits of paper flying.

"What are *you* doing?" Alia demanded, her heart pounding. Someone must have found out about Alia's reading material and told Kalisfena. There was no other reason why the woman would have barged into her room unannounced in the middle of the night, but she acted almost as if she suspected Alia had transgressed a far more important rule.

Kalisfena closed her eyes and lifted her chin toward the ceiling. "You have tainted yourself," she whispered. "Why, after everything we've offered to you?"

"They're just books," Alia said, shocked to see tears trailing down the envoy's cheeks.

"You told me, over and over, you did not sense your Ability, and I believed you. I thought they must have been wrong about you. Instead, you lied to me. You lied to all of us, even to your companions. And now you've found a way to use it. The taint of Ability exudes from you."

Alia scrunched her brow, not quite comprehending the implication of her words. "How could you know if I've used Ability?"

Kalisfena sank into the chair next to the table as she wiped the tears from her face. "I am a Guardian," she said in a raspy whisper.

"A what?"

"A Guardian. I can detect when someone uses Ability, you see. Protecting Xeydeya from the scourge of Ability is my highest duty —and my greatest burden."

Alia snorted. "Are you trying to tell me you're Sempiternal, too?"

"Of course not!"

"Only those who can use Ability can detect Ability. Everyone knows that."

"It is not so, though I can understand why you would believe it to be." She tapped the book's deteriorating leather cover. "How much of this did you read?"

"As much as I needed to."

"Did you read Aynira's dissertation on the Great Uprising?"

"No." She'd noticed it, but skipped it in her search for more of Lilla's work.

"Do you know anything of that time?"

"Only that it was over three hundred years ago, and that after, the Conclave eradicated all Sempiternals—or so they thought at the time," she said ruefully. "What does it have to do with anything?"

Kalisfena stared up at the ceiling with a slight shake of her head. "Your Masters have kept you all so ignorant. It is no wonder things are as they are." She folded her hands before her, her composure recovered. "I will explain."

"By all means." Alia couldn't help but be curious as to what Kalisfena would say to explain away her claim of being able to detect that Alia had used Ability, especially when she hadn't yet admitted she had. At this point, though, Alia could believe most anything, as it had become quite clear in the last few days how little she really understood about the power that had been a part of her since the day she was born.

"After the Great Uprising, some Sempiternals escaped to Xeydeya, whose citizens welcomed them graciously on the condition they never used their Ability. It was an easy condition to accept, because although they could feel their Ability, they could not put it to use. Most eventually learned how to ignore the constant pressure within their minds. Others, however, could not let it go, and the research compiled in these books was the result.

"Those who followed the methods described here, including its founding scholars, soon burned away what remained of their Ability. In so doing, they finally realized how it felt to be truly free. They helped others reach the same edification and ultimately became some of the fiercest defenders of the Xeydeyan way of life. They, better than anyone, understood the harm Ability caused. Their descendants became the Guardians. We are not Adepts, as we are not the product of two people who possess Ability, yet our unique heritage allows us to detect it all the same. And to this very day, Guardians serve Xeydeya by protecting its citizens from anyone who might seek to use Ability against them. People such as yourself."

Alia's mind was spinning. "If this is all true, and you knew all along there was a way for a Sempiternal to use Ability here, then why did you agree to take me off the rebellion's hands?"

She raised her eyebrows. "Ahh. So you know of that arrangement as well. I should not be surprised. You are a clever one."

"You're not answering my question."

"No Sempiternal has existed in Xeydeya since the time of my ancestors. When we entered into the agreements long ago, we did not anticipate your existence. Even once you became known to us, we remained uncertain if things would be as they'd once been. Our plan, if it came to be that history repeated itself, was to assist you in finding true freedom, as our ancestors had once assisted others."

She leaned forward, her expression one of earnest belief. "It is not too late for that, you know. You need only say the word, and we will help you eradicate the taint of your Ability. You have seen the full lives the other Adepts lead now that Ability no longer weighs them down. Think of little Tovi. She shines here, in a place free of strife and sorrow. Why would you not want that for yourself?"

"Why do you care so much?" Alia asked, discomfited by the intensity of Kalisfena's words.

"Xeydeya was founded in response to the abuses of the Masters. We've experienced enormous success, and through our trade, we've spread our way of life far and wide. Corinas is an anomaly, stuck in the past with a culture based on a tragic fallacy. All Adepts are victims of this, and we will not see you suffer. We once believed the rebellion shared that goal," she said with some bitterness.

"But that's why I wanted to use my Ability," Alia said, still refusing to admit she'd actually used it no matter what Kalisfena thought she'd detected. "I can't believe the rebellion would help the Conclave take back its Adepts. I wanted to speak with someone in Corinas who might know what's going on. I never would have used my Ability against anyone in Xeydeya."

"Did you know they've already tried, the rebellion and the Conclave? Our ships were waiting for them out in the ocean. So, you see, it is no matter what anyone might claim of their motivations. We already know the truth."

"But—"

"I'm sorry," she interrupted, her eyes narrowing, "but we simply cannot allow you to use your Ability again. A Sempiternal is a weapon, whether you appreciate that or not. So. You have a choice. We can either help you burn away what remains of your Ability in an instant, or we can implant you. Which would you prefer?"

29

MATHIS

HE RUBBED AT HIS RIGHT EYE WITH HIS FIST AND STIFLED another yawn as he walked down the corridor. Mathis had stayed up for hours last night waiting to see if Alia would contact him again before succumbing to sleep. She hadn't sounded quite right, and he could sense the effort the contact cost her. Had she returned to Corinas injured? When he heard nothing from her that morning, either, he wondered if it might have all been his imagination.

Still, he could only wait so long in his rooms for a communication that may never come. Someone would notice eventually and question his absence at the training grounds. At least Enece, who'd been his ever-present shadow, no longer lurked around his door. Mathis hadn't seen him in days; the aftermath of the riot must be keeping the eunuch busy with other duties as it had for so many others. It seemed half the Guard units in training within the Conclave were now tasked with maintaining order in Corval.

It didn't seem their commanders were particularly happy about these new assignments, though it was far better than the alternative. After news spread of the Masters' disastrous attempt to go it alone against Xeydeya, he'd overheard their speculation about what was to come next, with most believing their own half-trained units would be sent out to fight before they were ready. Mathis had little doubt that would eventually happen; battles required bodies, and the Conclave was now well short of those. Still, that the Conclave's loyal commanders would question the Masters' choices was a most interesting development.

Even more, the Guards in those units spoke of traitorous whispers in town suggesting that maybe, just maybe, the Masters didn't have the right of it. Zevon and Silar had shared with him what they'd heard. *Why did so many people have to die? Don't they have enough Adepts as it is?* If that's really what people were saying—in Corval of all places!—then now was not the time to capitulate, no matter what the Masters might have promised.

"Lieutenant Mathis! Lieutenant Mathis!" For a moment, Mathis thought his good luck had come to an abrupt end, but the eunuch at the end of the hall, frantically waving, was not Enece. When Mathis paused, the eunuch jogged toward him. "Lieutenant Mathis," he said, slightly out of breath.

"As you've said, several times," Mathis muttered, eyeing the newcomer.

"A member of the rebel delegation seeks your audience. Would you be so kind as to follow me?"

Fortunately, the eunuch turned around so quickly he wouldn't have noticed Mathis's befuddled expression. Why would a Conclave servant be delivering him this message? Was this a trap of some sort? Or had Alia's communication been real, and someone had noticed? He stood in place, debating what he should do.

The eunuch turned back around with a curious expression. "Lieutenant Mathis? Are you not coming?"

"Who wants to see me?" he challenged. He couldn't appear too eager to meet with whomever it was lest the Masters know he'd played them false.

"It is the older representative. Kelda, I believe, Lieutenant."

"What does she want?"

"I'm afraid I don't know, Lieutenant. The Masters only asked me to find you right away."

"Go on, then," he ordered, as if the eunuch were one of his trainees. He wasn't at all sure what was going on, but he wouldn't find out from here.

The eunuch led him toward the front of the complex; the corridors were much more trafficked than when the rebel delegation had first arrived. With a quick bow, the eunuch left him to wait in a small chamber Mathis judged to be near the Public Room. It was warm, although there was no fireplace, and the tapestries hanging on the walls complemented the rug on the floor. In the middle of the room, two blue, padded chairs faced a short sofa in the same color, with a low wooden table in between them. On the table, two short glasses and a pitcher filled with water rested on a silver tray.

Kelda walked in, unaccompanied by anyone from the Conclave—not even a eunuch. She wore the same brown robe he'd seen her in before, and her familiar bun was slightly crooked on the back of her head. Her eyes lit up when she saw him standing there.

"Mathis! I am so glad they found you. They promised they would, but, you know how it is…" She laughed as she pulled him into an embrace.

"I'm glad to see you, too," he said, disentangling himself. "I take it you spoke to Lieutenant Elcy."

"Oh Mathis, my dear boy. Yes." She gripped both of his hands with more strength than he'd expected. "I was so pleased to learn our first meeting was not as it seemed. I had been so worried."

She spoke at a normal volume, giving him some comfort that no one was listening at the door. He supposed the Masters had other ways to eavesdrop if they were so inclined. That Kelda didn't seem worried about that possibility must result from whatever rules of negotiation they'd agreed upon. "You shouldn't have been. You know me better than that."

"Yes, but seeing you, next to her, I…" She gave a little shake of her head as she sat in one chair. He took the other. "I confess I did not know for certain. She has always been skilled in her manipulations of people. But none of that matters now. I have the best news. The Directorate has agreed to allow you to leave with us!"

"The Headmaster went along with that?" He'd known Gersemi's last, desperate attempt to win his loyalty had been nothing but a lie, and this only confirmed it.

"I imagine so. She wasn't there when they told us of their decision, but nothing happens without her go-ahead."

"Huh. Well, good, then. She seemed pretty determined to keep me here. Would you believe she tried to claim me as her own?" he scoffed.

"She told you that? That…surprises me." She scratched the side of her head. "I wonder if the others know."

"It's a lie, Kelda," he said, amused she would believe such an obvious untruth.

She pulled her lips back, revealing her teeth with a slight hiss. "I'm not sure it is. No, no—hear me out. There is a resemblance, present even when you were a child. I've always suspected she might be your true mother, and when we first arrived, and Gersemi stood next to you, it was my very first thought. That she knows you are hers is surprising, yet it would explain why she spared your life after your capture. Leyta must have told her despite the prohibitions against it. Have they known all along, or is this—"

"Kelda! Now is not the time for one of your musings. This is ridiculous. If I really were who she claimed I am, she'd never let me go."

"I suspect it is more a sign of their increasing desperation. Given their loss at sea, they had no other choice to cede to our remaining demands—for you, for the Captains' involvement in our governance, and for our preferred territories. We will be well-positioned to continue reaching for our ultimate goal."

"I'm not sure I know what that is anymore."

"The end of the Conclave's power over Corinas, of course. That has not changed."

"Then these negotiations make no sense at all. Listen: I've been thinking. Instead of negotiating to help them, we should be taking advantage of their weakness. Even citizens here in Corval are dissatisfied and critical of the Masters now. It has never been a better time for us to strike."

"Mathis—"

He pressed on, certain he could convince her that his plan was more sound than whatever could come of cooperating with the Masters. "It seems to me the Xeydeyans have done us a favor, even if they messed up by taking Tovi. I'm sure they'll release her once they know she's ours. Lieutenant Elcy told me Alia was there looking for her, so when Alia reached out to me last night, I thought it might be bec—"

Kelda held out her palm, and her head twitched. "I'm sorry. Did you say *Alia* reached out to you? Are you sure? What did she say? Did she say where she was? Has she returned?"

Her rapid-fire questions made it difficult to keep them all straight. "Yes, it was her, but she broke it off before she said much of anything. She did say she was still in Xeydeya."

She chewed on a thumbnail. "How can that be?" she mumbled past her fingers.

Mathis frowned. "I don't know. She and I share something I can't explain that makes it easier for us to connect. She sounded strange, though, and like I said, she didn't say much."

"But it's not supposed to be possible..." She sighed and dropped her hand back into her lap. "Mathis. We must talk."

"Isn't that what we're doing?" he joked half-heartedly, trying to break the sudden, unexpected tension between them.

She gave him a small, sad smile, then circled around to sit on the sofa across from him. "I've known you a very long time, have I not? Since you were but a scared and lonely child."

"Yes." He thought back to the first time he'd met Kelda, after his parents' execution. He and his sister, running for their lives with nothing more than the clothes they wore, had somehow made it to an inn somewhere in the middle of nowhere. They had no coin to pay for food, let alone a room, and he'd resigned himself to spending a cold, hungry night in a field when Kelda had appeared like a benevolent apparition. She'd brought them into her room at the inn, fed them, clothed them in clean garments, and pretended not to notice when he, a boy of thirteen who thought himself as strong as any man, cried himself to sleep.

"Back then, our rebellion was still in its infancy. We had struggled for years with few resources—certainly nothing close to what we needed to have any chance of success. When you joined us, we'd recently come into an arrangement with the Xeydeyans, and things began to change. It was only through their assistance that we were able to grow into what we are today. Xeydeya has been part of the rebellion for over twenty-five years, yet even today, we remain subject to the terms of the agreement we signed in the beginning."

"I knew they helped fund us," he said, though Lieutenant Elcy hadn't mentioned the arrangement had been going on quite so long. "What about it?"

"Yes, well—the background of our relationship is important in understanding what I'm about to tell you."

"I get it," he said, impatient and not in the mood for a history lesson from his old instructor. "It's been a long time, and they've given us a lot of money. So why are you breaking your contract with them now, especially when we're so close to winning? I can't imagine they wanted this result from their investment."

"I don't think they care much who governs Corinas. Their reason for helping the rebellion is far more self-centered. Did you know Xeydeyans have an irrational fear of anything having to do with Ability? They despise the Conclave's use of it. In that, they were our natural allies. So, in exchange for their assistance, we promised that when the time was right, we would help to re-home Adepts in Xeydeya, where Ability does not work. That time finally came about last spring."

Mathis frowned. "You helped Xeydeya steal Adepts?" He ran both hands through his hair from front to back, trying to dislodge a creeping sense of foreboding. "Then why send me and Lieutenant Elcy to go investigate that one missing from Valen? And why send Marta and Tovi to do the same?" Everything that had happened in the last six months had stemmed from the questions surrounding that single Adept.

"It was at the very beginning of the Xeydeyans' efforts to transfer Adepts out of Corinas. We needed to make certain the girl's disappearance wasn't some trick of the Conclave's." She lowered her gaze, breaking eye contact. "But it did provide us with a convenient excuse."

His muscles tightened involuntarily, as if he were preparing for a fight. "What are you saying?"

"We had to uphold our end of the bargain," she insisted. "The Xeydeyans were quite clear there could be no exceptions. They knew we had Tovi and Alia, and their unusual natures only made the Xeydeyans want them more. We had no choice."

Mathis felt as if all the air had been sucked from the room. The woman sitting across from him, whom he'd known and trusted most of his life, was describing a nearly incomprehensible web of lies. "You let me believe the Conclave had taken her, knowing how I would respond," he said through clenched teeth. "People *died*, and I've been sitting here for *months* because I thought Tovi was in danger."

Kelda shook her head. "No. No. We did not know you would go after her. That had not been our intent; we needed you out of Brome before we sent her away, but we expected you to return once she was gone. You went after her on your own, remember? And once you were at sea, there was nothing we could do to stop you."

"Lieutenant Elcy was with me!" he nearly shouted, not caring who heard. "Why didn't she stop me?"

"She didn't know."

"I don't believe that." He tried to remember back to that time, wracking his brain for any hint of deception, but it was nearly impossible through his cloud of anger. "How could you expect me to believe anything you tell me now?"

"It is the truth. Our agreement with the Xeydeyans was closely held, and the triggering of this specific provision even more so. Levina and Jana knew. A few of the other long-time Captains. Hasso. And me. That was it."

"If Hasso knew, Ciara must have." That she would sell out her own daughter...

"No, not until very recently. Hasso had important contacts in Xeydeya, former Extirs who themselves were connected with people in the Xeydeyan government. That's the only reason why we told him—and we didn't tell him everything—and we also swore him to secrecy. Levina only told Ciara because she wanted her to know Marta was safe."

"And Nyona did not deserve to know that about her child?"

"Nyona had already left with Alia for Xeydeya by that point. By now, she's reunited with Tovi and knows it firsthand." She leaned forward, clasping her hands between her knees. "Mathis. Please. Know that everything we have done has been for the sake of the rebellion and all of Corinas. We did not expect Tovi or Alia to come into our lives. I love them both, you must know that, and I would have fought against sending them to Xeydeya if I thought their safety was at all at risk. We had to hide the truth from you, from Nyona, from everyone. We knew there probably were spies in the rebellion, if not in Brome itself, and we could not allow the Conclave to catch any hint that we were helping Xeydeya take their Adepts. That would have brought immediate retaliation down on us, which we weren't yet ready to defend against no matter how many people we'd gathered to our cause."

"And you think Xeydeya won't do the same? They decimated an entire fleet of Guards. If they can manage that, I doubt Brome stands a chance once they learn of your perfidy."

"They won't, because they know we're not really helping the Conclave," she said in a near-whisper. "Those weren't true rebels we sent to man those ships, but Guards who'd only very recently claimed to cross over to our side. And anyone we send to staff new ships for appearance's sake will do nothing to help return those Adepts to Corinas. We sent a message to the Xeydeyans explaining all this."

"Why bother with this charade at all, then?" he asked.

She looked tired—infinitely so. She sighed, then continued. "Because we're done with hiding. It is time for the rebellion to show the citizens of Corinas what we can do for them. And once we establish our governance, it will be that much easier to send even more Adepts across the sea. So, Mathis, you might be angry now, and you have every right to be. But your plan is not much different from our own, and we always meant for you to be a part of it. Please do not let what has happened change that."

She took his hand, and he did not resist.

30

ALIA

ARE YOU THERE? SHE ASKED MATHIS.

Yes. Continue.

I was starting to tell you that the Xeydeyans did not take Tovi on their own. The Captains *arranged it, and they sent me here on false pretenses, too.*

I know.

In her surprise, she dropped the connection again. "Fires!" she said out loud. Her communication with Mathis improved with each attempt, but she remained frustrated at the arduousness of doing what had once been as simple as breathing. It had taken half a morning to get through half a conversation that should have taken no time at all, in part because of the especially convoluted masking she overlaid to hide her efforts. She might have bought herself some time to answer Kalisfena's contrived question, but that would end in a moment if she or any other Guardian noticed her continued use of Ability.

"What happened?" Nyona asked. Tovi sat on the ground at her side with her head on her mother's lap.

"I lost it again. He said he knew about the Captains' plan!"

Nyona's jaw dropped. "That can't be right. He would never lie to us like that."

"I don't think he meant he'd known all along." Strangely, however, she'd not detected any anger from him in his brief response—merely a calm acceptance.

Hasso turned around in his chair to face them. "Kelda probably told him."

"I'm sure she disclaimed any responsibility for it when she did, too," Nyona said darkly.

"Mama…" Tovi said, rolling her eyes. For someone who'd been the target of the Captains' schemes, she'd been remarkably forgiving when it came to Kelda's involvement. She simply refused to believe that her former teacher would ever lie to her.

"I'll ask him more about what he knows, but I need to take a break before I try again. The masking technique I'm using takes a lot of effort, especially at the beginning."

"I wish I could help you like I used to."

Alia exchanged a surprised glance with Nyona, as it was the first time she'd heard Tovi express any desire to use Ability since they'd arrived in Xeydeya. *Kalisfena better not get wind of that*, she thought ruefully.

Nyona ran her hand over Tovi's dark curls. "I know, love. It is what it is." She stood up and walked back over to the table. "Do you want something more to eat?" she asked Alia. "We still have some bread left over, and a little cheese, too."

"Which one?"

"The goat."

"Then yes. I didn't like that other one at all," she said, wrinkling her nose at the memory of the pungent, blue-veined cheese.

As she nibbled on her snack, Tovi joined her mother at the table to tackle what the Xeydeyans referred to as "homework." Most children probably would resent being forced to read lecture notes and work figures on their own time, but not Tovi. Even if she'd had the choice not to take part, she would have chosen to learn. She loved the structure of the Xeydeyan education system, something that did not exist in Corinas, and she gobbled up all the instruction provided to her with vigor.

Alia could only imagine what it must be like to have all the knowledge she could ever want available at Tovi's age. The Conclave afforded Adepts the barest hint of an oral education that focused solely on those things bearing on an Adept's duty to the Conclave and Corinas. She hadn't even known how to read until Kelda taught her. The Masters had kept her and her peers in an appalling state of ignorance, something she wasn't certain she'd ever be able to overcome no matter how hard she might try.

No wonder Kalisfena is so desperate to save me. Maybe I need it.

Next to Tovi, Nyona flipped through the one ancient tome that had somehow escaped Kalisfena's notice when she'd scooped up the rest. At one point, Nyona paused, then leaned forward, frowning. Her lips moved silently as her finger moved over the page.

"Did you find something?" Alia asked, intrigued by her friend's befuddled expression.

"I'm not sure. Maybe."

"What's it say?"

"*These devices, what we've come to call 'implants,' are designed to prohibit an Adept from using her own Ability. To that end, they work as expected. However, repeated experiments have revealed an unexpected benefit. We can now report with confidence that the devices also prevent others from using the Ability stored within an implanted Adept for their own purposes. This is quite unlike the scenario in which an Adept's Ability is inaccessible due to disability or location.*" She looked up at Alia. "This suggests—"

"That Tovi might be able to help me, after all," Alia finished, having immediately recognized the consequence of Nyona's find.

"Yes, but this is only one account."

"Who's the author?" Alia asked.

Nyona turned back a few pages. "Someone named Lilla."

Alia sat up straight. "She's the one whose work showed me

how to use my Ability here. If she wrote that paper, then I have no doubt what she wrote is true."

Tovi bounced in her seat. "Oh, can we please try?"

"I don't think that would be a good idea, love. Kalisfena is watching."

"Can't you mask the both of you?" Hasso asked Alia.

"It would be an extension of what I'm doing now, I suppose, as Tovi would not be actively using it herself." Having only recently re-learned how to use her own Ability, she was a little anxious about trying to use someone else's, but she couldn't deny her curiosity. In the past, having access to Tovi's Ability greatly reduced the strenuousness of her own efforts, and there was no reason to think the same would not happen here. "But remember," she warned, "Tovi has a very small store of Ability compared to me. I could burn away all she has left."

"That's okay. I don't want it anymore, anyway."

Tovi's declaration surprised Alia. "Five minutes ago, you were sad about *not* being able to use it."

Tovi shook her head, sending her long curls flying. "Only because I wanted to help you. I wouldn't want to use it for anyone else."

Nyona squeezed Tovi's shoulders with one arm, then nodded toward Alia.

"All right, so long as you're certain."

"I am," Tovi said confidently.

"Okay. Let's go sit on the sofa. We'll be more comfortable there. Hasso, could you keep watch, just in case?"

"Sure." He sauntered over to the door and leaned against it. She wasn't certain what he would—or could—do if Kalisfena were to arrive, but it made her feel better to know he was there.

Tovi and Alia faced one another on the sofa, both seated with their legs crossed together in front. "I'm not sure how this will work," Alia said. "It might feel strange to you, or you might feel nothing at all."

"I understand." She reached out her hands.

After Alia ensured the masking of her own Ability so Kalisfena could not detect her activities, she took Tovi's hands and sent a tiny ball of Ability questing for the child's own. It took longer than she expected to find it, and when she did, she was shocked to find how little Tovi had. Compared to the pool of Ability Alia herself maintained, Tovi's was a mere puddle.

Alia gathered up Ability from Tovi until she had a ball large enough to send toward Mathis. For a moment, she hesitated. Once she sent this away from them, that portion of Tovi's Ability would be lost to her forever. *She said she didn't care*, she reminded herself, and Tovi was grown enough to know her own mind. *She'd be happier without it.*

She thrust the ball away from her.

I'm here.

Mathis's response came more quickly than it had before, and the connection felt more solid, yet there was no time to marvel over how much easier this was with Tovi's assistance. *What do you mean, you know?* she demanded. *Who told you? When?*

Kelda, just the other day. She said the deal with the Xeydeyans was made long ago, before you and Tovi joined us, and that they had no choice but to follow through.

So she knew this was happening when we were in Brome? And lied about it?

Yes.

At his simple affirmation, an immense sadness draped over her shoulders. Nyona was right. Kelda's friendship had been nothing but a falsehood from the start.

No. That's not true at all. Mathis's forceful rejection chased away some of her despondency. *I don't agree with what she's done at all, but I understand the why of it now. She thought it would help the cause. We've probably all done things we thought would help that didn't.*

She should have told us.

His attention drifted away momentarily, as if he were

distracted by a separate conversation. *She's here. You should talk to her directly.*

She grimaced. *It will take too much effort to establish a new connection. Tovi is helping me now, which is why I've been able to keep this up as long as I have, but I dare not risk losing it by switching to someone else.*

Then use me to talk to her. Alia winced. Even from this far away, he could tell when she dissembled.

Even that might be too much.

You'll feel better if you do.

She sighed. *Fine. If I can manage it, let her tell me to my—your —face why she lied.*

It took even more effort than she expected to twist her ball of Ability to gain access to Mathis's physical senses, something she hadn't done often even in Corinas. She drew a bit more Ability from Tovi to make sure her mask remained intact, and the child didn't seem to notice.

Mathis sat in a chair in a small room with no windows and a single door. His stomach rumbled. Kelda stood in front of him, dressed in a brown robe edged in a ribbon with a silken sheen. Her gray hair, free of its usual bun, fell past her shoulders.

Mathis nodded. "Go ahead. She can see and hear you now."

Kelda squatted down and rested her hands on his knees, peering up at him with teary eyes. "Alia. I'm so, so sorry. I wish there had been some other way, or that I could have told you what was going on. I thought you would be safer not knowing. I was wrong."

A mental shrug was all Alia could muster to that.

"She says she understands," Mathis said.

I did not!

We have more important things to worry about. You see how she is. She truly is sorry.

Kelda lowered her head for a moment. "I'm so glad. I thought she might never wish to speak to me again."

I'm not sure I do, Alia objected.

Mathis ignored her. "Well, she's speaking to you now, but I don't know how long she can keep this up. We've had trouble keeping a connection all morning. Tovi's helping her, but you should probably hurry, anyway."

"Yes, yes." Kelda said, pulling away from him to stand. "Alia. My, this is strange, talking to you yet talking to Mathis. But that's neither here nor there. How are you using your Ability? It should not be possible."

"I told you about Marta and Hasso's friends. They helped her find a way."

"Yes, I understand that, but how, physically how? She is much too far from the Provenance, with an ocean in-between."

She knows of the Provenance? Hearing Kelda speak so casually of something she'd only recently learned of excited her despite her distrust. *What does she know about it?*

"Alia wants to know what you know about…whatever that thing is you just mentioned."

"The Provenance? She knows that name? Oh, of course, she must, if she's somehow managed to overcome its limitation. I'm afraid she probably knows more about it than I do, then. No one outside the Directorate is even supposed to know it exists—for good reason, I suppose. It wouldn't do if people knew that Ability does not come fully from within." She snapped her fingers and refocused on Mathis's eyes. "Alia—you said Tovi is helping you? Did she find a way to use her Ability, then, too?"

No. I can access it, but she cannot use it herself. She cannot even feel it. To her, it is as if her Ability does not exist. Mathis relayed her answer.

"Oh my, that is very interesting, very interesting indeed. I wonder…" She chewed on her thumbnail. "Tovi proves the truth of the Provenance. Yet it cannot be the complete truth, as Alia is not drawing her Ability from it right now. What, exactly, about being Sempiternal makes this possible? And what if—*what if*—we can use that to our advantage?"

"What do you mean?" Mathis asked.

She pressed her fingertips together and rested them under her chin. "I'm not quite sure, my dear boy, but I mean to find out."

31

MASTER GERSEMI

THE FACE IN THE TINY MIRROR REFLECTED SOMEONE unrecognizable. Her silver-gray hair was in disarray, and dark circles under her eyes were set starkly against the pallid skin of her cheeks. Had it been six days since everything had gone wrong? Or only five? It felt nearly a lifetime. All she really knew was that she hadn't slept in days.

Gersemi shuffled back to the narrow bed situated underneath the only window in the room, inset high in the wall. Dark clouds filled what she could see of the sky, and rain pattered against the glass panes. She leaned against the headboard and pulled the blanket over her legs, covering her plain, gray robe. It wasn't a sleeping robe, but it might as well have been given its lack of ornamentation.

All this—still—was something she found difficult to accept. A vote of no confidence was an ancient rule, only meant to provide a check on a despotic leader. She might have been headstrong, and confident, but she had never, ever been that. No Directorate for centuries had even tried to use the mechanism, and Gersemi couldn't recall the last time such a vote had resulted in a Headmaster's removal.

Is this how her name would be remembered, then? Gersemi, the first Headmaster in modern times to be removed. She could hardly bear the thought.

They'd not even given her a chance to protest their decision before they'd moved swiftly to divest from her everything associated with her rank and thrust her into this cell-like room. At the memory, her lips curled into a snarl. Leyta must have been planning her move for weeks, poisoning the minds of the others. There was no other explanation for it.

An intense desire for revenge pushed past her misery. The other Masters, those not of the Directorate, must be fuming at this transgression, especially at a time of such uncertainty. They needed strong leadership to deal with the combined threat of the rebellion and Xeydeya. Who was going to provide that? Leyta? Gersemi snorted. The woman couldn't even handle what limited responsibilities she already had. No one else had the necessary set of skills. Gersemi was the only true choice to lead the Conclave in such difficult times.

She was still a Master of the Conclave. She had rights, and a voice. They couldn't keep her here forever.

Could they? Unused to second-guessing herself, that tiny voice of doubt now carried great weight, and her rage dissipated into frustration. How had it come to this? She was supposed to be the one to lead the Conclave into a new, awe-inspiring epoch. Mathis was the key to that, and those idiots wanted to send him away in exchange for a few extra bodies they didn't truly need.

The latch on her door clicked, and Enece entered the room unannounced. "Good morning, Master Gersemi. I have brought your morning meal."

She waved a hand, refusing to look his way. "Set it down and be gone." He was as much of a traitor as the rest, acting as her jailer at the behest of the others despite everything she'd done for him. She should have never appointed him as her personal servant. It had placed him far above what he deserved.

Dishes clanked as he set a tray on the square table tucked

against the corner opposite the bed. He turned, and for the first time, she noticed the plainness of his own black uniform, the sort reserved for the lowest ranking of domestic servant. "Is there anything else you need?"

"Besides wanting you to leave me in peace? Yes, there is plenty I need, but you lack the power to give me any of it." She eyed him up and down, making obvious her recognition of his diminished status.

His expression remained impassive. "Perhaps, but we won't know for certain unless you ask."

She scowled. Did he want her to *beg* for his help? That was something she would never do. "I demand a bath. Some new clothes. To get out of this squalor and into proper chambers. To speak with other Masters not of the Directorate. And to see Mathis. I'm sure all of that is well within your capability," she ended sarcastically.

"There should be additional clothing in the wardrobe, and I will have bathwater brought to you right away."

She closed her eyes and shook her head in derision. "I thought as much."

He left her then, but not long after, he returned, ushering in a train of eunuchs. The first two set a round copper tub in the middle of the room, and the rest poured into it bucket after bucket of steaming water until it was half full. The last set a few towels and a bar of soap on the chair before retreating.

As soon as the lock clicked back into place, Gersemi nearly leaped out of the bed. She grasped the bottom of her robe and pulled it over her head, dropping it and her smallclothes into a pile on the floor. Used to bathing nearly every day, being without a bath for this long left her feeling disgusting, which contributed to her malaise. She lowered herself into the warm water, sighing with near ecstasy as it lapped over her thighs, stomach, breasts, and arms.

By the time she'd finished scouring her body and hair clean, the water had cooled enough that it no longer remained comfortable to linger. She patted herself dry and selected fresh garments from the wardrobe. All the robes folded on the shelf were the same, as plain a gray as what she'd worn before, but after the pleasure of a bath, she cared less about the lack of silver trimming.

Standing in front of the mirror once again, she wrapped her hair into a wet bun at the nape of her neck and smoothed down the sides. She examined her profile. Her cheeks were flush with the heat from her bath, and it seemed as if the circles under her eyes had diminished. Funny how much something as simple as a bath could recover so much of her sense of worth—and her dignity. *I am a Master of the Conclave. They cannot treat me like this.*

The lock clicked, but this time, a knock accompanied it. "Are you finished with your bath, Master Gersemi? We can remove the tub if so."

"Yes. You may enter," she said graciously. She sat in the chair as the door opened. Four eunuchs labored to lift the tub and its contents out of the room.

"My apologies, Master Gersemi, but there is no way to drain it in here."

"I understand." It didn't matter if they took it away; she did not intend to remain here much longer. "I appreciate that you brought it at all," she said, a little surprised to find she meant it.

His eyebrows raised slightly. "You are welcome, Master Gersemi." He leaned back into the hallway and glanced to the side, beckoning with his arm. "I have also brought you something else you requested, but you must keep it brief. We have little time."

"Oh?" He was acting rather mysterious. It must be a Master, one of her many defenders, come to seek the confidence to challenge the rest. Gersemi straightened her back, lifted her chin, and rested one arm along the table, as if she were used to receiving guests in this squalor.

Yet instead of a woman in a gray-and-silver robe, in walked Mathis, tall and strong in the black-and-silver uniform of a Guard commander. She brought both hands to her chest with a sharp intake of her breath. *My Son.* Relief washed over her. He must have refused the Directorate's attempts to send him away from his new home. Away from her.

His dark emerald eyes traveled over the room. "Why did you bring me here?" he asked, and not even his suspicious tone could steal away her excitement at his presence.

"I wanted to see you." He was magnificent, her Son, and she drank in the sight of him. In retrospect, she wished she'd spent more time with him over the past few months, but she hadn't wanted to tip her hand. Maybe that had been a mistake. Maybe if she'd told the others from the beginning why Mathis was so very important to the Conclave, they would have understood why they had to keep him here, no matter the cost.

"But why in this place? Whose room is this?"

"I'm afraid it is mine, at least, for the moment."

"What?" His brow furrowed. "What is going on?"

She tilted her head. "You don't know?" If he didn't, then that meant the Directorate must not have announced what had transpired yet—and there was still time to reverse this travesty before Leyta's attempt to displace her became widely known. Her heartbeat quickened. It was now even more imperative that she get out of this room. Mathis would help, she was certain. He would not have come to her, otherwise.

"Obviously not," he said. "Whatever it is, it doesn't seem pleasant for you."

"It is but a temporary setback, I can assure you," she said, pleased at his concern for her wellbeing. "There was talk of sending you away at the rebel delegation's demand. I voiced my dissent, and the others threw a bit of a fit. I will take care of it all, now that you're here. I am so glad to see that you chose to remain."

He drew back his chin. "I did no such thing."

"What?" she asked, confused. The rebel delegation must have left days ago, yet here he was, in uniform.

"I'm not staying. I thought you knew that."

"What?" she cried, unable to hide her shock at his declaration.

"No—no, you can't leave. You said it yourself that this was your new home. You said it in front of everyone."

He shrugged. "I lied."

His admission, expressed so coolly, made her feel as if her heart had shattered into a million pieces. She clapped a hand over her mouth as her eyes unexpectedly filled with tears. She felt an absolute fool, especially with Enece standing right there staring at her, but she couldn't help herself. Mathis was supposed to be the answer. He was supposed to stand at her side as she pronounced that he, her Son, would ensure the future of the Conclave. Without him, the Conclave stood no chance of survival.

Without him, neither did she.

32

MATHIS

ONCE THEY GOT CLOSER TO MATHIS'S OWN QUARTERS, HE abruptly turned on Enece and hoisted him up against the wall by the front of his jacket, leaving his feet dangling.

"What…is the meaning…of this?" the eunuch gasped.

"I could ask the same of you, you lying little sneak. What in fires is going on around here?"

"I…can't entirely say…"

"Mathis!"

At Kelda's shout, Mathis released his grip, and the eunuch fell to the ground. "Get up," he muttered, nudging him with the toe of his boot as Kelda and Lieutenant Elcy rushed their way.

"What are you doing, Mathis?" Kelda asked with a look of dismay. "He's but a house servant."

"This one?" Mathis said incredulously. "He's much more than that. He's been spying on me since the moment I got here."

"And you're surprised by that? They couldn't have trusted you completely no matter what they said." Lieutenant Elcy helped the eunuch to his feet. "Our apologies for Mathis's behavior…oh! You're Gersemi's assistant, are you not?"

"Yes—or, I was. I am Enece."

"Don't believe him," Mathis warned. "He's still working for her. He just took me to see her in some hidden-away room, claiming she wanted to see me before I left, and I figured, why not? But she seemed rather surprised to hear I was leaving with you, and it didn't seem like she was faking it. Didn't you say nothing happened here without her say-so? How could she not know?"

Kelda exchanged a glance with Lieutenant Elcy. "You saw Gersemi?"

"That's what I said."

"Gersemi is no longer the Headmaster. They just announced it."

Mathis raised his eyebrows. "She said there'd been some disagreement with other Masters about letting me go with you, but she didn't say that. Is that why she's in that room?" Enece nodded. "Huh. I thought a Headmaster was Headmaster for life."

"Normally, yes, but there are procedures in place for unusual circumstances where the Headmaster is no longer capable of serving in the role. It's not been used for hundreds of years. I'm surprised they even remembered it, frankly. No one in the current Directorate is particularly interested in scholarly pursuits, and—"

"Kelda," Mathis and Lieutenant Elcy said simultaneously.

"I'm sorry. I know. Point being: The Directorate used this procedure to remove Gersemi as Headmaster, though they didn't give the reason. We were coming to tell you."

"Who's Headmaster now?"

"The former Principal Master of Security. Master Jeyne."

"Wow," he said. Things could be worse, he imagined. Master Jeyne had always been skeptical of him, yet had allowed him more freedom in his command than he'd expected. "Do we still have a deal?"

"Yes. I spoke to Master—Headmaster Jeyne immediately after the announcement. She assures me that nothing has changed, and that you are still free to leave with us."

"That's good." He scratched at the back of his head, still trying to wrap his mind around this development. "What happens to her? Gersemi, I mean."

"They suggested she might be banished, but I don't know how they could do such a thing. She hasn't left the Conclave in decades; she has nowhere else to go." Kelda wrung her hands. "Sending her away would seem a little dramatic. They should allow her to live her remaining days here, out of the public eye."

"Why do you care?" he said, though it seemed he could ask himself the same question. He'd gone to see her today because he thought that maybe, under the circumstances, she'd admit she'd lied to him. But her reaction to hearing that he would leave with the rebellion had been more than a bit disconcerting, and he found himself wondering if what she claimed might be true, after all. *Don't be ridiculous*, he thought. *She meant to manipulate your loyalties, and nothing more.*

Kelda lifted both palms toward the ceiling. "This is unprecedented. Why would they do this, especially now?"

"Because of him," the eunuch said, pointing at Mathis. "Gersemi refused to let him go, even when the others threatened her with removal if she did not."

Lieutenant Elcy wrinkled her nose. "She gave up being Headmaster over him? She must really believe you are her Son."

Enece nodded solemnly. "She does."

The Lieutenant tilted her head as she peered at Mathis's face. "Now that I think about it, the relationship seems pretty obvious. You really do look like her."

"I do not," he objected.

"It all fits," Kelda said, "and not merely because of your resemblance to each other. Since we were children, Gersemi has always wanted nothing more than power, and she's been willing to do whatever she felt was necessary to secure it for herself and the Conclave. Yet she has consistently set aside her ruthlessness for you —and only you. And now this? She would never risk her hold on the Conclave for just anyone."

"So what if it is true?" Mathis snapped, annoyed that everyone concurred with something so outrageous. "It changes nothing—we're still leaving, and soon."

"Yes, but—"

"It doesn't matter. I'm going back to my room. I have other things to see to." Alia was supposed to be contacting him soon, and that was far more important than standing around out here while they debated his parentage—something he would rather they all forget. "Are you coming?"

Kelda took the hint. "Oh, yes, of course. Thank you, Enece, for this information. You may return to your duties." He inclined his head, almost as if Kelda were still a Master, then turned and walked away.

~

Mathis?

I'm here.

We found something. Alia's excitement radiated through their connection.

What?

Kelda was right. There may be a way to destroy the Provenance from here.

His eyes flickered open, and the break of concentration almost caused him to lose the connection with her. *Really?*

That last book Lora Stretyn found for us had a trove of information about the Provenance in it, including a lengthy discussion of an attempt by a group of Sempiternals to destroy it. Essentially, they used their Ability to turn the Provenance's own against it. They weren't successful, obviously, but it sounds like they came close. I think we can replicate what they did.

How, if they failed? We have only you.

Yes, but they were doing it from Corinas, so their Ability was not fully disconnected from it. We also know more about how Ability works now than they did then. I can use mine, and Tovi's, and maybe even those of the other Adepts here.

She'd told him how hard it had been to figure out how to use her Ability from Xeydeya, and what she was describing sounded incredibly difficult. How could she possibly manage something of this magnitude from afar?

You will have to help me. Maybe Kelda, too, though our bond isn't as strong as the one between you and me.

What would you need us to do?

A hint of uncertainty tinted her thoughts. *When they tried this before, they made physical contact with the Provenance. You would need to do the same, and I would have to channel an enormous amount of Ability through you. It will be dangerous.*

Isn't everything? You know I will do whatever you need me to do. He suddenly realized his assumption about her concern might be misplaced. *Or do you mean dangerous for you? What happens to you and Tovi if this works? Or if it doesn't?*

Nothing, I think, except we won't be able to use Ability anymore.

Can you live with that? She might not have been an ally at the time, but he remembered how disconsolate she'd been back when Hasso had temporarily implanted her. And Tovi, under similar circumstances, had been in a near-stupor.

That won't happen again, Alia said, once again understanding his thoughts without him expressing them. *Tovi can't feel her Ability as it is, even now when I'm using it to augment my own, and she is completely unbothered by it. And I—well, when I first crossed your path, I thought my only purpose was to be an Adept of the Conclave. Things are different now.*

Her reassurance felt genuine, and it eased his mind some. *All right, then. So where is this thing?*

I don't know. Somewhere in the oldest parts of the complex, I imagine, and deep underground.

Your books didn't say?

If a sigh could transmit as a thought, then that was the impression that appeared in his mind. *I was hoping Kelda might know.*

I doubt it. She said she didn't know much, other than that it existed.

Ask her anyway?

I will.

I must go. This has gone on too long already. Speak again soon. Her presence retreated from his mind.

Lieutenant Elcy and Kelda sat on the edge of the bed, staring at him. "Well?" Kelda asked. "What did she say?"

"She thinks she's found how we can destroy the Provenance."

Lieutenant Elcy's eyes opened wide. "Kelda wasn't making that up, then?"

The former Master chuckled. "It was only a theory, though I'm more than pleased to hear Alia has confirmed it. Can you imagine if she were successful? Adepts would cease to be Adepts, and we would achieve our goal of denuding the Conclave's power—and, in a way, that would satisfy our agreements with the Xeydeyans, as well. Alia and Tovi could come home." She hugged her midsection. "So tell me. What did she find?"

"I don't know all the details, but apparently some Sempiternals tried to do this a long time ago, and she wants to do what they did, using me as a conduit. I would have to be touching it, though, so we need to find out where it is. Do you know?"

"I don't." Kelda paced a few steps away from the bed before pivoting back toward them. "I'll bet I can find out, though. In the meantime, Elcy: could you be a dear and fetch that new book I found, the one with the green cover? Its focus is the Great Uprising; perhaps there's something in there that might help Alia. Mathis: if she reaches out again, tell her we will need to know the specifics of her plan, and quickly. We're supposed to be leaving soon, so we have little time if we're going to try this."

"Where are you going?"

She brushed away something invisible on the shoulder of her robe, then fidgeted with her bun, setting it more askew on her head than it had been originally. "To do some convincing."

~

Mathis jerked awake at Lieutenant Elcy's sneeze. "Sorry," she said.

He lifted himself onto his elbows, somewhat disoriented. "How long have I been asleep?"

"About an hour."

"Kelda isn't back?"

"No. That's why I'm still here."

He glanced at the clock. "It's been three hours."

"You know how she is; she's probably lost in whatever library she talked herself into."

"I suppose."

"Don't worry. I'm sure she'll be here soon."

As if she were clairvoyant, a single tap at the door was followed by Kelda's entrance.

"Problem solved," she announced. Enece followed right on her heels.

Mathis scrambled to his feet. "What's he doing here?"

"He's helping us."

"Like fires he is!"

"Oh, stop it, Mathis. He already has." She patted the eunuch's shoulder. "He took me to see Gersemi."

"Why?"

"He was being helpful, as I said."

"No. Why did you want to see her?"

"She's one of the few people alive who would know where the Provenance is—and the only person with any chance of telling us."

"So when you said the problem was solved…" Lieutenant Elcy said, leaning forward in her chair.

"Yes. She agreed to lead us to the Provenance."

Mathis let out a short burst of laughter. "Just like that?" he said sarcastically, snapping his fingers. "And you believed her. You're acting a damned fool, Kelda. Why would she ever agree to do something like this?"

"Don't you speak to me like that, Mathis," Kelda snapped. "I am your elder. And your teacher. And your *friend*. I would not have approached Gersemi had I not believed there was a more-than-reasonable chance she would help."

He felt somewhat chagrined, yet he still found it difficult to moderate his tone when what she spoke of was so absurd. "A few weeks ago, she was your enemy, and now you trust her to take us to the Conclave's most closely guarded secret?"

"Circumstances have obviously changed. There's nothing left for her here, and she would do anything for you." She took his hand. "Mathis. I know you don't believe what she told you, but what you do or don't believe is irrelevant in this. *She* believes it, and from what she told me, it's based on sound information. You might see her decision to help us as irrational, but it's not like she's been particularly rational when it comes to you."

"I still can't believe she got the others to go along with making a man, and a rebel besides, an officer," said Lieutenant Elcy. "She must have amazing powers of persuasion."

"They were only trying to get me over to their side so I'd give up more on the rebellion," he said, though her rote dismissal that their agreement could be premised on his talent stung somewhat.

She shook her head. "Still, that they would casually toss aside tradition, especially when they had more immediate ways to find out what they wanted to know, is pretty amazing."

"Indeed," said Kelda. "And that goes for Gersemi's irrationality, as well. She had to know you were privy to a great deal about the rebellion, yet she wouldn't let them perform more than the one truth assessment on you. If her first concern had been with the Conclave rather than the preservation of her own child, she'd not have done any of that."

"She sent a spy to watch me from the beginning," Mathis said, jerking his chin toward the eunuch. "So she obviously didn't trust me the way you all suggest."

"I was not a spy," Enece objected.

"Not a great one, that's for certain," Mathis muttered.

"I was to watch you in the training grounds, yes, and I reported to her about that, but if she distrusted you completely, she'd have had me follow you everywhere. She even let you go into town that one time completely unsupervised."

"Well, that's neither here nor there," said Kelda, putting an end to their argument. "Did Alia contact you again?"

"No."

"Oh, I wish we'd figured out a way for you to reach her! When she does, tell her we have no time to waste. Now that they've announced a new Headmaster, Gersemi doesn't know how much longer she will have access to the Provenance. Normally the transition doesn't occur until the former Headmaster's death."

"Are there Guards or something?"

"Of a sort, though she said they're more intended to keep out Adepts—Sempiternals, specifically. Still, we do not know what changes are forthcoming. If we are going to do this, truly do this, we need to get our plan ready without delay." Kelda opened the blue knapsack on the table Lieutenant Elcy had brought back and fished out the green, leather-bound book. "I'm sure there is something in here that will help us. Now, where did I see that reference…"

As Kelda became lost in her research, Mathis shared a smile with Lieutenant Elcy, who was regarding Kelda with fondness. With all the madness surrounding him, it was comforting to see that at least some things would never change.

33

ALIA

A LAMP FLICKERED AGAINST THE DARK STONE, DRAWING Alia's eye to the side for a moment. *No distractions*, she reminded herself. *You must block everything out and focus.* She could not think on how stuffy this tiny room was, or the cobbles that protruded through the rug they'd placed on the floor, or the fact that her cushion needed to be twice as thick. And she could not worry about what might, or might not, come of this attempt.

Tovi faced her, their knees nearly touching. Alia reached for her hands. "Are you sure you're ready for this? I don't know what to expect," she warned.

"I'm ready."

Nyona squeezed Tovi's shoulders. The wrinkling at the corners of her eyes evidenced her own lack of confidence, but at least she had not tried to prevent Tovi's participation in this plan. She understood it was not something Alia could do on her own.

"And the others?"

"I think so. They told me they would be waiting."

"Hasso, are you ready?"

"Yes." He stood next to the bolted door, a long knife unsheathed at his side.

She nodded. What she was about to do would draw Kalisfena to her in no time, but there was no help for that. At least they'd bought themselves some additional time by sneaking Tovi out of the building she'd lived in for months through a service lift and coming here to this hidden room in the underground cellar of Marta's friendly wine merchant. When Kalisfena inevitably arrived, Lora Stretyn, Mila, and Kieran would block her way, and if she somehow got through the three of them to reach this room, Hasso would make sure she did not disrupt Alia's work, no matter what.

And if this worked—well, Kalisfena would thank her, she imagined.

Focus. "Okay, then let's begin. I will keep our efforts masked until it is time." She squeezed Tovi's hands.

Tovi gave her a smile of such conviction that it bolstered Alia's own certainty. They could do this. They *would* do this. She closed her eyes.

She took a little longer to find Mathis than she expected. *There you are. I was starting to worry.*

Is everything going as planned?

So far. She seems to be true to her word.

Where are you? You feel...heavy.

Underground. It's hot here. And humid.

Are you ready to let me in?

Always. A hint of humor carried in his thought.

Her own lips curled into a small smile as she altered their connection in a way that was likely imperceptible to him. A subterranean world sprung to life through his eyes, accompanied by the sounds of drips of water falling onto the stone, the shuffled steps of his companions, and his own measured breaths. Ahead, she spied Kelda, who herself trailed a tall woman in a plain gray robe. *Headmaster Gersemi?*

She's just Gersemi, now.

His comment was clipped and strangely angry, but she had no time to investigate his mood. *That's right,* she said instead. How strange it was to see this woman, who'd controlled so much of Alia's life and exerted such force over all of Corinas, reduced to helping the very people she'd once vowed to defeat.

The rocks beneath Mathis's boots were damp, and a few times he caught himself from slipping. He turned to look behind him. Two boys trailed him, along with Lieutenant Elcy and someone dressed as a eunuch, though if he was truly one, he was by far the shortest she'd ever seen. *Who are they?*

The eunuch's Gersemi's. The boys are from my unit—extra bodies in case there's a fight.

Extra bodies meant extra responsibility. She was already uncertain if she could keep those she'd expected to be here safe, and now there were three more people to look out for.

They came voluntarily. We all did. Don't worry about us; worry about what you have to do so we can get out of here. This place gives me the creeps.

She breathed in and out slowly, regaining her calm. He was right. She couldn't let things outside her control distract her, and the sooner she finished, the sooner everyone could return to the relative safety of the surface.

Up ahead, what had seemed like a distant light revealed itself as a large, silver door. Two pale creatures stood on either side, tall and muscular. Gersemi held a hand out behind her, then turned to face the group. Alia was immediately struck by how much she'd aged since she last saw her only a few years ago. "Remember, no one speaks but me," she whispered. "Even if the Wardens still see me as Headmaster, I don't know how they will react to all of you. Once Kelda, Mathis, and I are inside, stay close by."

"We'll protect you," one of the boys said, his bravado broken by a strange chirp in his voice.

"I'm sure," Kelda whispered. "But don't come inside unless there is no other choice. It isn't safe for people like you."

Gersemi looked right at Mathis then, and his heart skipped a beat. Her emerald eyes were almost a twin of his own, though his were darker. Alia wondered why she hadn't noticed that before. "Is she ready?" Gersemi asked.

Are you?

Alia breathed in deeply through her nose, then exhaled loudly through her mouth. *Yes.*

"She's ready."

Gersemi nodded. She approached the door.

"Headmaster," the Wardens uttered in a singular voice. Mathis's relief at their continued recognition of Gersemi soared into her.

"Open the door," the former Headmaster commanded.

"We sense the presence of those without Ability."

"They will not attempt to enter. Open the door," she repeated, and this time, they obeyed.

Mathis followed her and Kelda past the Wardens, and the hairs on his arms stood erect. They were taller than him, and a milky film covered their eyes. Who had these poor creatures been before they were cast into the earth? If they sensed Ability, they must be Sons. Had they ever seen daylight, even once, or were they like those Adepts who spent their entire lives in Generation, never knowing what lay beyond their cramped confines?

They entered a small, dark cavern. In its center, an enormous, jagged stone, much larger than Alia had anticipated, thrust out from the ground. It pulsed with a reddish glow, revealing a more crystalline composition. This thing, this ancient piece of the earth, somehow was the source of all Ability—though it would not be for much longer.

All right. Let's get this over with, he said, a thread of anxiety belying his cavalier words.

Mathis, I… She desperately wanted to say something, anything, before this all began. It might be the last chance she would have. *Thank you for being my friend.*

What kind of talk is that?

The truth.

I know. Amusement colored his thoughts. *I never thought I'd be pals with an Adept.*

I never thought I'd be pals with a rebel Son.

So let's do this, then. Together.

He stepped toward the Provenance. Kelda placed her hand on his right shoulder, and Alia quickly sensed her presence, just like when they'd practiced yesterday. *I feel you, Kelda. Are you ready?*

I am ready, she said, her warmth and encouragement flowing toward Alia, augmented by Mathis.

Gersemi gripped Mathis's left shoulder, and the link between her and Alia established itself nearly as quickly as it had with Mathis. Alia had expected it to take longer given that she'd never once connected with the woman who'd been the Headmaster her entire life. *I feel you, Gersemi. Are you ready?*

I am ready.

A puzzling mixture of fear and devotion swept toward Alia. If she'd had the time, she would have loved to fish through it to better understand whatever was going on in Gersemi's mind. *Focus*, she reminded herself, then, to the three anxiously awaiting her go-ahead: *give me a minute to gather the others.*

Keeping a tight hold of the connections she'd made in Corinas, she returned a portion of her attention to Tovi. Through her, she reached out toward Khyana, the blonde-haired Adept who lived next door to Tovi. The child was waiting as promised, and she didn't even seem to notice when Alia connected to all that remained of her pool of Ability. She moved on to the next Adept in Kalisfena's care that Tovi had somehow convinced to take part in their mad plan, then the next, and the next. They all understood, and accepted, that if she used their Ability, they would lose it forever—even if she failed.

After repeating this process nearly thirty times, Alia's skin burned with the heat of holding together such a large web of Ability over such incredible distances. The need to hide what she was doing from Kalisfena or any other Guardian only compounded her efforts, and it was quickly becoming too much to bear.

She dropped the mask that concealed her use of Ability from detection. *Now!*

Mathis stepped forward and placed both hands firmly against the Provenance. The rough stone warmed at his touch. A shock of Ability coursed through him, and he threw his head back in a silent scream. Alia shuddered at the onslaught, and her confidence momentarily faltered. *I know you,* the Provenance seemed to whisper to her. A tide of comfort rolled into her mind, with promises of well-deserved rest if she were to only let go, of a future without worry—

ALIA!

She shook her head. Who was she to think she could destroy such a thing? This was the source of all Ability, the power of the Conclave, the reason for her very existence—

ALIA! ALIA! ALIA! Tovi's shouts finally penetrated Alia's fog of confusion, allowing her precious seconds to reclaim her sense of self and purpose. The research she'd read had warned that the Provenance possessed mechanisms of self-defense, yet she hadn't expected anything to happen from a mere touch, and certainly nothing like that.

Hardening her mind against further insidious attacks, she returned her focus to the task at hand. Mathis still leaned against the Provenance, refusing to break his contact, but his body trembled with the effort. If this was going to work, she couldn't waste any more time.

Alia gathered up an enormous ball of Ability, greater than any she'd used before, and lobbed it through Mathis into the Provenance. Over, and over, and over, as quickly as she could, she sent a cascade of projectiles toward her target. Each contained the maximum amount of Ability she could muster. As she continued, the pool of Ability she'd gathered from the other Adepts diminished, and when she inevitably used up all the Ability an individual Adept had to contribute, her connection with that girl fell away.

By the time she'd burned through half her available Adepts,

something seemed to be happening within the Provenance itself. A pressure point, a sense of pliancy in an otherwise inflexible stone. Energized, she increased her pace. Sweat dripped from Mathis's temples. Another Adept dropped from her consciousness, then another, and another.

A tiny crack appeared right above Mathis's hands, and it quickly extended toward both the ceiling and floor. Another, and another, and another.

A long, thin piece of red crystal flaked away from the stone. Another, and another.

Suddenly, Mathis's knees buckled, and he dropped one of his hands to the ground. The Provenance's defenses roared back to life, pushing its energy back toward Alia. In an instant, she burned through the supply of four more Adepts in a desperate attempt to keep it at bay.

"No!" Gersemi wrapped her arms around Mathis and struggled to hoist him back to his feet. He tried to regain his balance, but his exhaustion was too great. Gersemi, wild-eyed, slapped her own hand against the Provenance in his stead.

Mathis…stand up, my Son…together…

Another, and another, and another, and then even Tovi dropped from her mind. Left with only what remained of her own Ability, Alia funneled it in a constant stream though both Mathis and Gersemi. The Provenance retreated, and what had been a small crack opened into a larger fissure. As she maintained that effort, she spun together a massive ball of her Ability, everything she had left. She hoped it would be enough.

Child! Now! Finish it now!

Alia jumped to follow Gersemi's command almost as if she were still an Adept under the Headmaster's control. She hurled everything she had toward the Provenance. When it made contact, the stone first seemed to contract within itself, then burst with an explosion of red light, throwing Mathis clear. The walls of the cavern flashed by before darkness overcame him.

34

MATHIS

A HINT OF LIGHT PENETRATED HIS CRUSTED EYELIDS. AS HE started to lift himself up on his elbows, a sharp pain shot through his temple, and he fell back against the pillow with a low moan.

"Don't move like that!" a woman yelped. A pair of hands pressed against his shoulders unnecessarily; he wasn't about to try sitting up again.

Mathis squeezed his eyes shut against the lingering pain and brought a bandaged hand to his forehead. The uncovered tips of his fingers touched fabric, which continued to wrap around his head. Had he been in a battle? Or some mission gone awry? He searched his scattered memory. There was a red glow, and an energy that burned away at his very core—nothing that could be real.

A smattering of voices drifted into his consciousness. "Is he awake?"

"Yes, but he shouldn't be disturbed. His situation is still quite delicate."

"All the more that I see him!"

"I understand, but I really think it will be best for him if you wait—"

There was a thud, as if someone had bumped into a heavy piece of furniture, followed by soft footsteps that grew louder. A cool hand rested against his cheek. He opened his left eye halfway.

Kelda peered at him as if he were an artifact in some museum. "Mathis, my dear." She brushed her hand over the top of his head. "I'm so, so happy to see you awake."

"Where am I?" His throat was dry and raspy, and his words sounded strange to his ear.

"You're in the infirmary. You've suffered a terrible injury. I wasn't certain you would—well, never mind. You're awake now, and that's all that matters."

"How long?"

"Nearly three weeks. You've been in and out of consciousness that whole time. This is the first time you've been fully awake."

"What happened?"

Her eyebrows raised. "You don't remember?"

"No, not really. I see bits of…something, I think, but every-thing is…scattered, I guess." It was almost as if a part of him had disappeared.

Kelda frowned. "Some of that likely is from your injury, but some might be because of what you went through, too. What is the last thing you remember?"

He closed his eye and grappled with the fragments of memory. "Redness. Darkness. Pain. Love."

"Oh, my dear boy."

The sadness in her voice set him on edge. "What happened?"

"You helped destroy the Provenance. Do you not remember?"

The Provenance. That name meant something. Something important. "I'm not sure," he said slowly. "Tell me."

"We were in the cavern with the Provenance. Gersemi and I were there to help you, to give you strength when Alia cast her Ability through you. And it *worked.* The Provenance is no more. Ability is no more. The *Conclave* is no more. Please, do you remember any of this, anything at all?" she pleaded.

Her words dredged up additional images from the depths of

his mind. Two tall, pale beings stood post before a silver door. His boys, looking fierce yet certainly scared to death. Kelda. Lieutenant Elcy. Alia, watching through his eyes, and doing the impossible.

And Gersemi. Gersemi, urging him on and giving him strength. Gersemi, exposing her regret for all that had passed, and all that never would. Gersemi, placing her hand on the Provenance when he'd fallen away, right before the world exploded into a wave of red.

He remembered, now, how it had felt when her raw emotion, a mixture of love and sorrow, had poured into him. That was not something someone could ever fake. She had not been playing him false, then. He was her Son.

He pried open both eyes. "Gersemi helped me."

"Yes. All that Ability flowing through you, in both directions —it was too much for you to bear. She took your place somehow; without that, we'd have failed. I will not pretend that what she did in the end made up for everything that had come before, but I will be forever grateful to her."

"I suppose I should thank her, too," he said begrudgingly. "Tell her I'm awake the next time you see her."

Kelda pulled her hand away from him, then returned it a moment later. "She's dead, Mathis. I thought you understood that. If she'd not stepped in when she did, likely none of us would have survived."

He blinked a few times, processing this news on top of all his slowly returning memories. It seemed he should feel...*something*... for the woman whom he'd just accepted as his mother. Yet all he could muster was a vague sense of relief. With her gone, he'd not have to pretend she was anything more than what she'd always been to him: the Headmaster of the Conclave, the woman responsible for years and years of tyranny.

The woman who'd given him a command—the one thing he'd wanted more than anything.

The woman who'd saved his life, and that of all his friends.

This confusing swirl of thoughts did nothing but make his head hurt more than it already did. "So what is happening now?" he asked, seeking to distract himself from his contradictory emotions.

"We've taken control of Corval. We had moved a large contingent of Guards in position across the strait in case things went south during our negotiations, and they moved in right away. You should have seen it around here. The Adepts, poor things, were lost, unable to understand why they no longer sensed their Ability. And the Masters—oh my, well, let's just say that the Directorate is no more, and we are in the process of making sure we have nothing to worry about from the rest."

"And the Tribunals?"

"Without Adepts, they were already barely hanging onto control. In the east, we've already taken over governance of most of the major cities—Quental, of course, Valen, and even Aldham. Soon enough our people will reach the cities in the west. The Conclave will be fully displaced."

"The citizens have accepted this?"

"Yes. Despite all those nasty rumors, we've been around a long time, and more people trust us to do what's right than not. It will take some time to transition everyone to a new form of governance, and I'm sure there will be some who will miss having Adepts to clarify the truth when things go awry. We will deal with those issues as they crop up. But for now, especially here in Corval, things are relatively calm, all things considered."

Never in his wildest dreams had he expected the Conclave to fall so quickly. Adepts, and Ability, had been the crutch propping it up this entire time, and now…that was no more. All thanks to Alia. *Tovi!* He grasped onto Kelda's arm. "What about Alia and Tovi? Are they okay?"

Kelda patted his hand. "I don't know. I hope so. What happened to Gersemi was because of her immediate proximity to the Provenance, I think, and whatever she did to take on your burden. We've sent a message to Xeydeya, but I doubt it has reached them yet, and then we will have to wait for a response. I will say, now that we lack Ability, we have got to come up with a better way to communicate over these long distances."

As she continued on about all the changes the Captains had planned for this place, his stomach tangled into a knot of worry. The rebellion had cast both Alia and Tovi away, yet they'd still helped. Would he ever know why? Out of habit, he opened his mind like he did when Alia wished to communicate with him, just in case—and he felt nothing, not even the hitch that normally came when he stumbled into the bit of Ability he'd inherited as a Son.

So, that was that, then. He'd have to wait along with everyone else to learn the fate of his friends.

∽

"Look out below!"

A large section of yellow stone from the Conclave's only remaining tower fell through the air. It crashed into the ground, throwing up a plume of dust that drifted toward the training grounds. Mathis was mildly surprised that in the frenetic efforts to tear down the physical representation of the Conclave, no one had been crushed to death.

Elcy leaned casually against the railing of the training grounds, which purportedly served as a barrier to protect passers-by from inadvertently wandering into the deconstruction zone. "Did you see the new design plans?" she asked, waving away the dust from her face.

"No." He shaded his eyes against the sun to watch the workers scurry over the diminishing heights of what had once been the seat of all power in Corinas. His head wound might have healed, but too much light tended to give him a splitting headache if he wasn't careful.

"It's nearly as big as what was already here. Seems a waste to tear it down just to build it back up."

"Symbolism, and all that," he said with a shrug.

"I know. Still."

"What does Kelda think?"

"She's ecstatic. They've added enough room for hundreds of students while keeping the space for the new public archive."

"Did they take away what they'd allotted for us?"

"No."

"Good." What they'd proposed as the expansion of the training grounds would help to ensure that every new member of the Guard received the training she or he needed to become a competent fighter. The existing space was much too small, especially if they wanted to bring units back from the field for re-education. In the next twelve months, the plan was to have every Guard member, whether formerly aligned with the Conclave or the rebellion—now styled as the Governing Coalition—cycle through the new training facility. The Governors thought it would be a good way to develop camaraderie amongst those who, not long ago, had fought on opposite sides.

There was so much to do, and at times, he wondered at the enormity of it all. Yet he was a part of the Coalition's command structure now, a real part of it, and he would do whatever he could to ensure their success. The Governors had granted him this opportunity, and he would not let them down.

Across the way, he spotted Zevon. "Captain Mathis!" the boy called, waving something small in the air. Mathis beckoned him over, and he ran up to them, slightly out of breath. "Captain Elcy," he said in acknowledgment, then he held out an envelope toward Mathis. "Captain Mathis, there's been a message from Xeydeya. Kelda asked me to bring it to you right away."

Mathis took the message from the boy, his palms suddenly sweaty. *If it were bad news, Kelda would not have let you find out this way*, he reassured himself, yet his hand trembled slightly as he slid his index finger under the lip of the envelope.

Before he'd read much of anything, Elcy leaned over his arm, trying to read the message, too. He elbowed her away as he scanned the remaining words. "What's it say?" she demanded.

He looked up, and Elcy responded with a ridiculous grin he was certain was a twin of his own. "She's alive, and well. They both are." The weight of weeks of worry lifted from his shoulders, and for the first time since he'd woken up in the infirmary, he finally felt free.

35

ALIA

WITH A NEARLY IMPERCEPTIBLE LURCH, THE LIFT BEGAN ITS ascent. Alia stood by herself in front of the doors, watching the sequential numbers tick higher and higher. She sighed as it stopped on the thirty-second floor, and she moved back into the corner. The doors opened, and a Xeydeyan woman, tall and elegant like all the rest, raised her eyebrows at the sight of Alia. After the briefest of pauses, she stepped inside with a polite nod, then turned around to face the doors. The rest of the ride occurred in semi-awkward silence. Alia knew the woman must be burning with curiosity, but would never speak to her without a proper introduction. Xeydeyans could be strangely polite.

"Pardon me," Alia said when the lift arrived at the fifty-first floor.

"But of course." The woman stepped to the side.

Out in the corridor, Alia resisted the urge to check over her shoulder to see if the woman peered after her. It was common knowledge that the new Ambassador lived in this building, and the questioning eyes were always there. Was it true she'd once had Ability? Had she really forsaken her country?

Alia fished a key out of her bag and unlocked the door to her apartment. Once inside, she tossed her bag on the small table by the entrance and crossed over to the floor-to-ceiling windows. Below her spread the city of Amrava, her home now, and no longer a stranger. To the west, the rolling green hills were awash in a sea of pink from the fruit trees that had recently exploded with springtime color. South were the docks, filled with merchant ships bearing the green-and-black livery of Xeydeya as well as those of other nations she was still learning to identify. None, however, showed the bold yellow-and-red stripes the Governing Coalition of Corinas had adopted as their own.

She let the curtain fall away with a small sigh. What would it be like, to see her friends again after everything that had happened? The stack of messages on her desk from Mathis and Kelda held no hint of condemnation, yet she still couldn't help feeling guilty at leaving them to the task of rebuilding Corinas on their own.

"We *are* helping," she reminded herself aloud, using Nyona's oft-repeated words. Nyona had joined Kalisfena's educational program for former Adepts, with a focus on teaching the new arrivals corrections to the Masters' many lies. She had so much material to work with that it had taken her no time at all to develop an entire twelve-week course. Tovi had become fast friends with several girls about her same age, and she had enthusiastically taken it upon herself to show them how they, too, could enjoy life without Ability in a place that held no reminders of what they'd lost.

As for Alia, her official role here was that of Ambassador to Corinas, and she spent most of her time trying to explain to the Xeydeyans what they might expect from the new Governing Coalition. Some of what she told them was guesswork—Levina and the other Captains hadn't exactly shared all their plans with her, she thought wryly—but she certainly could identify where she expected their actions to contrast with those of the former Conclave. In this role, she also served as the Governing Coalition's primary contact in Xeydeya. Once things settled down more, she might even travel to Corinas to see the changes for herself so she could report back to the Xeydeyan government.

For now, however, she worried about this upcoming meeting, the first between the two nations since the fall of the Conclave. As an advanced country with more than its fair share of natural resources, Xeydeya held the upper hand in any negotiations, and it was part of Alia's job to see their interests maintained. With all the recent turmoil, Corinas was ripe for the picking by other competitor nations, and they'd much rather have a partner to their immediate south than a foe.

Still, it would be more than passing strange to be on the opposite side of the table from people who'd once been her friends. *Stop it,* she berated herself. Mathis and Kelda and many others were *still* her friends. Just because she hadn't wanted to subject herself to life under the governance of those who'd betrayed her so completely didn't mean she didn't care about the future of Corinas. She wouldn't have risked everything to destroy the Provenance if that had been so.

A graceful chime notified her of someone at her door. She didn't move. She'd come straight to her apartment after a long morning of meetings rather than returning to her office so she could have a little time to herself before her next appointments. After three more chimes, each one coming quicker on the heels of the one before, her patience ended. She stomped over to the door and yanked it open. "What?"

Mathis stood in the hallway, wearing a wry grin. "I see that for all their education, they haven't taught you manners."

Alia couldn't believe her eyes. "Mathis!" she cried, pulling him into a long hug. "How are you here? I didn't see your ship. Is Kelda with you?"

He patted her back, then held her at arm's length. He looked much the same as she remembered, though he'd shaved off his beard and he seemed to hold himself with greater confidence. The black jacket of his uniform bore a circular, red-and-yellow striped emblem, with three white stars above it on the left side of his chest. "We got in this morning. Kelda's off with Nyona some-where, but she should be by later. We went by your office earlier, but someone told us you were busy and could not be disturbed. Tovi said I might find you here later. So. Here I am."

"I can't believe no one told me of your arrival. Oh, but I am so glad to see you. Please, come in, come in."

"Some place you've got here," he said, looking all around as he walked up to the window. He peered outside, then let out a slow whistle and took a step back. "We are really, really high up."

"Yes. It takes a little getting used to. What did you think when you first saw the city?"

"It's amazing. You weren't exaggerating."

"And the lift?"

"I almost didn't get inside it," he admitted sheepishly.

"It's better than walking up fifty-one flights of stairs every day. We do have them, in case of an emergency, but I'm happy I've never needed to use them." The door chime sounded again. "What now?" she said with exasperation.

"Maybe it's Kelda?"

When she opened the door, a young woman wearing the green-and-black jacket of a Xeydeyan courier bowed her head slightly. "Ambassador," she said, holding out a brown envelope with a red label. "I have an urgent message for you. I apologize in advance for the delay; I tried several times to deliver it to your office, but I could not leave it there as I was instructed to deliver it to you personally."

"It's fine. Thank you for bringing it."

The courier bobbed her head and dashed off to her next assign-ment. Alia used her foot to close the door behind her as she tore open the envelope. "Here's the announcement of your arrival," she said, waving the message in the air. "Three hours ago. This place, sometimes." She'd have a word with those that ran communica-tions down at the docks; they had what seemed to her nonsensical rules for when they required personal hand-delivery.

"You're clearly a very important person, *Ambassador*, if they dare not interrupt your meetings with paltry messages." The lines around his eyes deepened with his grin.

"As are you, *Captain*." She'd forgotten how much fun it was to exchange friendly taunts with him. Of all there was about living in a foreign land, she missed their banter the most. "I still can't believe they actually did it. Corinas is changing faster than I ever imagined."

"So far I'm the only one, though they have made a few other men Lieutenants. I guess they decided I was a safe bet for trying something new."

"Possibly, but I think there is more to it than that." She sat down in a chair in her living area, and he sat in the one next to it. "I get reports all the time about the Coalition's work to rebuild the Guard, and you've featured prominently in several. You seem to be one of their rising stars."

He scratched at the back of his head and grimaced slightly. She needed no Ability to see how uncomfortable her praise made him, yet from what she'd read, it was all true. The Conclave might have made him a Lieutenant in an attempt to influence his loyalties, but the new Governors of Corinas had made him a Captain because he deserved it.

"What about you?" he asked. "Are you truly happy here?"

She leaned back in her chair. "Yes. I admit to being a little surprised by that myself, seeing as how I wanted nothing more than to leave when I first arrived." She put out her hand. "Not to say there aren't things that drive me crazy at times, and things that are strange, but—*everything* is a little strange now that I no longer have Ability. In Corinas, I would have been reminded of that every day. And to be honest, I wouldn't have ever been completely comfortable living in the company of Levina and Jana and all the others who lied to me so thoroughly. I was a pawn to them. I probably always was."

He frowned. "Do you feel that way even about Kelda?"

Alia sighed. "Yes. I understand she meant no harm, and I believe her, but—" she shrugged. "Maybe after more time I'll feel differently. It took you a few decades to get over Hasso, if I recall correctly," she teased, not wanting to linger on what remained a painful subject.

He leaned back and lifted both hands behind his head, his elbows spread wide. "Yet you trust Kalisfena Tatyn, even though she was part of their scheme?"

"I'm not claiming to be consistent."

"You are claiming to make sense, though, and this surely doesn't. She threatened you directly."

"Yes, she didn't want me using Ability, and yes, she was willing to force an implant on me if that's what it took to get me to stop, but none of it ended up mattering once we destroyed the Provenance."

"And she knew that right away, you said?"

"Yes, through whatever it is within her that allowed her to detect my use of Ability."

"Think that's gone now, too?"

She shrugged. "I have no idea. No way for me to test it," she said with a small laugh. "Still, after all that, I didn't expect her to advocate for me to become their Ambassador. It was as if our little dispute had never occurred."

"Dispute...that's one way to put it, I guess."

"Yes." She crossed her legs, arranging the legs of the flowing pants she'd yet to become used to so they did not bunch strangely against her thighs. "Okay, enough about me. How are you? Are you still getting headaches?"

"Sometimes, in the bright light. The medics say it might take a while for that to go away. I slammed into that cave wall pretty hard." He twisted around and pointed to the back of his skull, where a long, red scar was visible amidst his dark hair.

"I'm so sorry that happened," she said, reaching for his hand, which fortunately showed no signs of injury.

His jaw clenched. "You didn't know what to expect. None of us did."

Alia let it drop. This first meeting was not the time to probe how he felt about the fact that Gersemi—his mother!—had died to save him. "How's the transition going?" she asked instead.

"Are you asking me as a friend or as the Ambassador?"

"Does it matter?"

He smiled lazily. "It might. Now that you can't jump in my head whenever you want, I can keep our secrets safe."

She rolled her eyes. "I never pried into your thoughts and you know it. But I'm asking as a friend. I promise not to use anything you say against you later. I'm just an arbiter in these discussions, anyway."

"It's going surprisingly well. There have been a few problems with some holdout cities closer to Corval, but we've sent in units to keep the peace. I think things will settle down soon enough once people understand that this is for real, and that the Masters aren't coming back."

"Do you really think you got them all?"

"Even if some are in hiding, they can't do us any harm. They're completely useless without Adepts."

Alia wondered what had become of those she'd once known, including those of her Initiate. Had they been executed with the rest? She'd not asked. It wasn't her place to question the decisions of the Governing Coalition. It wasn't as if they'd done anything more than the Masters would have done, had the situation been reversed.

At least they'd allowed the former Adepts to live. Kalisfena had insisted on it, though Alia doubted the Governors would have objected, as it solved the problem of what to do with them. She was glad for it. Those girls were blameless, and they deserved a chance at a better life. Kalisfena was thrilled to give it to them.

"And the construction of the new university?" she asked, wondering how long it would take Corinas to develop anything even remotely like the educational system of Xeydeya.

"It's progressing, though not fast enough for Kelda. She's already enrolling students."

"Men as well as women?"

He nodded. "Like I said, they want to try new things, now. Maybe you'll even decide one day to come back."

"Maybe." How she lived her life from now on was completely up to her, and she didn't try to anticipate what the future might bring. Anything was possible, she supposed, even a return to Corinas. Or, perhaps, she might go somewhere else entirely. There was an entire world out there she knew little to nothing about. What might it be like to explore all that had been hidden from her for most of her life?

A flutter of self-doubt crossed her mind. She looked past his shoulder at the puffy clouds in the distance, cast over with pink and orange from the descending sun. "Do you think we've made the right choices, you and me?" she asked. "When it's all said and done, do you think we'll be happy?"

The corners of his lips twitched into the faintest hint of a smile. "I guess we'll find out."

SPECIAL OFFER

Craving more from the World of Corinas?

Visit Beth's website to get a FREE short story prequel only available at the link below.

www.bethraymond.com/offer

ACKNOWLEDGMENTS

Thank you to my beta readers, David and Kristin, for your invaluable comments. The story is far better as a result.

Thanks also to Sylvia Cottrell for your helpful editing assistance and suggestions and to Andrew Brown from Design for Writers for yet another great cover.

And finally, thanks to my fans, especially those of you who told me you needed to know what happened next.

ABOUT THE AUTHOR

Beth Raymond practices law by day, but in the quiet, pre-dawn hours, writes fiction from the comfort of her leather armchair. When she's not writing or working, she enjoys traveling, playing video games, knitting, and organizing things that do not particularly need organizing. Beth lives in Portland, Oregon, with her husband and two cats.

If you liked this book, please take a moment to leave a review at Amazon, Goodreads, or the retailer where you purchased this book. All reviews are appreciated, no matter how brief.

Thank you!

www.bethraymond.com

facebook.com/BethRaymond.Author

twitter.com/Beth_Raymond

goodreads.com/Beth_Raymond

amazon.com/author/bethraymond

ALSO BY BETH RAYMOND

The World of Corinas

Secrets of the Conclave

Decisions (a short story prequel)